My First Wife

# My First Wife

# JAKOB WASSERMANN

*Translated by* MICHAEL HOFMANN

PENGUIN CLASSICS
*an imprint of*
PENGUIN BOOKS

PENGUIN CLASSICS

Published by the Penguin Group
Penguin Books Ltd, 80 Strand, London WC2R ORL, England
Penguin Group (USA) Inc., 375 Hudson Street, New York, New York 10014, USA
Penguin Group (Canada), 90 Eglinton Avenue East, Suite 700, Toronto, Ontario, Canada M4P 2Y3
(a division of Pearson Penguin Canada Inc.)
Penguin Ireland, 25 St Stephen's Green, Dublin 2, Ireland (a division of Penguin Books Ltd)
Penguin Group (Australia), 250 Camberwell Road,
Camberwell, Victoria 3124, Australia (a division of Pearson Australia Group Pty Ltd)
Penguin Books India Pvt Ltd, 11 Community Centre, Panchsheel Park,
New Delhi – 110 017, India
Penguin Group (NZ), 67 Apollo Drive, Rosedale, Auckland 0632, New Zealand
(a division of Pearson New Zealand Ltd)
Penguin Books (South Africa) (Pty) Ltd, Block D, Rosebank Office Park, 181 Jan Smuts Avenue,
Parktown North, Gauteng 2193, South Africa

Penguin Books Ltd, Registered Offices: 80 Strand, London WC2R ORL, England

www.penguin.com

First published in German, within *Joseph Kerkhovens dritte Existenz*, by Queredo, Amsterdam, 1934
This translation published in Penguin Classics 2012

001

Copyright 1934 by the estate of Jakob Wassermann
Translation and editorial material © Michael Hofmann, 2012
All rights reserved

The moral right of the translator has been asserted

Set in PostScript Adobe Sabon
Typeset by Palimpsest Book Production Limited,
Falkirk, Stirlingshire
Printed in Great Britain by Clays Ltd, St Ives plc

A CIP catalogue record for this book is available from the British Library

ISBN: 978-0-141-38935-6

www.greenpenguin.co.uk

MIX
Paper from
responsible sources
FSC
www.fsc.org FSC™ C018179

Penguin Books is committed to a sustainable
future for our business, our readers and our planet.
This book is made from Forest Stewardship
Council™ certified paper.

ALWAYS LEARNING     **PEARSON**

# Contents

## My First Wife

*Mirror of Youth*

## Six Sisters

She had five sisters – four older, one younger. The six Mevis girls were known all over the city. Whenever they appeared together, they were like a sealed phalanx, from the classically beautiful Lydia to the graceful Traude, a sealed phalanx. Their father and commander-in-chief, Professor Gottfried Mevis, shining beacon of the law faculty, a striking-looking man, was their Barbarossa. Six daughters and no sons – that was some freak of nature. Ribald commentators predicted a whole tribe of grandchildren. Frau Mevis, given name Alice, *née* Lottelott – one of the Düsseldorf Lottelotts, of Lottelott & Grünert, Consolidated Steel – had inherited a large fortune. The family, respected and envied, lived comfortably in a spacious villa.

## Duckling

No question: where physical attributes were concerned, Ganna lagged some way behind her sisters. She had become aware of the fact very early, to her chagrin. Mirrors proclaimed it, the expressions and reactions of others confirmed it; she was the ugly duckling among five swans. Therefore it was her task to clear a path for herself through the five arrogant swans. Nor was that enough; Ganna wanted to outdo them. She was endlessly ambitious. She dreamed of a glorious future. Hers weren't the usual banal girl-ish dreams, they were scenarios and imaginings of an unusual definition. She felt chosen, even though she couldn't have said in what way.

Even as a child, she had been hard to manage. I have heard tell that she was repeatedly the subject of scenes and commotions. In her tenth year, Professor Mevis took to giving her twice-weekly prophylactic beatings, to get her out of the habit of lying. A barbarous measure, which failed to achieve its purpose, and only caused Ganna unnecessary suffering. Because surely these childish lies of hers were only self-protective fantasies. Beatings only made her more wilful, and drove the badness further into her. When she was beaten, she would scream like a banshee. Sometimes she would throw herself to the ground and thrash about with her arms and legs. That would only provoke the Professor further. Once, her mother sent for the doctor, because Ganna wouldn't calm down. Irmgard, her next-older sister, shrugged her shoulders and said it was play-acting, Ganna was putting on an 'epileptic fit'; she had seen another girl at school have one a few days before.

So I was told. Also that on another occasion the Professor had lost his temper with her, and in his rage – which, like all tyrants, he enjoyed – shouted the words in her face: 'You're the nail in my coffin!' Whereupon Ganna is said to have fallen to her knees and raised her arms to him imploringly. A number of the sisters were listening at the door, with gleeful expressions. Ever since, when they were among themselves, they referred to Ganna as the coffin nail. All of which goes to show that a duckling has no easy time of it among swans. Swans are cruel and snobbish birds.

She thinks she's better than us, said the sisters, and from time to time they would rise up and make common cause against her. Ganna refuses to do any chores, so she's responsible for all domestic mishaps. She is so highly strung that she often breaks things, therefore she gets the blame for anything and everything that breaks in the house. A carton of expensive laid paper goes missing; the bathtub overflows; a china vase is found in pieces on the carpet; little stick-figures have been scratched in the cream gloss on a door: who is the culprit? Ganna. Look at her standing there, said the sisters, refusing to defend herself, eyes lowered like a good girl, every inch a martyr; it's no good, Ganna, we've seen through you!

## They want you to lie

Punctuality was enjoined in the Mevis household. The paternal rule decreed that lunch was on the dot of one. Time and again, there they all were sitting at table: Lydia, Berta, Justine, Irmgard, Traude, the Professor, Frau Mevis, their old nurse, Frau Kümmelmann – only Ganna's chair was unoccupied. Ganna's deeply ingrained objection to time-keeping was another of the family traditions. Professor Mevis pretends not to notice Ganna's absence, but his brow is twitching ominously. Frau Mevis keeps looking anxiously at the door; she's suffering agonies. Finally a creature bursts into the room in a mad rush, her face puce, her eyes wide with dread, her hair a tangled mess; and while the wrathful father, strangling his red beard in his fist, glowers at her, the sisters, five models of virtue, titter quietly to themselves, because there can be no doubt that Ganna is about to tell one of her famous stories that don't have a shred of truth in them, however masterfully she tells them. Poor Ganna. Don't you feel sorry for her. She stutters, she stumbles over her words, poor mite, she's so moving in her plight one should take her and pet her a bit; eight pairs of eyes are levelled at her, not one of them kind, not one of them encouraging, and there is nothing masterly about the story either – quite the contrary, her excuse gets snarled up in itself, and in the end she falls silent and starts eating her soup. Having witnessed similar scenes myself later, I can be fairly sure that they will have passed off in this way.

At any rate, Ganna comes to see that it is necessary to lie in order to save one's skin. It's what they expect. Really, they made her do it. Lying becomes an indispensable weapon for Ganna, like the black liquid into which the cuttlefish disappears. The plain truth doesn't work on them, you don't get your peace that way, you have to make things up. Experience becomes a sort of semi-scandalous adventure, and by and by her spirit is no longer content in a rather colourless reality.

## Several of the swans leave their home pond

Round about 1895, when Ganna was seventeen, her older sisters started marrying. One after the other, as though by some contagion, they fell in love, became engaged, married, started a home, and from that time forth were only ever seen at the side of their swains, with whom they behaved with unseemly displays of intimacy. The experience of three weddings in next to no time was decidedly difficult for Ganna. It was the combination of love and settling down, of dowry and secret and blatant necking that offended her idealistic sense. At least that's what I assume to have been the case. She did not trouble to hide her contempt: the noble swans had soiled their plumage. I remember reading a passage in one of the diaries she kept as a girl. There she protested: I could never give myself to a man who wasn't my intellectual equal. Once, when Lydia's consort, who was a professional seducer, attempted a tender advance on Ganna, she bit him on the thumb so hard that he had to wear a rubber fingerstall for days afterwards. 'Satanic little minx,' he would say furiously, when her name came up later.

The three most stainless of the swans had cleared the field, but there were still two left, who were more irksome, being closer to her in age. Also, the married ones continued to show off their exemplary lives and characters in the face of Ganna's loneliness, in which enterprise they had the support of their contented, beaming husbands, who had every reason to be proud of so much honour, intelligence and domestic virtue.


## Ganna lives in a world of her own

She did not know the meaning of obedience. Whatever she wasn't allowed to have, she would purloin for herself secretly. She was full of cunning. If asking isn't enough, and a person is driven to plead for something, it will tend to make them devious. She even used her absent-mindedness as a way of securing small advantages for herself. If you can make people laugh, they will be more lenient in their judgement of you. I know fools who are so diligent in their folly that they can quite comfortably live by it. The confusion that Ganna wrought kept her family and friends continually amused. Misplaced letters, garbled names, forgotten appointments, muddled dates and places, forsaken umbrellas, lost gloves, attempts to leave by the wrong door, inappropriate replies, pointless errands: it was one continual comedy of errors. 'Have you heard the latest about Ganna Mevis?' was a standing question in her circle. And some story would follow about how she had gone out into the woods one summer morning with her hairbrush wedged under her arm, firmly convinced she had *Beyond Good and Evil* with her. Priceless, people said, and they laughed till they cried. It was all very innocent, very adorable. And the most delightful thing of all was that Ganna herself could laugh at her innumerable slips, with a winning laugh that even made up for the coarse indiscretions she was often guilty of in her absent-mindedness. She lived in a world of her own that seemed to have been designed especially for her.

## Her father's daughter

Professor Mevis didn't lose too much sleep over matters of upbringing. If shouting didn't work, there was always violence. Ganna annoyed him. The spirit of rebellion with which she was imbued turned him against her. 'If only we were rid of her,' he said to his wife, 'if only she were safely married off.' Whereupon Frau Mevis would shake her head in a worried way. It was her view that with Ganna's rather indifferent attractions, there was little chance of him finding a suitable man to do him such a service. She told me so once, much later, laughing.

Nevertheless, the Professor sometimes was of the view that she was more flesh of his flesh and spirit of his spirit than the other girls, who were more *réussies*. The well-set figure, the stubborn brow, the bold expression; that in addition to her insistence on entitlement, actual or notional; her wilfulness and hot-headedness: it was as though Nature had had half a mind to make a son of her and only decided otherwise at the very last moment. None of the others could match her for toughness and strength. All that spoke for her. And there was something else too. Often, when he thought he was about to burst with rage and impatience, she would strike him as so irresistibly droll that he had to run to the nearest room to keep her from noticing his hilarity, and his own authority from being impaired.


## What her father means to her

She for her part feared him. He was the black curse and cloud overhanging her youth. Fear was allied to profound respect. Basically, his iron hand felt like happiness to her. In childhood she was more aware of this than in subsequent years. Perhaps it was an instance of that mysterious instinct that shields the kernel of the spirit till it is eventually subsumed by will and necessity. But even as a growing girl she would sometimes feel the dark threats emanating from her own character; she required this master, this powerful fist, to keep everything within her from collapsing in unruliness. She had a dream once of a flaming whip rushing down from the heavens. The mortal fear with which she tried to evade the lash helped her across an abyss she would otherwise certainly have fallen into. Regardless of the continual uprisings against his authority, the many trivial deceptions she regularly practised on him, she acknowledged his power unconditionally, and with her whole body. However much the physical chastisements outraged and upset her – she underwent them into her eighteenth year – a mysterious little pleasure did quiver in her when he beat her. He alone had the licence to do that. In all the world, he alone was in the right against her. When his great voice boomed through the house so that everyone flinched, then, underlying her own fear, there was a strange feeling in her of satisfaction, something that hailed the master, how good that the master is there. His fits of rage seemed to her to be splendid elemental events, as impressive as a spouting geyser or a forest fire. Can qualities be used up? Is there only so much submissiveness in one's heart that it might trickle away or evaporate if not resupplied? Never again, I think I am right in claiming, in no other association or relationship, did Ganna encounter a being whose presence and influence compelled her to the feeling: how good that the master is here, my master. And that was the ruin of her.

## Foolishness of literature

I come now to a delicate subject. At that time, the educated classes were pleased to take an interest in writing and in literature. It was a part of the *bon ton* to discuss the 'modern movement', to have read *Germinal* or *The Kreutzer Sonata*, and to have witnessed the latest theatrical scandal/sensation, although it was *mauvais* to overdo it and to take an excessive interest in such things. It was good to know the names of certain works and their authors, you had to be able to keep up your end of a conversation; though beyond that it had no more significance than knowing the names of the dishes on a menu. Young people liked to talk about 'life' without actually confronting it; while they feigned an enthusiasm for art, their real effort was to secure some vain ascendancy by parroting views they picked up in the papers, or had heard from some impeccable authority. A man who worked in one of the professions was only expected to show a limited interest in literature, otherwise people would stop taking him seriously. That left the field open for women. And, since they were the ones who determined taste and set fashions, they made their contribution to a fairly comprehensive debasement, because, just like the men, they gravitated quite naturally to the second- and third-rate; first-class things they ignored. It was the age of paste diamonds and shallow minds.

But with Ganna, things were slightly different.

## She writes her own world

She was convinced she was marching at the head of the true cognoscenti, right in the van, where the new world would heave into sight, where the youngest, tenderest reputations were just beginning to sprout, before they could be ferried into immortality by doting hands. And it's true, there was something smitten about her. She was capable of being enthused by a work of literature. She roughly understood the categories. She despised mediocrity. Once a fortnight she gathered faithful young male and female friends about her who were of the same persuasion, and then she would rapturously share her finds with them, but also read excitedly and blushingly what she herself had penned. Her otherwise clear and piercing voice would sound dark and hoarse, as if she had powdered her throat with flour. When it got about that a critic for a major newspaper had said of her philosophical essays that they bore the stamp of an unmistakable if undisciplined genius, her acolytes cheered, though she herself with modesty and agitation tried to mute the acclaim. These literary sessions took place in the small drawing room at the Mevises'. They had something of an occult character. None of her sisters was allowed to enter the room; Ganna, like a priestess protecting the godhead from profane disturbances, took steps. If an outsider had violated the presence, she would have pierced him with a look. Everyone in the house knew it, and they let her get on with it.

It wasn't a pastime, not something frivolous or pretentious. It wasn't possible to say at the time how far and how deep it went. For Ganna it was the 'higher reality', an expression of ridicule in the circles in which she moved. But was this 'higher reality' real? Was it a force for purity and nobility? Hard to say. Normally it's the case – and this casts an odd light on human nature – that a love of literature disguises a vacant inner space, so that where you might expect to find principles or high-mindedness, often you only meet with gush. If the enthusiasm is real, then a pact is made with it, and the ethical implications are quietly avoided. Whether this was the case with Ganna was, as I say, not yet ascertainable at the time. One day she was bound to reach the parting of the ways. In those early years she was still unsteady, still groping, looking for her law, looking above all for a mirror. People couldn't be a mirror for her, nor could the real world; it was only in books that she encountered a being like herself – so she thought – a trusting being full of earnestness and passion. She was delighted by the likeness, yes, that was her own poem, her own creation, she fell in love with it, and in her eyes it made her truthful and good.

It is therefore almost inevitable that a writer, a certifiable writer, would come to hold the meaning of the universe for Ganna, to save her from the repellent superficiality of the Mevis empire, the tarn with the five exemplary swans. She dreamed of the role and the mission of an Aspasia. But to be an Aspasia, you needed a Pericles and an Athens. Even to be a Rahel Varnhagen, you still needed a Goethe. But where was there a Pericles, or a Goethe, in the humdrum world of 1898? Well, that's what dreams are there for, for changing phantasms into reality.

## Yours truly

In May of that self-same year, it so happened that I left Munich for Vienna. I had just published a novel called *The Treasure Seekers* and the book had not gone entirely unnoticed. Some experts were even pleased to praise it at over its worth, and call its author a shining new beacon of light on the horizon, a rather tawdry form of words that was much in vogue at the time. Perhaps they were impressed by the darkness of the material and the seemingly inspired chaos of the narrative; today I can only say I am surprised by the many friendly voices and respectful opinions this unripe product of a twenty-five-year-old tyro managed to garner.

It remained a so-called *succès d'estime*. My grim financial situation was unaffected. I left Munich in a hurry, firstly to get away from creditors, secondly because a love affair had stirred up so much gossip and odium towards me that my closest friends deserted me and respectable citizens crossed themselves on the pavement when I was pointed out to them. I knew hardly anyone in Vienna, half a dozen admirers, that was all, and admirers are only useful to you so long as you don't need their help. I had no idea what I was going to live on, since I had only random earnings, and arrogantly rejected the idea of employment. Luckily, I met rich people here and there, who not only had some sympathy for me, but who also had a degree of snobbishness about them; they allowed me from time to time to borrow money from them.

In a quiet part of town behind the Votivkirche, on Lackierstraße 8, I rented an enormous room for myself, furnished, it would appear, from a junk shop, and rather negligently at that. I slept through my days and spent the nights with professional colleagues either in cafés, or else (it being summer) in the Prater, home at the time of a curious institution called Venice-in-Vienna, a ridiculous aping of Venice's bridges and canals. I walked home in the wee hours, singing loudly to myself in the deserted streets, or, like a drunken student, running the end of my cane clatteringly along the metal shutters of the shops.

Then one day I had enough of the city, and I picked up my rucksack and went a-roving: over the Moravian plain, into the mountains in the south, into the Bohemian Forest, along the Danube, always on Shanks's pony, rarely with more than ten crowns in my pocket, enjoying my own company or that of some comrade I found myself with. For instance, there was a young man by the name of Konrad Fürst, who had joined forces with me early on in my Viennese time out of a kind of fealty; he had writerly ambitions, though he was a pretty superficial fellow who liked best to play the cavalier, and had little going on upstairs but womanizing. I was impressed and somewhat surprised that he agreed to go on the road with me, and put it down to his admiration. I have always been vulnerable to such an approach. Then there was another man, David Muschilov, a red-haired Jew, who wrote theatre and exhibition reviews for the papers, and took himself for a witty writer, and oh-so incorruptible. He was by no means as incorruptible as he thought, and his wit soon got on my nerves. I have always been chary of witty people. But they were good companions, both of them, and I won't forget them; they had faith in me, and were happy to share their bread and their money with me, and were always up for pranks of one sort or another.

Overall, then, I was content with the change in my circumstances, and in the more relaxed atmosphere, and among the friendlier Austrians I felt myself reborn. When autumn came and put an end to my gipsy existence I returned to my uncomfortable quarters, which the landlady had let me keep in return for a small deposit, hired – on top of the sorry furniture I had –

an old pianino with brown keys and, to the dismay of sensitive ears, would bang away on it for hours on end. Then, all of a sudden, I felt in the mood for another prose work. I had supposed my little rivulet had run dry, but now when I came home at night from the society of my motley friends, I would stay up and write for two hours each night and give myself over to my creations.

## The effect of a book

Oddly it was through her father that Ganna first got to know about *The Treasure Seekers*. One of Professor Mevis's colleagues had pressed my book into his hand, and told him this was something he absolutely had to read. The Professor growled back that he didn't read novels, but agreed to take the book anyway. Reluctantly he started to read it, was captured in spite of himself, and when he had finished it he was forced to admit that it 'had something'. So he said to me afterwards. A crime story was professionally interesting to him as a lawyer; admittedly, that was just the frame for a deeper narrative that was inaccessible to him. He had no feeling for the artistic qualities the book certainly possessed; the impassioned diction and the grim atmosphere of the whole were disagreeable to him. Even so he is supposed to have remarked to the colleague who recommended the book to him: 'Not bad; someone worth keeping an eye on.' Quite some praise from a constitutional lawyer.

Ganna happened to walk into the room and saw the book on the table. She had heard about it, of course, it had been on her list for a long time. She picked it up; it was seven at night, and by three in the morning she had finished it. Gobbled it up. Avidly, the way you guzzle an elixir, for fear of losing a single drop.

What was it about it that so got to her? Why was she compelled to imbibe it so hungrily? I often asked myself that, later. After all, it was incredibly remote to her, it must surely have alienated her, been more off-putting than attractive to her – if beguiling, then only in a technical way, accessible only to one who had dwelt in a similar state himself. Whichever, her sense of the book was indelible and unquestionably genuine. She often talked about it afterwards, and it is not impossible that each time she slightly overstated her initial response, in roughly the way a lottery winner might, when describing the prophetic twitch in his fingers. Certainly, some sixth sense was involved, some sense of affinity. Shortly afterwards she came across my picture in a publisher's catalogue. She cut it out and pinned it up on the wall next to her bookcase. As she did so, she claimed (and others of her literary set confirmed it) she swore not to rest until she had met me in person. The picture, I have to say, was rather flattering. It's gone missing since, but unless I'm mistaken it made me look every inch a robber chief.

## A go-between is found

Things developed as follows. In the summer of 1899, Ganna learned from one of her friends that I had been living in Vienna for more than a year. He is intensely private, though, she was told, and it's not easy to get to meet him. Ganna had rather overblown ideas about writers, and her first notion was of a sort of court, surrounding some heir to the throne. When people in a better position to know broke it to her that I was a poor wretch, she ignored them. She hated to be disturbed in her fantasizing. She would have written to me had she not supposed my flat was awash with such letters, like a post office. If her letter remained unanswered, that would mean she had no chance of getting to me. She researched my circle and sought the acquaintance of individuals who had been named to her. She told me once she had no doubt she would be singed by a ring of fire that surrounded me. She heard more and more about me, met people who knew people whom I saw on a daily basis. She envied these people, she was jealous of them. In the first letters I got from her there was a lot about that. One day – by now it was the middle of winter – she happened to visit an old friend of her mother's, one Frau von Brandeis. This lady kept a salon, as the expression goes, albeit in a rather modest way. I had taken a few meals there. Ganna's mouth always spilled what was in her heart, and so she confessed to the old bluestocking what she so devoutly wished for. Frau von Brandeis said: 'Well, if that's all it is, help is at hand. I'll ask him round. Can you come to supper on Tuesday?' She told me herself that Ganna in her happy shock changed colour and silently kissed her hand.

## First meeting

An odd habit from which I still suffer compels me to follow each call, each summons, as if I was somehow afraid of hurting or even offending anyone who called out to me in vain. Sometimes there's nothing behind it but my inertia: you carry on in the direction in which you've been pushed. So I accepted unhesitatingly when Frau von Brandeis invited me, even though I had been horribly bored at earlier visits to her house.

I have no clear recollection of the impression Ganna made on me that first evening. I have a picture of a rather garishly clad, fidgety, restless young girl. I am unable to say whether she was well dressed or not. I didn't have a way of telling. She loved loud colours, and a picturesque framing of little scarves and flutter-ing bows. Over supper, with a sidelong look at me, she told how she'd almost fainted on the stairs. Her hasty and excitable speech was disagreeable to me, but Frau von Brandeis had prepared me for the degree of excitement she would be plunged into by my presence, so I took a clement view of her excessive vivacity. Two or three times I glanced at her fleetingly. She had a plain face with strained features, freckled complexion and intensely peering blue eyes; the cheekbones were prominent; very attrac-tive though were the sensuous mouth with splendid teeth, and a charming innocent laugh. Her uncommonly small, twitchy hands displayed recurring gestures that had something jagged and assertive about them, which she became aware of at inter-vals and tried to moderate.

This fairly accurate portrait was probably a composite, based on a number of meetings. To begin with, my interest in Fräu-lein Ganna Mevis was slight. I was more mindful of my work than of my surroundings. I am said not to have been prepossess-ing or entertaining myself – hardly a man of the world, then. At that time, when I went out, I wore a knee-length set of tails, with shiny cuffs and elbows and not all that clean either, an ancient garment that was not improved by a picturesquely looped black necktie. The meal over, I adjourned to the smok-ing room, sat down in an uncomfortable little armchair and soon found myself joined by Ganna. I had expected her. We started talking. Much of what she said astonished me. I forgot her excitability, her electric movements. I thought she was orig-inal. There was a mixture of foolishness and acuity in what she said. The charmingly innocent smile sometimes made me smile. I was most moved by the seeker in her, the pleading suit, the groping about her as in a dream. Strange creature, I kept think-ing. But by the time I was on my way home I had forgotten about her. And when I remembered her urgent words and looks, the burning devotion that imbued her whole being, I felt a pang of unease.

## Letters, hints, magical words

The next day, I got a *pneumatique* from her. Why the rush, I asked myself. There was nothing pressing in it. The letters were just as urgent as her speech. Big, jagged, impetuous characters that resembled a meeting of conspirators. I can't remember if I wrote back. It seems to me it was only the third or fourth letter that induced me to give her an answer. Because she wrote to me almost every day. Always *pneumatiques*. A few lines, with obvious attention to style. I thought sardonically: writing letters to a writer is surely an education in itself. And the content? Atmospherics: happy wonderment at the new turn in her life; a plea to me not to forget her; a friendly greeting because it was a nice day; anxious inquiries about my state, because she'd had a bad dream about me. She wasn't short of things to say.

And what possessed me to answer her? I don't know. If you feel vastly, boundlessly admired, you drop your guard. Even the most resolute misanthrope has a spot where he falls prey to vanity. And I was anything but a misanthrope. Even after numerous bad experiences, I only started to get suspicious of someone after they'd wrung my neck, metaphorically speaking. Perhaps Ganna had little hope that I would reply, but from the moment I first wrote back she had acquired in perpetuity a right to be answered. And so a man gets ensnared.

I had the bad habit of leaving letters carelessly lying about the place. At that time, I was involved with an actress, a nice, clever woman. One day she picked up one of Ganna's notes to me, read it in spite of my objections, smiled ironically and said:

'You'd best beware of her.'

'Why, what do you mean?'

'I can't explain, it's just a feeling I have. Watch yourself.'

She was the first to warn me. Many years later, I still think about that.

At a private view of the Secession, I ran into Frau von Brandeis. She asked me what I thought of Ganna Mevis. She sang her praises in the loftiest tones. A clever girl; ideal temperament; heart of gold; the family an impeccable collection of bourgeois virtues. She plucked at my sleeve and whispered that anyone who managed to land one of the Mevis girls was made for life; the Professor could afford to give each of his daughters a dowry of 80,000 crowns! I freed myself from the silly gossip, but I have to admit it didn't do me any good, the number caught in my brain. It's just the way it is: a man who doesn't know how he'll pay the rent at the end of the month can easily fall to calculating that a vast sum like that will keep him modestly in a garret for the next sixty or seventy years. A flip response, nothing more, and yet . . .

In the meantime I had had a few more meetings with Ganna in neutral places. Complaisance breeds complaisance. But I must confess I liked her better with each further meeting. There was something irresistibly impetuous about her that appealed to my own rather viscid nature. I thought she was an uncommonly harmonious and consistent character. The only thing that bothered me was the continual hyperbole. One day she told me the reflection of the book I was working on was clearly visible in my brow. I replied chilly that I preferred people with dry hands and a dry manner, clamminess was apt to become slippery. She was alarmed – only to give me her rueful and passionate assent. Then that in turn became too much. It was like standing on the pedal while playing a simple folk tune. Another time, on a stroll together, I was thunderstruck when she told me about the book I was writing at the time. As I hadn't discussed it with anyone, I had every reason to be surprised. It was a story of decline, set in a particular social stratum, and carried by a contemporary Parsifal. 'Only you can write it,' she said stirringly, 'no one else.' I had the uncomfortable feeling of a housewife finding a cat in her larder. The door was shut, the windows locked, there was no hole in the walls, therefore something inexplicable has taken place. Divination? Maybe. With Ganna it would have seemed possible. It was her way of saying: I am inside your work, it's my destiny, it belongs to me. Perhaps I was overplaying some vaguer formulation of hers; also the exposé was in the air; conceivably she had drawn some hint of the contents from me, though I can't remember such a thing. Whatever, Ganna had something of a sorceress about her. I thought she was a white witch, or a strong, energetic and courageous little fairy. And the fact that she asked, with maidenly humility, to be close to me, my scant conversation, my austere instructions – that did me good, because I was not spoiled.

## What was bound to happen happens

She persuaded me to visit her at her parents' house. We agreed on a date and a time, and Ganna made preparations as for a visit from the Prince of Wales. She served notice to her sisters that her tête-à-tête with me was not to be disturbed at any price. Later on, I heard complaints from Irmgard and Traude about the quarantine that Ganna so rigorously imposed. They would have liked very much to meet me and talk to me, but Ganna hadn't allowed it. When I stepped into the hall, a figure vanished with lightning speed through an open door, but a split second was enough for me to catch the astonished flash of a pair of black eyes. And when, some time later, I was back in the hallway, escorted by Ganna, I caught a glimpse of another fleeing shade and another astonished pair of eyes, this time blue.

I became a regular visitor to the house. Ganna received me with delicious sandwiches and excellent tea. I had determined the episode would end by the time I set out on my next summer wanderings. But in that case I shouldn't have made Ganna privy to my plans; shouldn't have told her the names of all the places where I was planning to stay. Not just that either; in my mindless indiscretion, I also told her that I had arranged to meet a few friends at the upper Mondsee in early autumn, and then go to ground in a farmhouse, to finish my book. Hot with joy, she replied how wonderful, her mother had rented a small villa nearby, on the Attersee, where she and her sisters would probably be staying until October, and if she got on a bike it was only half an hour. I was alarmed. My gabbiness annoyed me. But what should I have done? You have to talk about something, and if you have a certain respect for big subjects and questions that – even if you ask them with childish circumspection – are not really answerable because they take you into personal realms, then all that's left are bald facts. Somehow Ganna always managed to draw me out; tears would spring to her eyes when I turned her down kindly or gave her an evasive reply. She had no one she could trust, she told me animatedly, she was a stranger in the bosom of her family, her sisters were her enemies, her parents didn't understand her, she was lost if I didn't give her more of the manna that was the only food for her soul. Such words moved me. I had seen that she was the Cinderella in her brood.

'Will you promise to write to me?' she asked with hungry, avid expression.

It was always all or nothing. I wavered. I ducked. She followed up. In the end I agreed.

'All right,' I said, 'I'll see.'

With a strange, predatory movement I will never forget, she seized my hand.

'Really? You will write to me?'

Suddenly I felt afraid, but the charming, innocent, beatified smile allowed me to think the promise was not dangerous.

## *Some rather belated glosses*

And then there were more letters. Express letters. The jagged, indomitable characters marched in. They formed up into words, and the words spoke of everlasting gratitude and obligation and inner kinship and a deep sense of belonging. I was startled. I wondered: are all these things so facile that they can be set down on paper so instantly and glibly? To tell the truth, my eye tended to fly over them. The sound of the big oppressive words loitered in my ear. Sometimes, when I was opening one of her notes, it was as though I had to push away her little hand that reached for me with greedy grasp. That summer I still had a way out, if only I'd been honest with myself about my situation. I wasn't. I deceived myself instead. Freedom is an inestimable thing; if you allow it to be tricked away from you, it means trouble, you will have to pay and pay until the bloody sweat spurts from your eyes. But then I had lost my mother when I was still a child.

When I look back at myself, it seems to me that a nature like mine can only be judged in its vertiginous dreaminess. All my flaws and good points are anchored there. I was always stood so close to reality – like a man working at a machine, in front of its wheel – and yet I didn't see it. I exhausted myself in the effort to see it, but the pictures I saw, the experiences I had, were utterly transmuted by the galvanic process that befell them in my imagination. Something light became heavy, something cheerful became murky, warnings found me deaf, even pain and joy were like two puffs of breath on a sheet of glass. I was so deeply caught up in myself, in my Rip Van Winkle-like sleep, that the need to act concussed my entire being, shooing my soul up out of its remote hiding-place, and demanding it set out on a hundred-mile march.

This may explain something. Because when, one September morning, Ganna jumped off her bicycle in front of the isolated farmhouse where I was staying in the attic, and I rushed down to greet her, I didn't see a flushed, purple face, a sweat-drenched blouse, a wild, almost fevered regard; to see that would have been disagreeable to me and would have repulsed me for a long time. No, I saw a being I had created and imagined. I felt pity. Perhaps it was the transferred pity of writers, when they turn a real-life character into a figure of their imagination and clothe it in the mystery that is the only quality that provokes and sustains them. Poor, tormented creature, I said to myself, and I could feel my heart beating for her. Here was a woman in flight, a lover, stepping up to meet me, a victim, a persecutee begging for shelter, seeking a shoulder to cry on, deeply inflamed, in need of a little tenderness and soothing. Should I have shut myself away, should I have remained aloof and said: begone, there is no room for you in my life? There was room. Of course, the fact that I saw and sensed her the way I did in my self-sacrificial compassion, this single pregnant moment that bore the seed of thirty years – that was also in part Ganna's doing, her over-powerful will, her dazzling sorcery. But I wasn't to know that, back then.

## Almost a confession

Rowing across the lake with her, strolling together through the autumnal woods, I talked to her about my past. I was now twenty-seven years old, and all I had experienced thus far were hardship and worry. To tell the truth, every single day had been a struggle to get food, to find a bed to sleep in, to put shoes on my feet. I omitted the details, the humiliating wealth of tawdriness. Why spread it out at her feet? I felt too ashamed. It would have sounded somehow accusatory. Perhaps I had a sense as well that she wouldn't take it the right way, someone like her, grown up in luxury. Moreover I had a dim notion she liked such confessions, as though they reinforced her in a hope I didn't mean to encourage. But I must have gone beyond what I had it in mind to say, because at times I caught her looking at me like a mother her sick child. I talked a lot about my wanderings and about how it was only in the countryside that I could stand my isolation, which in the city crushed me; all I got from the city was a crust of bread, and sometimes not even that. How did I avoid despair? What kept me going? Where does a perfectly irrational tinge of optimism come from? What sort of inner light shows me the way? Why didn't I let myself slip into the darksome river where I was cowering in my fear of mankind? Why do I not curl up and die when my brain can produce only revulsion and dread? Well, you see, Ganna, I will have said, it's strange, something quite unaccountable happens. Even those moments of wanting to die come with a small flame that causes the heart to flicker into life. Then a friend shows up, whom you'd forgotten all about. Then you meet a girl for the first time, and she looks at you, and smiles at you, even though she knows everything about you. The least happiness is something so exquisitely precious in the lower depths. At such a moment I fell into the love affair for which I gave up three whole years of my life, as into a bottomless well, and that, once it was painfully over, left me as poor in my soul as I always was in my flesh . . .

### How does Ganna take it?

These words, or similar, I will have spoken to Ganna; of course I no longer remember them exactly. What about her? To begin with, she was stunned. Here I must make mention of something odd. Ever since the first days of our acquaintance, she had kept a notebook about me. It was full of thoughts and reflections about my uninteresting person, complicated interpretations of my being, and pages and pages on the moral character of my work. I only heard about it years later, and I won't deny that I laughed heartily when she showed me the volume. Typical Ganna, I said to myself; falling in love and writing a thesis about it at the same time. But at the point when I came up with such a response, I was already more critical of her. It was a fact with Ganna that her notions of life came out of books, and they stood to reality like a painted tiger to the beast that lays your shoulder open with a swipe of its paw. Still, my talking had stirred her up, and I had the feeling too that I wasn't as inaccessible to her as I had been previously. Her emotion was unmistakable. It dawned on her that she had something to offer me, which she hoped I wouldn't be able to dismiss out of hand. My surroundings, my life, were bound to let her know that my situation basically hadn't improved since. I was living off expectation, off faith in an inner source, off the charity of friends and the carefully measured generosity of my publisher. I had no financial security. My entire existence was speculative, was a matter of plans and schemes. My face was etched with worry.

The melancholy that from time to time would overwhelm me couldn't be plucked from my eyes. In Ganna's hot head that may have given rise to some serious questions. What did she have money for? Why had the Lottelotts worked so hard to amass their fortune? Let her have it. It's in her gift to help the person she loves. And not just help him, she can restore him to his correct, sovereign height. She is jubilant, she has the key to this man on whose behalf she is prepared to go out and conquer the whole world. I didn't misunderstand the shining eyes and the speaking looks. But patience, Ganna, patience: do you propose to take what you call your wealth, today or tomorrow, and merely drop it at his feet, unconditionally and impulsively and without regard to yourself, and without reference to any of the usual contracts and obligations? It would be a splendid impulse, whether it were possible or not. Or is some forfeit not required – in fact, wouldn't the person, the future, the whole man from head to toe have to serve as your collateral? Speak!

It's true, this question was never spoken out loud; it only hovered uncertainly over our conversations. But it seemed to me that Ganna didn't understand its deeper implications. Why should the man not furnish the security, the pledge, she clearly was saying to herself, since all his difficulties would be resolved at a stroke, all his darknesses dispelled? If he only declares himself willing, then she will make him deliriously happy, then she will guard him like the apple of her eye, then she will be his slave, his exchequer. His muse, the guardian of his fame, the proclaimer of his greatness. All for him, say her shining eyes and her imploring looks; her dreams, her ambition, her gifts, her life, all for him.

But really I was still clueless.

## *Because it's new*

Until one day she came out with it. Without preamble and with the same courage with which she plonked herself on her bicycle and pedalled off, even though she'd never properly learned how to. I was stunned. For the longest time, I wasn't sure what exactly she meant. She took care not to be explicit. She was nervous. But she kept going back and starting over again. Each time it was a shade more graspable, with more eloquent descriptions of the practical possibilities, more excited dwelling on the splendid prospects for my life and work that she was able to predict with visionary fire. When I think back on it today I have to smile, because by instinct she was doing exactly what a shop-keeper does, feigning reluctance to show his most precious stock, and only putting it out on the counter once he's worn the customer down with his patter. When I finally caught her drift, I had no idea what I could decently say. Nothing like this had occurred to me, not remotely. It was like someone suggesting I might like to move to the moon. I laughed. I treated the whole thing as an extravagant joke. I said that where marriage was concerned, I might just be the least suitable man in the whole of Europe.

In the way of these things, her arguments started getting to me after a while. If I was aghast the first day, by the second I was just annoyed, and by the third a little impatient. I couldn't always avoid her stuttering suit, her fiery offer, her willingness to make herself useful that caused her to tremble like a fever. Not always. After all, she had proved to me – though not ulti-mate proof – that she didn't hold anything back. It couldn't possibly be calculation. Her tenderness was gushing. Her desire to please me, to anticipate my every wish, was nigh on obses-sive. I regularly felt ashamed. If I'd only guessed that my shame was an unconsciously erected barrier, perhaps I would have behaved differently. I thought she was funny in her wildness and her muddle-headed dreaminess; funny but lovable. You can find a woman lovable without loving her; that's a dangerous grey area. When I gave her my hand, she could sit there charmed as though that moment was a singing eternity, then she would lean over and press her lips to my fingers with a reverence that sometimes made me say: oh, don't do that, don't bother. It hadn't happened to me before. The woman I loved before, the first time, boundlessly, to the point of folly and even crime – yes, crime – had coolly endured my passion, and shamelessly cheated and exploited me. The wound I received from her had continued to fester. What a tonic to receive, for once, instead of always giving, thanklessly giving, and being mocked for it.

## Will you have me or not?

For the moment I let things take their course. I didn't say yes and I didn't say no. Yes would have turned my life upside down. Think of a solar system where a pert comet suspends the law of gravity. And no . . . no was tricky. Not that I wasn't hungry for some of the fleshpots of Egypt. I wouldn't deny that I was tired. Tired of the unpaid bills, the sheepish faces of my acquaintances when I tried to pump them for a loan, the holes in my socks that no one darned, the frayed cuffs of my shirts and the daily humiliations I had to take from people who despised nothing so much as poverty. It would have been nice to have no more experience of bitterness and offence, to go to bed at night without racking my brain about how I was going to pay for the privilege. It would have been nice to be freed from worries. Ganna wasn't wrong when she argued that all these tormenting details would slowly wipe me out. But just for that, it didn't occur to me to squinny at the groaning tables of the rich, and their nicely stocked wine cellars, and their jealously guarded safes.

It was one of my most disastrous qualities that, faced with a self-willed person, I would lose out because the phenomenon of willpower in and of itself would put me into such a state of amazement that I could generally only come to the decision my opposite number had made for me. I would tell myself I had done my bit, and was glad that there was no more back-and-forth. And Ganna decided for me. During those days her eyes had the sort of tunnel vision of athletes so set on victory they can see nothing but the finishing-tape. What was she so afraid of, why was she in such a hurry? I tried to calm her down. She thanked me exorbitantly, but it looked as though, inside, she was hurt and sore. I sensed how very much she was at the mercy of her drives, and if I wasn't to stand in front of her as a poor bungler, I had to try and spring her from her jail. And, in so doing, I was clamped in chains myself.

One rainy afternoon she turned up on her bicycle again, panting and exhausted, flung herself at me, clasped my shoulders in her hands and stared at me as though she was on her way to the scaffold within the hour. I asked her in alarm what the matter was, but she merely closed her eyes and shook her head. Then she broke away, ran out to the little balcony, leaped onto the balustrade, turned round to me and, with a hysterical jingle in her voice, said:

'If you don't take me, I'm going to jump into the lake; I swear I will. Either you're going to marry me, or I'll jump.'

'Ganna!' I appealed. The house was on the lake. The water smacked against its western walls. A jump from twenty feet was no laughing matter. She was certainly capable of it. 'Ganna!' I called out again. She looked at me, half-blissful, half-fanatic, and spread her arms out. I caught her by the ankle and said reluctantly:

'Please don't, Ganna.'

And she: 'Will you have me or not?'

I didn't know whether to laugh or be cross. 'All right, I will, I will,' I said hurriedly, if only to put an end to the upsetting scene, but even as I said it I had the feeling I had swallowed poison. She jumped back, dropped to her knees in front of me and covered my hand with kisses.

Later, much later, I thought about that episode a lot. In one way, I thought, it wasn't all that unlike a stick-up with a revolver. Hands up or I shoot. Whether the gun was loaded or not was immaterial. It wasn't always possible to tell. Bad if it was, worse somehow if it wasn't. But at the time it all happened, I didn't have a clue. The notion that it might be a trick didn't occur to me. Trick was too coarse a word for what it was, too. I saw a woman in the grip of elemental feeling. I can't say whether it was vanity with me, or pity, but I said to myself I mustn't push her away from me, I might destroy her for good. I thought I couldn't be responsible if she came to some harm. I admired her bravery, her resolve, her bold all-or-nothing. And strangely enough, my blurted yes hung on a sensual appeal. As I clutched her slender ankle, I had the feeling I was holding her whole shaking, burning body in my arms. She seemed so frail to me, so delicate. Frailty and delicacy in women has always moved me and inflamed my blood. Hitherto, I had tended to duck my head under the storm of her feeling.

I don't know if it might have been wiser not to say the thing about the revolver. In her inner confusion, she couldn't distinguish between what was admissible and what went beyond. She was in the grip of passion, blind, animal passion. The stone tumbling down over a precipice doesn't think about whether it's going to strike some poor walker down below. And her passion, her dumb momentum, was like a force of nature to me.

## Fedora

There had been a little group of us there, which, because the season was advanced, had begun to dwindle. Now only my friend Fedora Remikov was left, a young pianist from Moscow, and, with her, Dr Eduard Riemann, an exceptionally clever and well-read man of my own age – philosopher, scholar, well-off playboy. I liked him more and more; rarely have I met a clearer head and a more unimpeachable spirit. Those two, who were close, had noticed my distrait and unhappy mood, and as they had seen me several times in Ganna's company, they thought she might have something to do with it. Fedora put it to me directly. I avoided the question, but one day I asked her whether I might introduce Ganna to her. I wanted to get her opinion. I wanted to know what impression Ganna would make on such a pure and unpartisan being. We arranged to have tea together. Riemann was to be present as well. The experiment went pretty badly wrong. Ganna was terribly excited. She had the feeling she was to be examined by my friends. When she appeared, her demeanour was like that of a defendant in court. In the effort to show her best, she cramped up. Fedora sensed the strain she was under and looked at her sympathetically. Conversation happened to turn to the then much-read book *The Rembrandt German* and a discussion developed between Ganna and Eduard Riemann, who had no great admiration for the work; if I remember correctly, he described it as a set of glib paradoxes to please a bourgeois readership. Ganna argued with him. Unfortunately, she was too vehement. She was no match for Riemann's knowledge and superior logic, but she was unwilling to face it, and talked like a teenaged philosopher. Riemann bounced good-humouredly back and forth on his chair. His replies were gentle but devastating. Fedora stayed out of it. When her eyes met mine, there was a questioning look in them. I admired Ganna's pluck, her reading and her ability to think on her feet. The disapproval of my friends upset me. It was as if I were being misunderstood, as if adverse circumstances kept Ganna from showing herself in her true light, and I identified with her.

Ganna had sensed that she was not making the hoped-for impression on Fedora and Riemann, and so she sought to do better. She shouldn't have bothered. God knows what made her think she had to gain a supporter in Fedora. That was already proof of her bad instincts. She always behaved as though she could force people to like her. She brought Fedora little bunches of flowers, and sent her notes with vehement declarations of undying love. To begin with, she had thought there was more between Fedora and me than mere friendship. When Fedora straightened her out with a few cool words, in more or less the way you correct something misreported in a newspaper, Ganna threw herself at her and kissed her. An unpardonable mistake. Shortly afterwards, on the eve of Ganna's departure for Vienna, when Ganna had come to say goodbye, it was Fedora's turn to make a mistake. She was foolish enough to counsel Ganna against marriage with me, and tried to talk her into giving up the idea.

She said: 'If not for your sake, then for his.'

Ganna replied with flashing eyes: 'What do you think you're playing at, Fedora? How can you talk like that? Alexander and I belong together for ever and ever.'

Fedora told me about it a few days later, with a cold chuckle. I can still see her, leaning against the grand piano, with her white handkerchief by her mouth. Because she suffered from morbid obesity, and was prone to asthma attacks while playing, she was in the habit of keeping a handkerchief impregnated with some solvent to her mouth. In spite of her fatness, she was an attractive person; on top of the outsize body there was a real Bellini head with clever, piercing eyes. She asked me what would happen now, how things stood between Ganna and me. I said Ganna was going to talk to her father. She wanted to know whether this step had my approval. And when I said it did, then whether my conscience was clear. I became impatient, and accused her of being unfair to Ganna, and of failing to understand her magnanimous nature, and of being peevish and feminine herself. She shrugged her shoulders and replied quietly: 'These are subtle matters, my friend, incredibly subtle matters . . . '

The next morning I got a note from her. I kept it for years and years, until I finally lost it during the move to Ebenweiler. She was worried about me, she wrote. I ought to consider very carefully the step I was contemplating. I should examine my reasons, wait, not hurry anything, she begged me. 'You must love your future,' she went on, 'you must love it the way a woman cherishes her unborn child. You are carrying a huge responsibility. You are taking an extraordinary risk. You must respect what fate has in store for you. I am very concerned. It is the bitterest of disappointments when a friend fails to keep what he promised to friendship, because he promised it also to the world. If you have already tied the knot, then that to me is a form of betrayal, and I don't want to see you again.'

The sentences stuck in my memory. But they didn't have the effect that Fedora meant them to have. I was cold inside. I looked for reasons that were nothing to do with Fedora's blameless nature. I put myself completely and not without anger on Ganna's side. It appeared to me that it wasn't enough to return her love; no, I also had to be her knight and protector. The next day, I heard Fedora and Riemann had left.

## Ganna swears

There's something I've forgotten to tell, although it has no particular importance. Only at the time it had a certain significance for me, who was so short of worldly wisdom. The last evening before our separation, we were sitting by the lake. After a long silence I turned to her and said:

'Well, all right, Ganna. We'll do it your way. But on one condition. You must solemnly swear to release me if I should ever ask to be released.'

Ganna, the innocent child, the offended and mistreated child, answered reproachfully:

'Oh, Alexander, how could you think I would ever refuse! I wouldn't be worthy of you if I was like that!'

She looked at me with her maidenly eyes and hand upraised, and swore to God. I was eased.

Believe it or not, I was eased. What a failure to understand the word, and the effect of the passage of time, and the meaning of God's name in a philosophically enlightened soul like Ganna's! It was a beginner's error. Would a man in love have required such assurance, and would a woman, wanting to keep him, not have given it by the sun and moon and God and all his angels? The passing years make a mockery of the gravest oath, and memory is an eager bawd.

Then, when she was gone, I thought of her very tenderly. There were moments in which I took my feeling for love, but then I would say to myself: love is a ball of mercury, the pursuit of which costs half a lifetime; if you try to pick it up, it breaks apart, you never get all of it. Comradeship appealed to me. Harmony of two souls, I tried to convince myself, makes love dispensable. It can't be a sin to obtain love, not if you're able to pay something for it. And what I was able to pay was in the form of tenderness, tender understanding, tender guidance, tender confidence. That was the way to go. I was convinced it was right. I didn't notice that I was losing myself in emotional casuistry.

## Astonishment in the Mevis household

Ganna had promised me she wouldn't talk about our engagement, but she couldn't control herself, and after three days everyone knew – her sisters, her mother, her relatives, her acquaintances. Frau Mevis made no secret of her grave doubts. Today I see things differently from thirty years ago; lots of things that were absurd looked all right to me. It was one of the tasteless absurdities of the time that in rich middle-class homes they would speak of misalliances, as if in the upper reaches of the aristocracy. The only person who was kept in the dark was the Professor. Frau Mevis trembled night and day. If he should withhold his consent, hideous scenes were bound to result, and she would be the one to get the blame. She bore some responsibility: she had failed to keep Ganna properly chaperoned. Her fear of her husband, which she had had from the beginning of their marriage, had by and by eroded her personality. She was under as much pressure as a sunken ship, under the water. It's only a matter of time till the hulk breaks into pieces. The more alert of her daughters had long observed the symptoms of mental illness in her. It was the illness suffered by maybe four-fifths of the women in bourgeois society, the illness of nothing to do, empty representation and constant pregnancies. The day Ganna went to her father to make her confession, and everything inexplicably passed off without *éclat*, the old lady heaved a deep sigh of relief. 'I thought he was going to kill her,' she said to Irmgard and Traude; 'an author; a man who is nothing and owns nothing. Truth be told, I don't understand my husband.' Irmgard reported it to me later.

How the Professor received his daughter's news calmly and without ire is something for which I have no explanation. For sure, he had read my book. He won't have taken me for quite such a hopeless and feckless individual as his wife did. But a writer of books with whom one might pass the time of day and an official son-in-law, those are two completely different human categories. Later, with deafening laughter, he assured me he hadn't believed a single word of what Ganna said to him; he was firmly convinced the fantastical creature was the victim of delusions, and he had first decided to wait to see whether I would turn up at all. 'Well, and then you turned up,' he crowed, and whacked me on the shoulder, making all my bones hurt. That gave him away. I could tell how delighted he was to be rid of Ganna. The other girls couldn't get over their surprise. They said: 'She's turned Alexander Herzog's head, she's turned Papa's head, she must have worked some magic.' In the swans' terms, working magic was what I felt to be Ganna's dark Pythian power.

## Celebration

I noted down the salient points of my conversation with the Professor in my diary at the time.

'So you want to marry my daughter?' he began, once I was sitting opposite him.

'I don't really want to,' I said, 'Ganna does.' He looked at me in astonishment.

'All right,' he conceded, 'then let's just say you have nothing against the idea in principle.'

'No, in principle.'

'Then we can move on to the practical side of the question. I assume you are able to provide for a wife.'

'I'm afraid I must destroy your illusions there, Professor. I can't even provide for myself.'

'Admirable honesty. But surely that's not an abiding inability?'

'You're wrong. I see no change in prospect.'

'Why is that? You are a well-known and much-admired writer.'

'But I still have no means.'

'Then what do you live on now?'

'Tick.'

'How high are your debts?'

'Around about 3,000 marks.'

'That's not so bad. You're still young. One day you will become successful.'

'Possibly so, but that would worry me.'

'Why so?'

'It would be a sign that I had compromised. With taste. With the fashion of the day. I don't want to make any compromises.'

'An admirable stance. But then how do you envisage a life with my daughter?'

'To be frank, Professor, I wouldn't be able to entertain the idea if I hadn't known she was well-off.'

The Professor laughed in his rackety way. 'You mean to say that *I'm* well-off?'

'Yes, I suppose so.'

'You're not afraid of the truth, are you?'

'That's my job, Professor. I don't care about money. I don't care about a certain standard of living. I want a life with Ganna. It's my belief that we're a good fit. But I would have to renounce her if it means I have to work for a living, in the bourgeois sense. Ganna understands that I must be free in that regard. Nor have I come to you to ask for Ganna's hand in marriage, as the expression goes, though that's maybe how it appears. I wanted to tell you frankly about my circumstances, because Ganna is utterly convinced that she will only be happy with me.'

'All right, that's Ganna. What about you?'

'I am extremely fond of Ganna. I have very high expectations of her. But for me marriage is not essential.'

'I understand. But you don't mean to tell me that you don't see yourself ever – even many years hence – attaining an income that accords with your gifts?'

'I don't think it's very likely. Not impossible. There are a few instances. The intransigence of a writer is sometimes not an obstacle. But we live in barbaric times, Professor.'

'I see. I didn't know that. I had the sense we were living in the lap of a happy, blooming civilization.'

'I'm afraid that's an illusion.'

The Professor got up. 'The interest on the capital sum I am giving my daughter should keep you both from starving. But that's all.'

'That's all we need.'

The Professor extended his hand to me and said warmly: 'In that case, we seem to be agreed. Welcome to the family.'

That same day he had a brief conversation with Ganna, at the end of which she left the room, laughing and crying with happiness.

## *Negro village*

Every family is its own hoover. Greedily it sucks into itself the stranger who has been enlisted into it and, inhibited by shyness, tries to resist. After I had met my five future sisters-in-law, my three brothers-in-law, all the various uncles and aunts, the grandchildren, the friends of the house, it took me a long time to sort them all out and remember their various names and titles. It was like a play with a large cast, where you have to keep the programme open on your lap to check who is onstage at any given moment. I forgot that I had a role myself. I had trouble with all this fraternization. I saw no good reason why I should suddenly be on 'Du' terms with people I didn't know from Adam. The automatism with which it was expected that I should astonish me. I learned numerous new customs. Most of what I did or said turned out to be in breach of these. They were supposed to be something sacred, but in the first days and weeks I thought they were more like the customs in a Negro village, and sometimes I had the feeling I was visiting such a village. The whole bustle intimidated me. The meals, the family days, the joint undertakings, the conversations were as noisy as they were arduous. Gradually, I became desensitized. Getting accustomed to something is generally thought of as a blessing, but myself, I'm not sure if it isn't rather a dulling of the senses and a blunting of the nerves. I was in their eyes a rough-edged individual and they enthusiastically went about filing me down. Eagerly and even a little flattered, they took me into the sacred ring of the family, but at the same time they were a little afraid of my stranger's ways and accommodated me in a sort of invisible cage, like an exotic beast that is shown to the public for money, no matter how tame it actually is and how little thought it has of running away.

These are all posthumous thoughts and I could add even more to them, were I not afraid that the roughness of my judgement today would contrast too much with the feelings and behaviour I had at the time. Because soon enough I completely belonged and was entirely theirs. In my new bod's naivety I allowed myself to be ensnared and filled full of their interests, woven into their relations, taught to like their tastes and actually to believe that their bustling Negro village was the whole world. I was thrilled with them. The luxury in which I was allowed to participate fogged my vision. Each of the magnificent villas where I was introduced seemed palatial to me. Every bank manager I met looked to me a man of limitless power. The tedium of their society somehow escaped me; the faces with the dull tension of people blowing soap bubbles with a straw and vying with one another who can make the biggest and gaudiest, escaped me. The fact that they were completely undiscriminating; that all their business dealings were somehow inconsequential; that they stuck together externally like burrs, while within there was no cohesion: I didn't see it, and if I did then I still allowed myself to be lulled to sleep by their lullabies. I didn't yet understand the law of the kraal, the mysterious power of the kraal, even though I was caught in its clutches. It was the same in every family: sisters, brothers, in-laws and their trail, nephews and nieces, more of them with each year – their weal and woe were the weal and woe of the kraal, the world outside was hostile, suspect and basically unknown. What was I so fascinated with? If you throw a lasso round the neck of a wild mustang, it starts to tremble and stands perfectly still. But was that really my situation? Was I not more of a deserter, a turncoat? I didn't account for myself. I can honestly say I didn't know. Of course, I was never entirely sure of myself either. This secret uncertainty will have been why I introduced my friend Riemann into the Mevis circle. The occasion was easy enough: I had promised

Ganna, her sisters and one of the brothers-in-law I especially liked that I would read them a few chapters from my new book. And so I did, and it seemed to me I could have no complaints about not being properly understood and appreciated. Or was it just Ganna's passionate rapture that blinded me to the effect on the others? Were they not a little like grown-ups listening indulgently to the breathless rigmarole of a small boy playing cowboys and Indians? Or like people watching the angels and devils projected by a laterna magica? Admittedly, there was one soul present in whom the seed unexpectedly took root: in Irmgard's. But that too I didn't know until years later.

## Gush

Ganna, meanwhile, was quite transformed. No more rebelliousness, no more tantrums, no more coffin nail. An obedient daughter, a loving sister. When her father came home in the evening she would run to his bedroom, pick up his fleece-lined slippers, kneel down at his feet and unlace his boots. In the morning she would stay in the kitchen, a place she'd previously shunned, the theatre of the anti-spirit, and try to learn what can be magicked up with flour, oil, green leaves, sugar and spices. It wasn't interesting, she was certainly never going to learn, she wouldn't even learn how to boil an egg; but it had to be done, it was the custom, those in the know insisted it was part of a good marriage. Under the influence of the literature of the day, as a faithful disciple of Nietzsche and Stirner, she had deeply despised family and family traditions. Now, though, the happiness that she carried in her breast like a sun gilded the least member of the household, the lowest servant. Even the old Kümmelmann woman, with whom she had lived in enmity ever since she had been able to think, enjoyed new-found respect from her. 'What have you done to our Ganna?' the sisters and the mother would ask me. 'She's unrecognizable.' When I was told stories of how disobedient, how difficult she had always been, of the mad pranks she would perform, I would assume an expression of disbelief, because I knew no other Ganna than the one I saw, my gentle, dreamy, smiling, mild and tender fiancée.

There was one thing that struck me as odd. How could it be that her brain, thus far crammed full of poetry, of famous names and idealism and ambition, now suddenly became a repository of twenty or thirty birthdays, deathdays, honorific days and family anniversaries? That overnight she found in herself a mawkish piety for the most distant of relations and would pay calls on obscure, long-lost cousins, twice removed, or on various mothers of various in-laws? The swans said: she is putting her happiness on display, she wants to show off with her Alexander Herzog. A malicious interpretation. Perhaps it was to make amends for past neglect. She had seemed to be a cheeky minx and an *enfant terrible* for so long that she was now compelled to try and make a good impression.

I don't know why this new trait bothered me. To me there was something cramped and driven about it, a bad mixture of piety and politicking. It got on my nerves. But I didn't have the courage to tell her. When she felt that I was displeased by something, she would lapse into despair and quiz me for so long until I chose to deny everything, so as not to see her woeful eyes any more. On one occasion, though, I was unable to repress my irritation. In a little lane in the old part of the city lived an ancient couple by the name of Schlemm, who in some hard-to-trace way were connected to a defunct branch of the Westphalian Lottelotts; there were other Lottelotts as well, but they hailed from Cologne. These Schlemms were incredibly dull; he was deaf and somewhat imbecile, she as chattersome as an old hen.

Ganna was courting them, agreeing with everything they said, patting their wrinkled hands, calling them Uncle and Auntie, raving about their wise serenity and their terrific characterful faces. One day I let her talk me into going round to see them. She said the dear old folks had only one wish left in this life, and that was to see me before they died. That was some line she'd got from somewhere. Well, I went with her, what was the big deal? It was like a puppet theatre, where all the puppets were talking gobbledygook. It was only half an hour but it went on for ever. But what tormented me was Ganna's absurd teariness. I just couldn't understand it. Where was the reason, the cause? Two soulless silly bags of bones, and all that emotion? 'I feel so sorry for them,' she justified herself later, when I was unable to repress my anger; 'Uncle has a bad liver and Auntie has been tending him for the past forty-three years.' She sent me a melting look from her big blue eyes and I felt a little scared, I don't know what of.

## The marriage contract

Between Christmas and New Year's Day, a few days before the beginning of 1901 and hence of the twentieth century proper, I was summoned by the Mevis family solicitor to his office at a given hour. When I turned up the Professor was already there, the solicitor, an efficient busybody with the face of a lance corporal, greeted me with a little show of ceremony, and on a leather sofa where he had cleared himself a little space free of legal files and law magazines sat the notary, with a Virginia cigar in a corner of his mouth. The last-named handed me a calligraphically perfect document – at that time typewriters were not yet in common use in law offices – and asked me to peruse it. I tried hard to oblige. The dowry was spelled out in figures; but the rights and duties of the respective spouses were described in utterly opaque legalese. There was also something about revocability in the event of a dissolution. I wasn't familiar with the word. Since I didn't ask, no one felt called upon to tell me. I was bored. I signed. I thought: the Professor is a man of honour, why shouldn't I sign? It seemed unreasonable to me to ask questions. Twenty-five years later, I understood what it was I had put my name to. A quarter of a century had to pass before the light went on and I saw I had been duped. In the spirit of family, of course, and loyalty. I could have asked. I could have gone to a lawyer myself. It never occurred to me to do so. It was my first encounter with a notary. A notary, I thought, is the embodiment of the law; this is all above board. I had to pay for thinking so.

## Riemann

With surprise and dismay I saw my friends begin to withdraw from me, Fürst and Muschilov as well, though they at least offered excuses when I suggested a meeting. I sensed the reason of course: they disapproved of my marriage, there were all sorts of gossipy rumours about Ganna going the rounds, one man even sent me an indignant letter in which – almost like Fedora – he terminated our friendship and made the absurd remark that I was about to throw my life away. I tossed the letter into the fire. What pained me more was that Eduard Riemann had been avoiding me for some time. I wanted to clear the air, and since I knew he went every evening to a chess club of which I too was a member, I went along there one night quite late, asked him into a room where we were alone together and had it out with him.

'I know what you hold against me,' I started violently, 'our mutual friend Fedora has set you against me. I don't understand. It's a conspiracy. What has Ganna done to incur your disfavour? Isn't it enough if I love her? Do I need your consent?'

'You're asking the wrong questions, my dear Alexander,' he replied with his strangely nasal, droning voice, 'that's not the situation. You have a couple of dozen friends, here and elsewhere, who are following your career with very specific expectations. High expectations, too. To them the thought of you selling yourself – I'm sorry to put it so bluntly – is just hard to take.'

'Me selling myself? Riemann! You're not serious. Selling myself! Think about what you're saying!'

'All right, what are we to think? It doesn't seem to us that Ganna Mevis is the right woman for you.'

'How not?'

'That's not easily explained. We're fearful for you. You're going off on a tangent. You're in the wrong setting. We're afraid you're acting against your better instincts.'

'Let me tell you, Riemann, there is no price for which I would, as you put it, sell myself. Don't you know me at all? Do I need to say that?'

'No, you wouldn't do it directly.'

'And how would I do it indirectly?'

'The forms are often veiled, but the possibilities of self-deception are limitless.'

'I have honestly and strenuously examined myself.'

'I believe you. Even so: undo what you've done. Go to India, go to Cape Town, go anywhere. If you don't have the money, I'll lend you whatever you need. I'll take the responsibility for settling the matter.'

'My God! What are you saying! What nonsense! It's too late for any of that.'

'I don't agree.'

'I . . . I can't live without Ganna.'

'That's a different matter, but I don't think that's true either.'

'What's this all about, Riemann? I'm not welded onto her. If things go wrong, I can always end it.'

Riemann looked at me with strange, benevolent scepticism. 'You never were much of a psychologist, Alexander,' he said. 'Do you really think you can get free of her?'

I was in consternation; I felt like fizzing up in rage, but he went on calmly:

'And one more thing, my friend. Did you ever take a good look at the mother? That woman is disturbed. And that's putting it mildly. With that in her genes . . . True, it's a large family . . . but Ganna is on the downward line. Her psychic balance . . . I'm not sure . . . if you had eyes to see . . . '

The innuendo was painful to me. I pushed the argument away from me. Unfortunately, that's always been my way with inconvenient arguments.

'I don't want to think about it,' I said, 'it's going too far, this is meddling in God's affairs.'

'We can't help ourselves, my friend; that's His way of setting us in motion.'

I didn't go to bed that night. First I walked the streets in wind and snow, and then I sat till dawn in a bar on the outskirts of town, among hauliers and market women.

## Wedding presents

I stood with Ganna in front of the pushed-together tables where our wedding presents were displayed. There were garish sofa cushions with Secession patterns, eccentrically shaped lamps, twisted bronzes, metal frog and dog candle holders, models of the Stefansdom and the Tomb of the Medicis as paperweights, nymphs with nozzles in their heads as perfume dispensers, Venetian gondolas as desk ornaments, gilded pine cone picture frames. And then there were useful, practical things, books, silver, porcelain, vouchers for linens and furniture. We weren't going to set up house immediately; we intended to go travelling for a year first. I was delighted with the presents. I had never had such a warehouse full of possessions, real possessions. All of it seemed beautiful and good. I didn't think it was real, but then what was real to me? Not even my shirt or my pen. The continual nodding association with people who took these fata morgana things for real was incredibly sapping. Not just that either. Sometimes I got the sense that it was killing something within me. I couldn't say what, but it was certainly killing something. It was no more than logical that they couldn't help taking true things for illusions; that was their nature. Here, at the present table, behind all this foolish pleasure in things, I was tormented for the first time by the fear that Ganna might have something to do with the little killings that I was supposed to agree to and introduce into my life. What else did the light in her eyes signify, or her jubilation? Certainly she lives with a divided consciousness, half among human beings, half up in the stars. A princess, getting hitched. A fairy-tale creature floating off into new realms of bliss. She no longer recognizes anyone. She mixes up faces and objects, and vice versa. If you wake up in the morning with the feeling that you're a rose, or a sunstruck cloud, then you can't speak in a normal way with human beings, then your speech is bound to be a little haywire. Pseudo Gothic, pseudo Baroque, pseudo Renaissance – what did it matter? They were proof of love, proof of victory. 'Look at this,' she said tenderly, 'this is from Auntie Jetta, and this is from Uncle Adalbert, and this is from Court Councillor Pfeifer, isn't it sweet of her to have thought of us!' And Ganna's delight communicated itself to me as though I'd been given a magic potion to drink.

## The wedding

And that worked on the day of the wedding as well, which was a snowy day in January. In my memory I have it as a day also of indescribable noise, for hours and hours. Squawking women, false male voices, clatter of plates, chairs being dragged, champagne corks popping, smells of meat, sweet and sour tastes on my tongue, incessant opening and closing of doors, and coming and going, dutiful telegrams, hands I have to shake, dry and moist, bony and fleshy, warm and cold, rough and smooth, supple and stiff. A humiliating and hurtful wedding, because official, formal language presumed to curtail personal freedoms: like reading a convict the prison rules. The image of Ganna, furthermore, done up in white, and seeming to float over the ground, and then sat at the table with the oddly shameful, conniving smile of a conventional bride. An image of her mother, wrapping her arm round my shoulder, pulling me over to a window seat where, surrounded by noise and bustle, with timid wandering eyes and an alarming laugh, she proceeded to tell me strange, unexpected things, a ghost at a party, heard by no one and ignored by all except me. This last was an insistent, drilling sort of impression.

Then the speeches. The brothers-in-law, showing off their culture and their reading; the friends of the house, who had taken pains to be droll; a colleague of the Professor's from the philosophy department, who in a thunderous voice, as for the opening of a monument, praised Ganna's virtues; a military man, an actual general – I had never yet shared a meal with a general – who toasted 'the splendid and promising young groom' and expressed the wish that he might 'continue to walk the paths of science and art'. All in all, when I think about it today, it was a concentrated parody of the social mores of the epoch. Life of a comfortable middle class condensed into a matinee performance, with musical accompaniment from a mildly soused four-piece band. But I didn't at all feel myself to be a dispassionate observer. No, I was in play, I was active and engaged. When at last the six daughters and the established sons-in-law plus half a dozen assorted grandchildren filed past the Professor's chair to kiss him on the forehead after his pithy concluding speech; when he then got to his feet, towering in their midst, the kingly patriarch and all-powerful overlord of the kraal, so that one imagined the future of the clan assured well into the next century, by which time his person would have become mythical and emblematic; and when Ganna, overcome by the greatness of the historical moment, sank against his chest and, sobbing, thanked him for everything he had given her, then I myself was moved, and looked at the red-bearded patriarch as if to my own patron.

There followed a hasty departure, drawing deep breaths of freezing air, the drive to the station in a bumping carriage, alone with Ganna, who was now Ganna Herzog.

*The Age of Certainties*

## Teething troubles of a couple

We travelled the length of Italy, with many stops, from the Tyrolean Alps down to Sicily. We were very happy.

I had never spent more than three days cooped up with another human being, male or female. Just as well I was used to small spaces and didn't feel constricted. We had agreed to travel on a very modest footing. Ganna thought it was wonderful to have a husband who carried his business around in his head and was able to settle his practical affairs in ten minutes or so at a restaurant table.

The new insouciance may have been a kind of dream; still, it entered my life as something unfamiliar. When a burden borne over many years suddenly slips off, one's state afterwards is not automatically easier. There is a period of adjustment. Different breathing is required. I had always had all the solitude I required; now I had none, neither by day nor at night. Ganna was always present, wanting to be seen and heard, protected and loved. And to love me back. If it were possible to dig love out of the ground, she would have dug it out, if only to prove to me how inexhaustible her supplies of it were.

But various things happen that are hard to avoid when your world is a room with two beds in it, and the space by the door and in the corners is all taken up with your suitcases. For instance, I'm sitting quietly reading a book. So as not to disturb me, Ganna creeps through the room on tiptoe. But then – oh dear! – there is a chair in her way, which she manages to upset. Crash. Or she knocks over a glass of water. Or a suitcase lid bangs shut. Thousand anxious apologies. She is a little unlucky. If she is unlucky, you have to comfort her. She lives in a permanent state of war with things. She loses her purse; horror. She drops a letter through someone's front door instead of in the letterbox; a mobile pillar of wailing. She needs comfort. It's not possible to be angry with her when she warbles up to complete strangers as if they were all her uncles and aunts; she's just made a mistake; she's absent-minded. Or when she takes as many books with her on a walk as you would need to pass a university exam. It's funny. You have to laugh. She sees that you have to laugh and she laughs along. But that doesn't mean that she does anything differently the next time. She lives in a world of Ideals. She's like the famous birds who try to peck at Apelles' famous painted grapes. I try to bring a little order to her being, a little consistency. It's hard. Ganna's is not one of those adaptive natures that are geared for experience. Experience is as baffling as, say, pain. I have a sense that I need to mould her. I ought to give her a form, because she has none. It took me a very, very long time to understand that it wasn't possible to form her. Not that she was too soft or too hard. Soft things and hard things can still be shaped. But something that is in between, that flows, that is jellied, that is forever changing its nature – that cannot be formed.

## Little soul

In her innocence she thought she just needed to give herself to the man she loved to make him happy. There wasn't much subtlety about her. She was incapable of giving herself completely, simply because her will was never entirely extinguished. She *wanted* to be will-less, but that was as far as it went: that was the seed of the calamity. By temperament, she was a force of nature, proof against any civilizatory intentions. All her life she took it for a brutal meddling in her character if anyone tried to rein in or refine the elemental strain in her. The very intention was baffling to her. And the drive, the blood was the only thing to keep in parlous balance her ethereal intellect and her earthiness. I understood intuitively that it would be wrong of me to rob her of its innocence.

Nor was I the man to tame her. I had such profound respect for the thus-and-thus-alone of any living creature that I couldn't summon up the courage to take the darkest innermost parts of a human and shape them and light them. It's not possible to be an educator if you have diffidence in your veins. Nor was I masterful in love, not least because my senses in their guilty darkness were unfree. All this requires to be said: it's the hidden source of all that follows, otherwise no one could understand how things took their subsequent course.

Guilt: the word makes me flinch, but from the very beginning there was guilt in my relationship with Ganna. I never felt any passion for her. I didn't realize it right away. It took me a while to understand. Once I had understood, I had to fight off Ganna's sudden surges of passion with secret dread. She misunderstood me. She had to misunderstand me, because otherwise she would have fallen out of the sky. I couldn't allow that to happen. I had to see that she stayed up there for as long as possible. It wasn't so terribly hard. She took refuge in fantasy. I was Robert Browning and she was Elizabeth Barrett. The model of a highly intellectual marriage made it possible for her to reinterpret my growing reluctance to give her the much-craved protestations of love as a metaphysical union. I had to admire the tenacity with which she managed to live in a fantasy. My admiration for her was altogether undiminished. I was able to discuss all my plans with her. Within a very short time she had mastered all the technical expressions of a hard-boiled novelist. When news I had from Germany left me in no doubt that my book was not only a critical but also a popular success (though that didn't lead to any great earnings for me, seeing as I'd changed publishers, and my former publisher was insisting on a large transfer sum and the return of unearned advances), I noticed that she lost the calm and equilibrium that had previously cladded her being like a sort of enamel. It appeared she was no longer so certain of me. I asked her directly if that was so. Reluctantly, she admitted it was. She thought it was her duty to keep the lures of the world and the blandishments of fame away from me. 'Whatever for?' I asked in astonishment. 'What are you afraid of?' She said she had no guarantees of a future. 'Do you need guarantees, Ganna?' Of course, she replied, the present wasn't enough. 'But surely,' I said, 'you can't carry me around with you like a kangaroo her joey?' Yes, she could, that was exactly what she wanted, she replied with her sweetly cunning smile. She wanted security. She hungered for more security. She admitted it. I stroked her hair. I called her little soul, the tenderest endearment the German language has to offer.


## Bank account and anangke

In Taormina we stayed in a hole-in-the-wall dive. There were bedbugs. The mosquitoes ate us alive, there were no nets. At night Ganna burned all sorts of incense, but that only made us choke with the reek and smoke. If we'd had just two lire a day more to spend, we could have lived somewhere human. Ganna didn't want to know. Keeping to budget was her biggest anxiety. Budget was one of the magic words that turned up on the horizon shortly after we were married, like so many glow-worms in the gathering dark. The concept 'budget' was linked to the concept 'bank account'. 'Bank account' was the biggest and mightiest of the glow-worms, and of course another magic word. Her father had dinned it into her never on any account to eat into her capital, not even to use a dime more than we had from the interest. 'Someone who eats into his capital will stop at nothing,' had been the Professor's awful watchword. Ganna was now parroting it. Her father, more revered the further he receded into the distance, was so to speak the high priest of 'capital', a revered fetish, and he kept his mighty hand over the mysterious institutions of those tamper-proof investment papers that were the basis of the bank account. So many securities.

Ganna knew of course that the majestically round figure of 80,000 crowns had already been reduced by the sum that had been necessary for the cancellation of my debts. She had come up with a financial plan to make good the missing amount. Following this plan, we were to use not the full four and a half per cent interest of 3,600 crowns, but only 3,000; the rest was to go to the capital, and any further expenses were to be defrayed from my income. I thought the plan was inspired. It called for extreme economies. Every bedbug and mosquito in Signor Pancrazio's wretched quarters was physical proof of the guarantee system of the head priest and the gilt-edged tabernacle. What touching lengths Ganna went to to prove to me that my ironic contempt for these divine securities was based on folly and ignorance. She spoke nobly of the ethos of self-restraint and the moral duty to twist the sword from the grip of fate, as it stood there menacing the noble-minded. Immersed in her Plato, the pencil in her hand to scribble in the margin of her copy, her girlish brow creased, she pointed to the irresistible force of anangke, before which everyone had to bow. I was impressed. I said she was right. Truth to tell, it wasn't me who was in charge of the money. Even if the bank account was kept in my name, I submitted to Ganna's economies without demurring. I was in the position of a man whom pride and self-respect kept from laying a hand on the preserve of others.

## A primal creature?

I undertook to climb Etna and had promised Ganna to be back by the evening of the third day. I got lost in the lava fields, moreover the weather turned and I was compelled to seek shelter in a shepherd's hut. That delayed my return by six hours. Ganna had been waiting for me in growing impatience. By six o'clock she had alerted Signor Pancrazio and his household. Two hours later, crying, she demanded that the police be notified and a detachment of carabinieri sent out to look for me. At eleven o'clock the pleading of the landlord's entire family and other German guests was not enough to dissuade her from pulling on her raincoat, and she sobbingly set off down the pitch-black lane, followed by Pancrazio's two sons, who were eventually able to prevail on her to turn round. When I arrived at around midnight she hurled herself at my chest with a piercing scream, like a madwoman. Pancrazio and his family, shaken by such a display of conjugal fealty, treated her thenceforth with an awed respect of which only Italians are capable. With delightful sapience, a fourteen-year-old girl expressed the supposition that the signora must be expecting. Which soon enough proved to be the case. Two days later, when a south wind flung the yellow dust of the Sahara over the island, shrouding the scene in eerie yellow twilight, Etna spat fire and the frightened populace organized propitiatory processions, Ganna, with wide Sibyl's eyes, intoned: 'Now do you understand my fear? I could feel it coming. It was already in me.' Oppressed, I asked myself how I was to cope with such lack of restraint in future. I really believed there was some connection between her and the dark forces of nature. I wondered how such a primal creature could have slipped out of the sober bosom of the Mevis family.

## Return

Pregnancy was not on the agenda. We had decided not to have children for another two years. You can't go gadding about the planet with an infant in tow. It was in Rome that, trembling with happiness, she came to me with the great news. A crowned head could not have been more diligent than Ganna in the business of making an heir. She sent for medical literature from Vienna. She observed a stringent diet of her own devising. She found a German doctor and consulted him for hours on end. She treated the temple of her body with loving care. Inside and outside, she went around on tiptoe. Her one and only thought was of the child. Her only concern was that it should be beautiful, beautiful and important. She was certain she had it within her power. Like a farmer's wife, she believed in the effect of transferred shock and so she avoided ugly sights. She spent her mornings in the Vatican collections and sat with avid, adhesive eye before the statuary. She bought a postcard of the Neapolitan fresco of Narcissus. She put it up over her bed and gazed at it with hypnotic devotion, before going to sleep and when she woke. She thought nothing was beyond her illimitable will – not even influencing an embryo in the womb. I wasn't allowed to say anything otherwise she would get angry. Ironic remarks annoyed her. She had no use for irony. She didn't think she was someone to be smiled at, she thought she was holy. And there was something else as well. The ultimate security she thirsted for – she had it now. Since she didn't want to have her baby in a foreign city, and she was missing her family, we went back to Vienna in the autumn.

## The yellow room

I was dreading it. I feared the claims of family, the utter automatic mindlessness with which I would be reclaimed. I was afraid of a life within walls. When I decided once and for all in favour of the life of the bourgeois and the tax-payer – with a bank account to protect me from every eventuality, newest recruit and pride of the Mevises, Schlemms and Lottelotts – that meant the end of poet's garret and Samson's struggle. Fedora and Riemann were right: I had sold myself and betrayed myself. But Ganna was able to talk me out of my worries. She spoke so confidently and enthusiastically of a life of calm domesticity that I complied and went quietly.

After looking for a long time, we finally rented a furnished garden flat far out in the western suburbs, far away too from the Mevises, that was free over the winter. Ganna wasn't yet ready to find somewhere permanent. The furnishing and equipping would have cost too much money. This postponement in her eyes doubled as an economy. The building faced onto a crooked street of bungalows and banal front gardens. Every twenty minutes a steam tram clattered past. There was a bell fixed to the locomotive that you could hear from a distance, and long after it was gone. The aspect of the lodging that had won Ganna over was a very large room with a glass wall at the back, the front extremity of which was flooded with light, but whose interior was so dark that we needed to keep the gaslights on during the day. This was our room of state where we did our receiving, our living and dining room, my workplace; and on top of all that it was where I slept on a sofa in a recess during the weeks before Ganna's due date. It was painted lemon yellow and divided in two by a cloth screen, also lemon yellow. On the left-hand wall we had the Dying Gaul and on the right the Thorn Remover, both set up on top of carefully draped crates, both in plaster of Paris; both souvenirs from Rome.

I dwell on it at such length because the room was important to me. We know so little about the influence of different spaces on one's mood, on thinking, on decisions. An inch more or less in height or breadth and life feels different. I felt as if I was in a suit that was too big for me, bought from some second-hand dealer. I never felt at home in the room. When I woke up in the night and the wintry light dribbled in through chinks in the curtains; then I felt like stepping out into the garden to do something loutish like throwing snowballs at the ridiculous room. Or I wished I could get leprechauns in to do my work for me, because my skull was full of the merry jingle of the tram. It's not good to be with a busy woman if you're trying to paint a delicate picture or weave a delicate tapestry. It's not just one woman either; there are many, as many as the day has hours, that's how many Gannas there are; and each of them wants to do something different, each one is full of herself, each one is happy, excited, has a plan, a wish; and some of them I don't even know yet – I would have to be introduced to them.

## I get pocket money

Baby clothes need buying. The rent needs paying. The servants need paying. I need a new suit for the winter. Ganna needs a coat. The interest isn't enough, we need – Ganna's nightmare – to attack the capital. We need to sell some of the tamper-proofed securities. Ganna's horror. The holy awe of money in the bank has by now infected me. There is nothing more odious than money and the spirit of money. On the first of the month I toddle along to the bank to take out the money we need for the household. I feel like a thief doing it. The cashier at the desk, a gaunt man with gold-rimmed spectacles, is old Mevis's viceroy on earth; he is certain to subject me to a thorough cross-questioning. A man who attacks his capital will stop at nothing. Ganna's tiny hands clutch the bank account like a legal scroll. The cashier lets the notes flutter over the marble till, the capital swishes. I count them shyly, and when I pack them away in my wallet I feel I have outwitted the man at the till and am about to leg it. I leave with the footfall of a fraud. I have no peace till I have handed the money into Ganna's safe keeping, every last penny of it. Ganna notes it down, Ganna calculates, Ganna doles out my pocket money. Yes, my pocket money, as if I'd been a boarding school pupil. It seems perfectly natural to me. What would a man need money for if he has board and lodgings? I have a good mind to say that to the man at the counter when I next visit. It may make him take a milder view of me.

## Not everything is as it should be

'Can't we eat soon?' comes my dejected question as the grandfather clock strikes two in the yellow barn. 'In a minute, Alexander,' Ganna breathes back anxiously, one of the many Gannas, 'in a minute.' And then see what the messy 'maid of all work' dishes up! Things that deny their nature. Meat that looks like charcoal. Cakes that look like book bindings. Soups of which all that can be said in their favour is that they are steaming. All of it produced by gigantic effort, with Ganna's endless trouble. Ganna's trouble is a chapter on its own. Imagine a great surge of energy followed by nothing, nothing at all, that disappears without trace. An almost scientific thoroughness, the most serious commitment, and the result more or less as if someone had taken a sledgehammer to a fly on a windowpane. It's all precisely calculated, it's a radical procedure, but the windowpane suffers, as anyone could have predicted except Ganna. Ganna doesn't understand. With her apron tied on she stands by the stove, stirs the batter in the pan, and open on the sideboard are Hölderlin's poems, which she sneaks a look at. When the batter at the bottom of the pan is charred, she can't help herself and scolds the maid. I see the real problem and tell her: 'But Ganna, it's not possible to read Hölderlin and cook pancakes at one and the same time. You have to decide which one you're doing.' Ganna concedes that, but it's difficult for her, she's so riven by the claims of utility and the spirit. You could say she sweats with effort. In her desire to please me nothing is too much trouble, no inconvenience is too great. But everything falls down because of the excess of fuss. Whenever she tries to see that I am left in peace for my work, she manages to knock over the metaphorical chair. The little domestic devils have it in for her. Her burning ambition melts everything she reaches out for. It's interesting, even at times breathtaking, but it's not what one could call a peaceful existence. It feels like being on board a ship that keeps being clumsily steered into the teeth of the gale.

And then there are the servants. The first maid stayed for six days, the second lasted just two, the third fourteen, and none of her successors was with us for longer than three weeks. Ganna is at a loss to explain it; I too am puzzled. Only gradually I come to understand. I discover that under Ganna's regime any flaw in a human being turns into a vice. It's quite something. If a girl comes into our house with a sweet tooth, she leaves it as a thief. An untidy girl becomes a whirlwind. Since Ganna doesn't have a clue about how you make a bed or polish a doorknob, her orders are heard with quiet derision. She hasn't the least idea how long it takes to do anything. Either she demands the impossible, or else she's diddled. She doesn't understand common people or their speech. Her somewhat pretentious idiom leaves people in the dark and they are suspicious of her. First of all she's sugar-sweet and then without any sort of transition she can become crude. The bourgeois conceit of the Mevis girls and her own literary education keep her from viewing people working for her as beings like herself. Sometimes she would like to, but it's more than she can do. At the slightest difference of opinion she flies off the handle and her eyes throw sparks. In the early days I am able to calm her down, but later her rage will turn on me, too. I am forced to leave her to it, otherwise the domestic strife just gets too exhausting.

There was one girl called Resi who managed to twist Ganna round her little finger, by the simple expedient of flattering her mercilessly; one night she plundered the linen cupboard and vanished. There was a Kathy, who had a string of lovers, and if Ganna ever caught one in her kitchen there would be a terrible yelling match on both sides. There was a Pepi, who was picked up by the police on suspicion of arson. There was a Hannah, who turned out to be in the advanced stages of syphilis; when we let her go her fellow sneaked into the house at night and threatened me with a revolver. There were temps who were as dirty and uncouth as if we'd got them from a holding cell. There were kitchen maids who made off with flour, rice and preserves under their skirts. It smells of burned milk all morning. Girls come, girls go. Ganna spends hours at domestic agencies. Come the evening she's beaming: she's come up with a 'pearl'. A couple of days later the pearl turns out to be just a rotten pea.

Ganna feels discouraged, and I need to comfort her. Every now and again one of the sisters turns up, to show some solidarity. With a little admixture of Schadenfreude, admittedly. They are pessimistic about the future. Ganna might know about books, their expressions say, but she doesn't have a clue about life.

## The Hermitage

When Ganna started having her contractions, I fled. I know it's a shameful confession to make, but I had had too much of home. I spent the afternoon with the big cats in Schönbrunn. Something cold and slick had got hold of me. I had heard Ganna's screams. Even her screams were louder and wilder than other women's. Her nature put up one hell of a fight against the pain. What, I, Ganna, am expected to suffer?! I, a Mevis, Alexander Herzog's wife, am expected to suffer?! Nothing helped, she had to suffer. I suffered with her, but I couldn't stand to witness it. Not out of the usual male cowardice and guilt, but because it wasn't through passion that I had brought her suffering.

When I got home, there was something dark and hairy in the swaddling bands. It was a son – Ganna had been right. (I couldn't see any resemblance to Narcissus, though.) In a pristine bed, her russet hair tied up under a blue cloth, Ganna with a blissful exhausted smile held out its little hand to me. I was deeply moved. 'Don't you think he's beautiful?' she asked. 'Yes, very nice,' I replied, and probably I looked a bit foolish as I said so. When the baby was put to her bosom, her eyes welled up. It was as though this particular show had never happened before, no woman had ever given birth before, or breast-fed her baby. Well, I said to myself, there are some people who experience life in a particularly primal way. We called the hairy amphibian Ferdinand, Ferry for short. He did turn out to be an uncommonly attractive child; here too Ganna managed to get her way.

I asked myself more and more why it was that I always submitted to this will. It's not that I am will-less myself; and weak-willed only inasmuch as my nature is opposed to pointless exertions. So, once it was spring and we had to leave the flat with the yellow room, I moved with her to somewhere at the back of beyond. The new place was an inn called the Hermitage, since (and deservedly) disappeared off the surface of the earth. It was a grim and sad abode, much worse than Signor Pancrazio's hole in the wall. It reminded me of the murderous inn in fairy tales, where the offed guests were interred in the cellar. It had one advantage: it was cheap. That was what decided Ganna. But she was also fed up with her sisters' condescension and even more with the hellish dealings with the servants. So, it was up sticks for the romantic ruin. Ganna said it was high time she returned to her higher calling. I agreed with her. I thought it was high time too. I didn't know exactly what she had in mind, but I let that go.

I worked in a gloomy cell that got wet when it rained, and when it was fine I heard the trippers carousing in the beer garden; and all the time I had Ganna's squabbling with the nurse-maid to distract me. What was it all for, I would ask myself periodically, to be living like an outlaw? A bank account, I thought, is obviously intended to be a type of conserve, like *foie gras*; not something anyone eats fresh. As for the nursemaid, Oprcek by name, she was a confirmed lunatic. She put the boy to sleep by singing him obscene ditties, and when Ganna quarrelled with her she would curtsey to her with a giggle, hoick her skirts up round her knees and mutter Czech oaths under her breath.

I remember one particular night when I was woken by my son's piercing wail. Ganna flutters and flusters round the room, and makes up some camomile tea by the light of a candle. The

Oprcek woman holds the pillow with the infant on it in her upraised arms and performs a sort of Negro minstrel dance with her hideous singing. Ganna begs me to call a doctor. It's a long way to the nearest doctor, but my tiredness is no match for Ganna's fears. I pull on some clothes and go out into the night. And while I walk down into the village, I am taken by a vague and bitter yearning that has me reeling through the stormy, rainy night . . . I never forgot that time.

## The new face

In autumn we finally settled. We moved into the upper storey of an imposing villa on the edge of the 13th district. Furniture, crockery, curtains and lamps needed to be bought. The bank account was ransacked. Ganna spent sleepless nights.

The house belonged to an old couple by the name of Ohnegroll.* Never was a name less deserved. The man was deceitful and malignant, and his wife was a termagant. Brightly coloured ceramic gnomes stood around in the flower beds in woolly hats. I had such a fury against these gnomes, it was as though they were the ones who had made off with my money. An attic room was my study, where I sometimes slept. From there I had a view over a moth-eaten meadow, where a carousel went round in the daytime, to hurdy-gurdy accompaniment. But in the evenings and at night it was eerily quiet, and I worked all through the winter undisturbed.

When spring came I felt restless. Ganna didn't want to leave the baby, so I got in touch with Konrad Fürst and we headed south. In Ferrara my companion ran out of money; by the time

---

* 'without spite' (Trans.)

we got home, he owed me 700 crowns. Barely a week later, Fürst met me in a café and begged me almost in tears to let him have another 1,000; it was a gambling debt, he had given his word of honour and if he didn't have the money by morning he would have no option but to shoot himself. I responded coolly that I didn't think it was his place to get into all this honorious behaviour; if he was in trouble, then I'd help him out, but I didn't think it was advisable for us to see each other for a while. It was a discreet sort of break with him. Fürst's fatuous lifestyle and his megalomania had got on my nerves more and more.

As I was expecting a sizeable payment from my publisher, I thought I'd be able to plug the hole in the bank account before Ganna found out about it. Unfortunately the payment was delayed, and I was forced to tell Ganna what had happened. I was prepared for an outburst of rage, but not for the torrent of bitterness and indignation that followed. To begin with, she just looked at me speechlessly. 'Well, really, Alexander,' she stammered with blue lips, and then a second time, 'Really, Alexander . . . ' like someone whose ideals are crumbing away before their very eyes. With stomping strides and tiny feet she walked up and down, yanked the tablecloth off the table, thrust the chairs out of her way with her knees, ground her little teeth, pressed her tiny hands to her temples and chuntered away to herself: some friend; nasty piece of work; outrageous, taking advantage of someone's kind-heartedness when he has children of his own to feed; well, she wasn't going to stand for it; she was going to write a letter to the slick con-trickster, and one that he wouldn't stick on his mirror . . .

She had every reason to be angry. After all, she was economizing the soul out of her body, turned every crown over three times before spending it, haggled with market traders over vegetables, wouldn't buy herself a new pair of shoes until the old ones were falling apart. Fine. But she still shouldn't have carried on like that. The wrong I thought I had committed suddenly didn't feel wrong any more. Even though she shortly after apologized to me in tears for her vehemence, a sting remained which drilled itself into my flesh. I had seen a new face to her. It was even there in her charming, innocent smile, the new face.

## At the concert

In the same way as strands floating in a murky liquid end up coalescing in strange patterns, so the continual strife gradually made Ganna's life opaque, and her relations with people and things unpredictable. There were recurring scenes which ended up forming a pattern. I bought tickets for an orchestral concert. It starts at seven. You need to allow three-quarters of an hour for the ride into town. At a quarter to six I go to Ganna to tell her to get ready. She is lying dreamily on the terrace; in her right hand a book on mysticism and the Pre-Raphaelites, and in her left the usual pencil. 'Oh, just a minute,' she gives back, startled, drops the book on the lead flashing where it remains, to be found sodden with rain the following day, and scuttles into the bedroom. Ten minutes pass, twenty; I'm in hat and coat looking at my watch all the time, then I pluck up courage and go and see what's keeping Ganna. She's standing in the bathroom, half-dressed, washing her hair, now, at ten past six. I am furious. Ganna asks me not to rush her, she's going as fast as she can. She's the victim of unlucky circumstances. Her best intentions are crossed by bad chances. Everyone tramples around on poor Ganna. Even me. Sighing and groaning and wailing, she's finished by half past six. Just a quick dash to the nursery, intense farewells with Ferry, some rushed parting instructions (because we do rely on her) to the nursemaid (don't ask me which number nursemaid), and we're running to catch the tram. We stand around waiting for the next ten minutes, Ganna with offended expression and pout. No sooner has she taken her seat than she realizes she's left behind her little purse with her opera glasses and her money. Reproaches. The only reason it happens is because she's been 'rushed'. She thinks she doesn't 'deserve' it. When she's trying 'so' hard. She complains and complains. I feel embarrassed in front of the other people in the tram; Ganna is quite unembarrassed in front of the other people in the tram. That's part of her sense of superiority. Why do I answer back to her? Why don't I keep my mouth shut? I feel sorry for her, that's why. She's tormented. I want to help her get over it. I don't like it when she complains and whines. Perhaps it's her magic arts that make me so yielding. Arrived at the concert hall, we are made to wait for a break in the performance. I am still reasoning with her, trying to prove to her that she's in the wrong, a sure-fire way of confirming her in her self-righteousness. Her anger continues as an empty babbling. Then she's sitting down in her seat with a rapt expression. Music affects her like strong drink. I've understood that she's about as musical as a piece of drift-wood, that she doesn't have the least understanding of the structure of a composition, the assembly, the interlocking of various motifs, the worth or worthlessness, content or vapidity of the whole. It would be a simple matter to sell her an operetta overture of the better sort as, say, Bruckner, and she would start to gush; but all that doesn't prevent me from believing in the sincerity of her response, the genuineness of her emotion. Ganna is like a part of me. I can't behave otherwise than as I do; if I did, it would be the end of me. Of course there are times when the sight of her intoxication offends my modesty and my judgement; then I need only remember with what flaming awe, what passionate support she listens to me, hour after hour, when I read aloud to her from my work, how I feel the sympathetic beat of her blood, and her whole being is enthusiastic assent. I like her drunkenness, then; so must I damn her when in another context she seems merely – disinhibited? But surely then everything would be deception and pretence.

## *In company*

I was no longer in touch with my former friends and associates. Either the relationship had come to a natural end, or they had jobs and offices to go to, or they had disappeared into an intellectual underworld. Many of them described me as a cold-hearted user of people. The ones who most especially said it were the ones who had used me almost all up. People are voracious. Give anything of yourself to them, they want to chew your bones; put up a fight, they call you inconstant or feckless. I had a reputation for arrogance. In fact I was excruciatingly shy and still am. But what I couldn't stand was the complacent ignorance of others with respect to my person and my work, a conceited tolerance, of the sort one might show to a neighbour who has put up a fortress wall round his little handkerchief garden.

Ganna preached worldliness to me. She said I should get down from my ivory tower from time to time. 'You need to see people and gain fresh impressions,' she said. I had nothing against going out and seeing people, but unfortunately the ones she had in mind were those who kept salons or gave parties and wanted to collect celebrities. It was her ambition to secure me an appropriate position in the world; but what she thought of as the world was just the financial-cum-artistic circle where she had spent time as a girl. She was proud of being Frau Alexander Herzog and wanted to enjoy her social status. Each and any invitation was an honorific confirmation of the fact. But for the rung of the ladder where she liked to be, she lacked a little discrimination. If she heard her name being whispered behind her, the pleasant sensation tingled into the roots of her hair. When a lawyer or university lecturer kissed her hand, she beamed. When she had a head of section presiding at her dinner table, she was as excited as a young actress being given a plum role. I was perfectly willing to allow all these various gentlemen the credit that Ganna so prodigally lavished on them. I was a little fish. My sense of self was poorly developed. Intellectual attainments have never let me become too full of myself. I thought Ganna, being experienced in the ways of her circle, would do the right thing. I allowed myself to be dragged along. I went solemnly into 'people's houses', as I sometimes sarcastically put it. From time to time I would suggest that really we ought to reciprocate. Ganna insisted that wasn't necessary, it wasn't expected from an artist. Since it suited me to believe that, I believed it, and thereby put myself on the same level as a tenor who was only invited because his name appeared in the paper – or even a little lower, because the tenor at least sang for his supper. Offering people hospitality would have been difficult for us; we ate so terribly badly. When Ganna organized a family meal, which was about the most we ever did, there would be strange giggles about the taste and the puzzling identity of a dish or other. Ganna had no idea how bad it was. She didn't care what was set in front of her. She would launch into a half-cooked potato and a pineapple with the same enthusiastic lack of awareness.

That evening we were guests of the bank director Bugatto, who at the time was a big wheel in the world of high finance. I can remember a whole series of unpleasant feelings besieging me, and I see Ganna in her element. She is forming a circle. A wreath of professors, doctors, lawyers, town councillors, manufacturers and some of their ladies surrounds her. She makes bold assertions and tries to back them up. They are shallow paradoxes, things she has got out of books, but she craves the attention; she pulls it off. Such an original mind, people say. I am happy for her; it means she will be in a good mood for days to come. I like it when her good qualities are recognized. I have an easier time with her. The only embarrassing thing is her way of referring to 'my husband' all the time. I hate that possessive.

I get unbearably bored. The sitting around; the stupid questions and answers, the vulgar gossip. And Ganna's ingratiating chit-chat – I can no longer deny that she is making an exhibition of herself; her warbling, her giddiness, her provincial coquettishness: I suffer, it pains me, can't she feel my shame, my ambivalent position, her own exaggeration, her prostration before this portfolio of pearls, dresses, investments and titles? No, she doesn't. She rises like yeast. She blooms. Two or three times I approach her and suggest going home. Mutely she implores me for leave to stay. She is having such a wonderful time. On the way home she asks me what I had against them. They had all been so charming to her, only I with my bad mood had spoiled the lovely evening.

She doesn't get it, what am I to do? She carries on digging around and complaining until I lose my patience and say something intemperate and find myself in the wrong. Ganna has been waiting for just that. She exploits her advantage to the full. She says I quite systematically go about making enemies, and that I therefore have no business complaining or being surprised at my lack of readers. A poisonous observation, which isn't any the less hurtful because it crudely conflates two separate categories. Riposte, counter, Ganna takes nothing back. It goes on and on, to the point that at two in the morning the Ohnegrolls bang a broom handle against their ceiling to get some quiet. Ganna ignores them. She sinks her teeth into every word of mine. This is no more warbling and fluting like there was in the plush halls of the dignitaries and the *rentiers*; this is anger and a vicious style of argumentation that will stoop to any rhetorical trick to force the opponent to his knees. The crazy thing is that I practically am on my knees. That always used to astonish me. When I think about it today I can't help believing that sensuality is somewhere involved, the blind urge that contains something of the desire to batter, and to stun.

## Hothouse of emotions

With horror I recollect the day little Ferry fell ill. At the least sign of fever Ganna would be beside herself. First, the nanny was subjected to harsh questioning. If she was guilty of some mistake in the care or feeding of the baby, the storm would break over her head and she would be dismissed on the spot. (When the temperature went down she was quietly reinstated.) In such instances, Ganna's brain would assemble all conceivable illnesses and they would race through her imagination in a terrifying rout. Every hyperbole was justified by the imagined danger. But the danger can be avoided if you recognize the cause early enough. A human being, Ganna likes to say, has everything in his own hands, happiness and unhappiness, life and death. If he sticks to the advice of doctors and the prescriptions of science, then not much can happen to him. The biggest threat are germs. The fight against germs, the way she sees it, is like hunting fleas. You're immune if you learn the doctors' and professors' trick of taming and dressing these wicked little creatures. Since Ganna is capable of saying in almost every instance where and how a certain illness was caught, there is always blame involved. If she feels a rheumatic twinge, she will remember weeks later that I talked her out of wearing her fur when on a certain day – I've forgotten all about it – we went to visit

Auntie Claire. Ganna doesn't let nature get away with anything. She believes in doctors the way a devout Catholic believes in Holy Communion. At the slightest suggestion of a symptom the doctor is sent for, a specialist even, for whatever it is. Any and every doctor in her eyes is a sort of all-powerful bourgeois God. But there's trouble for this Godhead if he doesn't bring about an instant cure. Then we get blaspheming and the daughter of the heathen kraal will send for a fresh god.

I often struggled against it. I lectured her, warned her, implored her. In vain. These are emotional excesses, I would say to myself then, she exists in a sort of emotional hothouse. The day-to-day is humdrum; emotions will eat it up. Emotion becomes the measure and mirror of the world. To impede Ganna and change the direction of her affect is as hopeless as it would be to ask a storm to kindly take itself off somewhere else. I began to be afraid of her lack of moderation. Since my strength was invested elsewhere, I didn't have it to draw on when I needed it with her. Sometimes I simply shut my eyes when I saw things that depressed or alarmed me to see. I tried to see the whole Ganna experience as my destiny in life. The more reality weighed on me, the more the picture I had made of Ganna took the weight from me. It was of brass, not readily destroyed. A demonic person, I told myself. That was the first flash of the insight that later, much later, came over me like a brand. Demonic; not a word one can do all that much with. An excuse word, a false coin. It's a facile explanation for the inexplicable, a charge of spiritual inadequacy or unrighteousness laid against the door of an unknown power. At that time, Ganna hadn't gone off the rails. I could still have got her in my power if I'd been careful, if I'd been alert, if I'd been tougher.

## A few snapshots of Ganna

But at that time it was still extraordinarily difficult to extricate myself from certain intriguing traits of her personality, her quirky absent-mindedness, her silly little mishaps, her dreaminess. All that had the charm of youth, and was further enhanced by the happiness in which she seemed to float.

She is lying blissfully spread out on the sofa in her hideously untidy bedroom, marking up Goethe's *Italian Journey* in pencil. In the nursery the baby is screaming her head off, because we have gone on to have a second child, my daughter Elisabeth; in the living room Ferry is banging around on the piano; in the corridor the cook and the maid are fighting a pitched battle; down in the garden patio, Frau Ohnegroll is yapping away like an unpleasant little dog. None of it reaches Ganna. She can't hear it. Her spirit is in heaven. Then a glance finds its way out to the rose I brought her the other day. She smiles, gets up and carries the glass with the rose in it to her dressing table. Now she has two roses, because there's a second one reflected in the mirror . . .

Or this. It's May. To Ganna the concept of 'May', regardless of the actual weather, is inseparable from 'sunshine' and 'blue sky'. So she goes out in a thin serge dress with a frail-looking parasol, where an icy north wind blows and a shower comes down every fifteen minutes or so. It doesn't matter. In her imagination it's 'May'. She passes a fruit stall and sees the first cherries of the year. How wonderful, she thinks, I'll buy some cherries for Alexander. She buys a pound of cherries. She is given them in a twist of paper. It has a hole, and while she wanders dreamily home (when she's alone she doesn't need to 'hurry' and is free to 'enjoy' her walk); so, while she's 'enjoying' the illusory May air, one cherry after another escapes through the hole in the paper bag. People stop and turn and watch her, and grin. The pavement behind her is studded with cherries at regular intervals. Finally a woman takes pity on her and tells her. Who could describe her shock! Thank God, there are not that many people out and about; she goes back and picks up the cherries, one after another . . .

Yes, an eccentric, clumsy, moving creature, Ganna. A Ganna that you'd want to try and protect from wounds and damage. If there weren't the seam in the surface, the crater from which the dark element bursts forth, of which you never know when it will be and how catastrophic its effect.

## Female Don Quixote

I had got to be close to Irmgard. Fleeting conversations had deepened, and then we had gone hiking together – because, unlike Ganna, Irmgard was a splendid walker and tourist. She had, again unlike Ganna, a low opinion of herself and was grateful to me for the lengths I went to to reinforce her sense of self. That was really what she most lacked, even though she had a solid and substantial character; as a woman, though, she had suffered various disappointments that had robbed her of courage. She had a particular sort of beauty. She looked like the statue of an Egyptian princess.

Things between us were such that we could have fallen in love at any moment. It didn't happen. The thing that stopped it was a sort of magic line drawn by Ganna. Irmgard had creditable old-fashioned notions of marriage and fidelity. Moreover: the husband of her sister – the thought made her shudder. I didn't dare cross the magic line either. To rouse Ganna's suspicion was to start an inferno. The suspicion was already lurking. Whenever Irmgard mentioned it she trembled like a child in the dark, and I wasn't much different. We kept on telling each other about the purity of our feelings and were so reticent that each pressure of our hands, each greeting, was managed with cautious attention; even so, Ganna had her eyes on us. Ganna stood unseen next to us and saw that nothing belonging to her was stolen. Not a look, not a breath, not a smile, not a thought.

Perhaps it was just feminine curiosity, a little jealous curiosity that prompted Irmgard to ask one day what it was that fascinated me about Ganna. She had thought about it a lot and had no explanation. At first I had no answer either. Then I talked about Ganna as a sort of ordering principle in my life. 'A sort of what?' Irmgard asked in bafflement, 'Ganna creating order, Ganna?' I could see that I would have trouble convincing Irmgard of that. After a little further thought, I found the way out, and for the first time articulated my sense of Ganna: I said she was a new type, a sort of female Don Quixote. Irmgard shook her head. It was too much for her. She knew Ganna, Ganna was her sister. The parabola from coffin nail to idealistic battler against windmills didn't make sense to her. Hesitantly she suggested I was being poetical. I denied it.

A few days later, Ganna went up to Irmgard, plonked herself in front of her and said, in the tone of a policeman undertaking an arrest:

'I forbid you to flirt with my husband.'

Irmgard replied spiritedly: 'I didn't know Alexander was your prisoner.'

'Find a husband of your own and stay away from mine,' Ganna went on.

Irmgard told me afterwards, bitterly, that she had sounded like a market stallholder, standing up for her veggies in a public spat.

'Your attempts to take up with him behind my back are unacceptable,' Ganna shouted.

She had a particular way of saying the word unacceptable –

the 'x' in it was painfully lengthened. Irmgard couldn't help herself, she began to laugh. She pointed to the door.

'If you want a scandal, you can have it at home. Talk to Alexander. I'm not his nanny.'

After a livid Ganna had left, Irmgard once again couldn't do anything about it; this time, she wept.

After she had related the incident to me, she asked me ironically:

'So where does that leave your female Don Quixote now? Can you tell me where you see her noble folly, my dear brother-in-law?'

I was stuck. I replied:

'One shouldn't judge Ganna on the basis of single incidents, you need to see her in the round, as the wild nature she is. Her errors, her passions, her mistakes, they are all founded on a splendid unity. What's wrong with noble folly? You always made fun of her. The ridiculous is very deep in her, where she fights with phantoms. Everything is a phantom to her: people, the world, you, me, she herself. She doesn't have a clue about reality.'

Irmgard looked me in the eye with her thoughtful gaze.

'Poor Alexander,' she whispered.

'What do you mean, poor Alexander?'

'Oh, I was just thinking . . . '

'What do you mean?'

'I mean, perhaps you're the one who doesn't have a clue about reality.'


## The 'human' side

I note that Ganna is very anxious about something. She is listening out, spying, she looks at me with the sad scrutiny that actors playing forsaken lovers have onstage. To get the better of me, she asks me little trick questions. If I manage to avoid her traps she tries a bigger, rougher calibre.

'Oh, I am the unhappiest woman in the world!' she cries out to no one in particular, and criss-crosses the room, as though she wanted to knock down the walls.

'You're seeing ghosts, Ganna, your unhappiness is all in your mind. Irmgard is much too decent to go in for any dubious escapades.'

'Irmgard? She's the most unscrupulous person there is.'

'But Ganna!'

'What about you? Would you deceive me?'

'I hardly think so, Ganna.'

She hurls herself at my chest. 'Really? Will you swear? Will you swear you haven't got a relationship with her?'

I have to laugh. It's so crude, the way she says it, you feel you've been punched on the nose; I'm not quite sure why I'm laughing. She holds my hand between hers, examines the palm and says with an expression as though she longed for me to contradict her tough judgement:

'Your love line is withered. Perhaps you haven't got a heart, Alexander?'

'That could be,' I replied, 'but the one you're looking at is understanding, so far as I know.'

'Oh, is it?' she says in relief. 'Thank God for that.'

Her conclusion is that she perhaps needs to offer me more, be more alluring. She buys a sophisticated scent for a lot of money and douses herself with about a teaspoonful of it (which is certainly too much).

'I'm not sophisticated enough,' she laments, with an undertone of pride, 'I have no gifts as a seductress.'

'No, you're right about that, Ganna,' I tell her, and take the opportunity to tell her she should stop slouching about the place as she does. She heeds my advice, and for thirty-five crowns buys a fake Japanese kimono that makes her look like Sarastro in *The Magic Flute*. The slippers she wears with this prize piece are ancient and filthy, and seeing that she also doesn't pull up her stockings until and unless she's getting ready to go out, they look like a pair of sausage skins hanging down her legs, where the kimono stops. When she gets wind of my disapproval, she says crossly: 'All right, the garter ribbons are torn, but surely that's nothing to do with the human side.' Of course not, I never said it was. But the 'human side' isn't a reserve fund that you can draw on in exalted hours, and at others licenses the fake kimono, ragged slippers and baggy stockings . . .

## The scream in the night

At this time, there is the following development with Ganna. If we've had a quarrel or difference of opinion in the day, her resentments and rancour, which are intensifying all the time, accumulate in sleep, until she frees herself of them in an eruption. Then she screams. Usually, a single, piercing, terrible scream, which rings through the entire house and wakes up all its inhabitants. By and by this scream becomes a fearsome event for me, something that cuts into and darkens my life. I wake up, when it rings out, as if to the feeling of a skewer being driven through my head, in one ear and out the other. I lean over her in the dark, I talk to her, I try to calm her down. (Later on, when we were no longer sleeping in the same room, I dashed into her room with shudders running down my spine; sometimes I had the suspicion that with that terrible screaming she was trying to force me back into her bed; not consciously; but so as not to be alone any more; so as not to let me forget that she existed in my life; from envy of my sleep; who could tell what it was with her?) She tells me the dream she awoke from. They are often strange dreams, dreams of a hopeless, betrayed, tormented soul; dreams with a quality of primal darkness, something bizarre like everything in her unconscious. For instance she once dreamed of Irmgard, standing before her with red hair and a bloodied mouth; her mouth was bloodied because she was holding Ganna's heart in her hand, and biting into it every so often, as into a red apple.

The person I am holding in my arms to comfort is the mother of my children, not a woman, not my wife. Her accumulated pains, complaints and reproaches are poured out over me in a flood. In her fevered eloquence she loses herself in detail, mixes up things that happened yesterday with others that happened long ago, imagined things with others that are true or half-true, and if I manage to refute one charge, she comes at me with another one that I've refuted three times already. It's as if someone, in ignorance of the pattern on the front side of a rug, were picking at loose threads on the back, and with a sore finger. Her brain is a reservoir for all the murky waters that have poured into it for days past, and are now threatening to overflow. Irmgard, always Irmgard. Where I saw her, how long we spent together, what we talked about.

'If you deceive me, Alexander, I don't know what I'll do, I think I'll kill myself.'

Followed by the accusation that I undermine her authority with the staff.

'But Ganna, you don't have any authority with the staff.'

I cancelled her instructions, she says.

'Of course I do, when they don't make any sense.'

Hadn't I calmly stood by the day before yesterday and listened to the impertinence from the Mam'selle?

'I couldn't very well take your side, you treated her like a dog.'

This drives her wild.

'Well, really, Alexander, really . . . '

The murky waters continue to spill out of her without cease; staring out into the darkness, I have the feeling my head is about to burst open. Now the subject has come around to money. That my pocket money is never enough for me; that the capital is dwindling from year to year like snow in the sun; that that bastard Fürst has yet to repay a penny of what he owes me. Did I want the children to live in penury? And my own coldness, my lack of love.

'But Ganna, Ganna, how can you! Cold, me?!'

Yes, wherever I could I would ignore her; accepted invitations from my aristo pals and went round to see them without her. Was it that I was ashamed of her?

'Tell me truly, Alexander, are you ashamed of me?'

My head is reeling. 'Go to sleep, why don't you,' I say, 'please, enough . . . '

## Death of her father, insanity of her mother

In summer 1905, Professor Mevis died of a coronary. Ganna's grief was dramatic. Thus far, she had been so spoiled by fate that she hadn't had to think about death at all. How could death suddenly intrude, and bring down the sacred paterfamilias? She embarked on a programme of idolatry towards the departed. She collected relics, pictures of him, sayings of his. She wove legends. She planned to write his life story. She claimed – to the annoyance of the sisters – to be his favourite; she believed it too, implicitly.

But the man himself was no longer there, the man with the iron fist. The one the mere mention of whose name had made her sit up. The dealing in images and idols was her last respect to him. Now, she need fear no other man.

Shortly after the Professor passed away, Frau Mevis needed to be institutionalized for a couple of months. The ancient hulk had given way to the pressure of the waters. The removal of the spiritual straitjacket had liberated the illness. Ganna would go and visit her mother once or twice a week. Every time, she pleaded with me to go with her. One day I went. We were taken to a room with barred windows. The madwoman sat in an armchair, furiously shredding a newspaper. She always needed to have something to destroy – letters, a book, an item of clothing. Sometimes she smeared the walls with filth.

She seemed to take no pleasure in our having come. With hectic shining eyes and hoarse voice, she complained that she was being unlawfully detained; she had written to the Emperor to let him know. Ganna addressed her tenderly; I couldn't manage to get a word out. Much as I'd sympathized with the old lady in quieter days, I found her repulsive now, really hateful in her illness. The sick spirit doesn't excite sympathy like the sick body, but fear and revulsion. The thought that some of the blood of this disturbed person was flowing in the veins of my children was appalling. 'Is he always so quiet, your beloved, or have you done something to him?' She turned to her daughter with a hideous grimace. Ganna took it as a cue to launch into a paean of praise of me and our marriage. Thereupon the sick woman started to rave about my latest book in embarrassingly hyperbolic terms and to assure me that all the denizens of the establishment had read it with enthusiasm. It was more than I could stand to hear. 'Let's go, Ganna,' I urged. As we stepped through the gate I mumbled goodbye and ran off.

## Two speeds

There is a lot to this. It reaches into the nerve endings, the mood, the sexual embrace. It's most clearly visible, of course, in walk and stride patterns. 'Can't we go for a walk,' begs Ganna, 'forget your appointments, go on, please.' I consent. But the gladly begun enterprise ends in strife and disagreement. She's not up to any physical exertion but won't admit it, and accuses me of tiring her out on purpose, so as to prove her unsuitability. I bite back a reply to the ugly accusation – I can't always take issue with her, this Ganna dialectic can drive you mad. To go for a walk with her – fine. But I go off the idea as soon as I witness her preparations. She's not ready in time. I prefer to be unencumbered, she lugs around everything she deems indispensable: a book, a heavy overcoat, a blanket to put on the ground, an umbrella in case it rains, even if the heavens are cloudless, a bag of provisions, notebook, salves and ointments, loose leaves of paper and a straw hat whose elastic she loops round her wrist. She can't carry it all, I have to help her. She wants to march, she wants to enthuse. I hate raving about scenery; she's in transports over every green or brown hill. In her delight she links arms with me, but as that compels me to fall in with her stride, which means setting one foot ponderously in front of the other like an invalid, I break free and hurry on ahead. (I walk fast, just as I breathe fast and eat fast and, yes, live fast; how could we ever fall in step like two of a kind? It's a physical impossibility.) Then Ganna's bitterness breaks out of her. A woman who has given birth to two babies and breast-fed them both for eight months deserves respect and not uncouth behaviour like mine, the long face, the merciless hurrying and geeing-up. She's right; I am not sparing enough of her; I let her sense her physical weakness; I am not courtly; it's all true. If only she hadn't said the thing about bearing the children, though. To her the bearing and feeding of children is what victorious battles are to a general – praiseworthy deeds for which she deserves a medal, as if children come into this world by some secret ruse of man, and woman, the innocent victim, needs to pay all her life for that vicious breach of trust. Once Ganna has taken a dialectical fortress, she doesn't stop. What has she done, she rhetorically asks the sky, what has she done to end up living with such a beastly egoist, she who is so absurdly modest, she who – God is her witness – has long ago given up wanting anything for herself, who sits around at home for days on end all alone while he diverts himself in all sorts of ways . . .

You may be right, Ganna, you may be right, but please, please stop, won't you, can't you see people staring at us? She doesn't stop, all the way home, over supper there's a zestful complaining, a simple shudder-inducing lamentation. Sometimes I keep quiet, sometimes I explode; I can't always control myself, above all I can't control Ganna at all, everything is twofold, two ways of feeling, two ways of looking, two sorts of speed. Finally I can think of nothing else but to sit down at the piano, open a score and with clumsy fingers approximating the trills, the allegros, knock out a Chopin Prelude or a piece from Schumann's 'Carnival'. All at once Ganna is transformed. Lying back in an armchair, she listens wide-eyed like a child praying. What possesses me to show off my dire musical gifts? Is it the way the two speeds give rise to discord and arrhythmia? Because she will then beg forgiveness and embrace me, and kneel at my feet? The difference between us was this: she forgot everything from one hour to the next, the way only angels or demons forget; I forgot none of it, for all eternity. And it grew darker and darker in my heart.

## The mystical union

From the time when Irmgard got engaged to a mining engineer by the name of Leitner, I find the following entries in my diary: 'For Irmgard I was merely a staging-post in the journey of her desire. Since giving me up, she seems to have given herself up, there is something ever so slightly wizened about her. But if you give yourself up, no God can help you, only the winged soul remains young and full of love, it loves without needing to be loved back, what it has it gives, and its grief comes from fullness, not lack.' And then again: 'There is a sadness so extreme, it makes you want to stretch out on the ground and wail; your tongue is sore when you speak; the very air is a crushing weight on your shoulders. And yet everything has merely taken its course. How nice that two people walk freely side by side, when they so clearly belong together. Even in the pain of loss there is a good and bitter taste, and something that so indefinably and lightly oscillated between passion and sibling affection didn't even shatter. Rather, it leaves a golden memory. My continual nightmares! Never forget last night in the park, our last conversation, the way she stood there, pale and still, and a meteor etched its great parabola across the sky . . . '

Since the youngest sister Traude has now also married – her husband was a Berlin manufacturer by the name of Heckenast – Irmgard would have felt unhappily alone on the shelf. And so, when Leitner, a nice and clever man, proposed to her, she accepted. My feelings for her had lost none of their original freshness, even though I had already started having relationships with other women. Her image was precious to me. I depended on women. Without the erotic trance, without the magical involvement of the senses, I felt I was only half alive. Irmgard knew it. She never laid a claim to me. The evening cited above, at the end of a long silence, I reached for her hand and pressed it to my lips. She was shocked and gave a little jump. Suddenly, as though talking to herself, she asked:

'How are things with you and Ganna?'

I replied: 'Nothing has changed. Nothing can change.'

And she: 'Did you never think of leaving her?'

I shook my head. I said it had never entered my mind; it would feel, I added, as if I were undertaking something against myself.

'But you continually deceive her,' she whispered with something like contempt, 'and you continue to sleep with her . . . She has one baby after another . . . How can you?'

'You're right,' I conceded glumly, 'but even so . . . my marriage with Ganna is not in question. Quite apart from the children . . . There's something . . . I can't explain what it is, it's a fact, you have to take it as it is.'

'So the other women, that's just a pastime?'

'Nonsense, Irmgard. You know perfectly well that I don't play with people. Please understand, it's a mystical union.'

Those were my words. Irmgard replied with a shyly questioning 'Oh?' She didn't believe me. But she had neither the strength nor the need to shake my faith in the 'mystical union'. Perhaps she didn't want to be in the company of those who eased my conscience by not questioning the 'mystical union'. But she was mistaken if she thought such a union didn't in fact exist. It did. It was put together from guilt and a fear of ghosts. It was steeped in the sense of imminent calamity, because I think I am one of those people who, half-knowingly, half-ignorantly, carry their future destiny around with them in the form of living substance.

## Ganna's tolerance

If I remember correctly, the time of my physical turning-away from Ganna coincided with our leaving the Villa Ohnegroll. The flat had got to be too small for us and we moved into a rented house on the northern edge of Vienna, among the vine-yards at the foot of the Kahlenberg. At first, only half of it was vacant; it was November when we moved, and for the next six months once again I had to retreat to the attic to work. I wasn't too upset about that. I lived and slept under the roof, in a sort of world of my own. The ceiling was so low that I could put out my hand and touch it. Once I had bolted the iron door behind me I was alone and unreachable, with only my creations for company. When I moved down into the Ganna zone at the end of that time I felt much less happy, even though I continued to occupy a remote part of the house. There was an ever increasing unquiet about Ganna. She was embroiled in conflicts with all and sundry. There was endless trouble with the couple who ran the house; either it was about the use of the laundry room or the time the front gate was locked at night, or the tyranny of one of the cooks, or some malicious local gossip. There was always something. I kept having to intercede, tone down, apologize. And when it was fine, the songsters in the local wine bars made an unholy racket. What could I do other than flee the house when I felt uneasy there?

When Ganna gradually came to understand that I was no longer faithful to her, she took it very badly. I was never able to discover just exactly what went on in her innermost recesses. Sometimes I would find her in tears, sometimes there were bitter outbursts, sometimes I thought she was adjusting and had decided to tolerate my escapades, in roughly the way some wives don't mind when their husbands go out drinking. Since I was usually terribly discreet – to spare her – it comforted her that in most cases she didn't know the identity of the woman in question. Then she would persuade herself that other people wouldn't know either. If this game of hide-and-seek couldn't be kept up, she had a further consolation: she said it was just a question of a 'concubine', someone on the side. She, Ganna, remained the lawful spouse. There was no changing that. Also the world had to learn that she, Ganna, so to speak, supervised my amours. As soon as a new female creature entered my circle of acquaintance, and captured my heart and imagination, Ganna sought as a matter of urgency to find out how much danger this rival could pose, or, to put it another way, the degree to which her own claims remained unaffected. Her overall behaviour then developed in a sort of domestic politics. It was quite extraordinary when she explained to her confidantes (often I would be told about this afterwards) that a man like me might become spiritually impoverished without fresh experiences; it was important for his creativity that he wasn't made to stick fast in his family, and besides he worked so hard that he had to be allowed the occasional diversion. The result, if I had been able to judge it clearly, as I was not, was a dispensation that sanctioned the literary reinvestment of amorous experiences. What was spent on one side of the ledger in terms of passion, time, even money, was earned back – with compound interest – as material for future books. Every movement of the spirit, every exaltation, was converted into subject-matter; then the book is printed and sold, and if it sells well, the expenses are easily covered. That was Ganna's calculus. 'You only need to have some insight,' she said, and all she told me was, for her sake, not to give too much of myself, as though the account-keeping might be affected by erotic waste; 'all these women are vampires, they want to suck the blood from your veins,' she warned; and to prove that degenerate women had at all times taken aim at credulous men and got away with it, she would sometimes read me lurid passages from Görres's *Christian Mystics*.

## The ethical imperative

Whether Ganna crossly gave in to the inevitable or turned a blind eye depended on who my current friend might be. Thus, the beautiful Belgian Yvonne enjoyed her particular favour because on the few times she visited me she had behaved with respect and forbearance. Something Yvonne had said was reported to Ganna, to her delight, perhaps because she didn't understand it properly. 'I would never dare to try and take this woman's husband away from her,' she said; 'that would give rise to the most awful calamity.' Yvonne couldn't have known how prophetic her words were. She said to me once, she thought Ganna was the most disturbing person she had ever met. On occasion she would recoil from my embrace in dread, just as if Ganna's tiny fist had choked her windpipe. When I suggested going away with her somewhere, for as long as she liked, she trembled and wheezed in panic: 'For pity's sake, no. You must stay with her. You'd still be with her anyway, so far as I was concerned.' That was an instance where Ganna could be sure of her ground. Her sister Justine told me mockingly one day that Ganna had told her with a half-subtle half-smile: 'Imagine, he's involved with a Belgian countess.' Even the slightly slow Justine was rather nauseated by this peculiar boast, while I was dismayed and a little outraged by it.

If my friends shake their heads reading this, no one will understand their surprise and disapproval better than I. I can hear them asking: how could you stand it? Were you blind to the terrible danger beside you, behind you? When you pushed the woman into ever deeper suffering and insecurity, how could you square that with your sense of truth and decency? Because she was suffering, no matter how she tried to get around it with her indestructible optimism. The whole relationship was based on a lie; there was something mouldy in your life . . . How could you carry on like that?

It's all not true. You mustn't confuse the picture I'm painting here with my perspective at that time of my life. It's difficult enough to exclude the experiences of the next twenty years, and frame the truth of those days in such a way that I might have recognized then. Fate deals with us like a thriller writer. Blow by blow and step by step it discloses its truth, which was kept concealed from us until the inevitable surprise denouement – a reflection on the skilful way the author has manipulated our judgement and sense of probability.

I have an unshakeable faith in Ganna. Even though I was increasingly drawn to other women, and was never able to resist sensual temptation, I did remain connected to her in a way that was mysterious even to myself; and this connection, which in her was like a force of nature, was an iron law that governed my existence. Impossible to shake it, impossible to break it. Everything else was just a temporary aberration. This I would insist on to her, and these repeated solemn insistences strengthened her feeling of security and made her tyrannical. But never mind how boldly she overstepped the boundaries that were drawn for her – and her boldness, her brazenness, increased year on year – it didn't change anything in my inner trust, my admiration for her truly exceptional character, my belief in her intellectual and spiritual comradeship; and the less so as I often wasn't aware of her oversteppings, or didn't register them as such. For example, it happened that without my prior knowledge she published a long article on me and my work in a German weekly, quite a clever and readable discussion, albeit studded with the modish critical terms of the day. Some of my friends pointed out to me the dubiousness of such an enterprise; a writer's wife shouldn't put herself forward as an interpreter of his ideas, they contended. I disagreed. The essay was well written, I claimed (which it wasn't), and how could you tell a man's wife not to write a dignified and objective essay on her husband's oeuvre? I wasn't all that convinced by my argument, but I couldn't very well leave Ganna in the lurch.

My friends were still more astonished when my book *The Seven Dances of Death*, on which I had worked for four full years, appeared with a fulsome dedication to Ganna, combining my thanks to my helper and exegete and my love for the wife and companion. This glorification of Ganna *in excelsis* was done with an honest heart. I have never written a single line in which I suppressed the truth, have never been able to prettify a feeling. It was my gift to her, freely given; and yet, such gifts may be compelled by discreet means, even if it's no more than the constant mute expectation of some sort of atonement. Also: the Ganna in my life and the Ganna in my imagination were two completely different creatures. They were fused together by my gratitude, or what I called gratitude, a dark, fluent sense of indebtedness and obligation. That was on top of everything else, and it never ceased tormenting me. Baffling to me why, if I had any sort of debt to discharge or thanks to convey, I should have done so day in day out, year in year out, with my whole person. It was as if a long-since acquitted prisoner doesn't stop supplying proof of his innocence to the prosecutor. This tormented state of soul led to my raising marriage to a sort of ethical postulate, completely cut off from reality; I idealized Ganna in a sort of lofty vacuum and from a distance, from my many trips, wrote her the most humble, yearning letters. I was hymning a perfectly unreal connection to her, and forgetting that the earthling Alexander Herzog had no terra firma underfoot. I exalted Ganna to a principle, an idea, she and the children together, three hearts beating within mine, to whom I had to remain of service till the end of my time. And Ganna knew that. She built on it. The ground on which she built struck her as solid enough for the heaviest load.

## The capital melts away

Ganna can't sleep for worry: the once-sizeable dowry is now a tenth of what it was. The slimmed-down bank account is like a fire banked up with the last remnants of wood, lighting a criminally irresponsible way of life, a frivolous trust in princely earnings to come, the speculative existence of a lottery player. The money from my books is not insubstantial, but it doesn't begin to stack up against our expenses. The hopes I pin on them are always far in excess of what happens. There is no prospect of my earning back the spent dowry money, as Ganna had tried to reassure herself at the beginning of our prodigality. The result is, I see her hunched over bills and receipts like a desperate treasury official, and with wrinkled brow filling in line after line of the enormous ledger she bought herself. In addition to sizeable sums for rent, wages, travel, insurance, food and clothing, there are endless small and trifling amounts for soap, thread, tram tickets, beggars, postage stamps, new soles; every penny is written down. 'Ganna,' I say, 'you're making so much work for yourself, why not keep the small sums separate?' But no, she doesn't want to do that. Her pedantic exactitude has a reason: Ganna has no overall view, and she hides this defect by stringing together details. She must keep a thousand trivial things in her mind; and if she gets confused, as is almost inevitable, isn't that pardonable in a woman who never goes to bed without a volume of

Nietzsche or Novalis, and must try to see that the daily round doesn't keep her thoughts from taking wing? Unfortunately, she loses the bearing she owes me and herself too. She bawls me out like a servant if I happen to spend money unthinkingly. The menacing spectre of the future is straight away there. The wolf is at the door. At the time I had a friend in Berlin I was very fond of, a gifted man of immense humanity. He was very hard-up. I helped him out from time to time, albeit with very small sums. Ganna resents even those. She can't 'accept it'. There are other people, better off, better able to afford 'such a luxury', in her view. Charity, she claims, begins at home. Blood is thicker than water. The 1,700 crowns that the wretched Fürst still owes would be enough to take the children to the seaside for the summer, which is something 'they badly need'. I deny that the children need a beach holiday; they are in excellent health. 'I see,' Ganna flashes back in fury, 'and didn't Dr Blau think Elisabeth had a tendency to bronchial catarrh?' I venture to object that the sum she spends on unnecessary doctors' visits would fund not only a trip to Biarritz, but also half a dozen Parisian gowns, so that she would no longer have to go around in picturesque drapes of her own devising. At that Ganna yelps like a wounded she-wolf. 'You're attacking my simple style? You want me to buy Paris fashions? Do you take me for Odilon or what? And not go to the doctor, when my children are ill? You would just sit there and watch the poor things suffer, wouldn't you?' What can I say? That I would indeed 'sit and watch the poor things suffer', because I have more trust in nature than I do in Dr Blau and Dr Grün? Ganna acknowledges no facts or experiences; all there are for her are momentary satisfactions of her instincts, inner short-circuits that wreck the whole of her internal lighting system. When she holds out the household accounts book to me in her extended hands like a book of laws, or recites the crushing litany of my economic sins, all at once I am no longer a creative person any more, no Pericles on the arm of his Aspasia; then I am the unscrupulous exhauster of her dowry, the sacred capital that the tribal chieftain Mevis in wise forethought set aside for her and her children in years to come. With passionate garrulousness she boasts about saving at least 100 crowns a month by having found a supplier of cheap fruit and vegetables, but overlooks the fact that such savings are used up perhaps three times over by the folly and indiscipline of her staff. But I am not allowed to say that. She would go wild. I don't know what to do. Oh, Ganna, I often think, what can I do to help you find peace, and to help you see things more clearly? There was little prospect of either, and the following events buried my faint hopes once and for all. Ganna was now thirty-two, and if people in general are past changing at that age, then she, by constitution and genetic make-up, was even more so.

## A meadow appears on the horizon

At that time, it was the fashion for the wives of the bourgeoisie to parade their devotion to their children. So-called toughening measures, hygienic principles, pedagogic instruction – all that was bandied about with a solemn seriousness, talked about in meetings and pursued in the most modern way. One might have supposed the offspring of these well-off ladies, who could afford any extravagance, would grow to be a morally and physically perfect race of beings, equipped to transform the prospects of human society. Unless I've missed it, this has not proved to be the case.

Ganna was resolutely against sending her children to an ordinary school. They were home-taught, which, over time, turned out to be an expensive business. Every classroom, according to

Ganna, was a toxic dump, rife with infectious diseases, an inferno of germs, as she put it. Further, she was dead set against conventional methods of teaching and child-rearing. She favoured special treatment, respect for the individual, holistic development of the personality. Splendid – but where were the institutions where such things were promulgated? I was suspicious of the theories of the latest wave of pedagogues, whose child-worship laid the foundation for the brutalism of a later era.

I put it to Ganna that children needed to be taught to exist in a community; that they would turn into selfish anti-social brats if they were not made acquainted with self-sacrifice, adversity and shocks; where would they end up if not with the millions of others, what remorse and revenge were lying in wait for them when the day of reckoning and levelling finally arrived? I was wasting my breath. To a spirit like Ganna's the state of the world in which she moved must seem unalterable, since she herself harboured no possibilities of change either. She embarked on lengthy fantasies on the cruelty of schoolmasters, who had no interest in knowledge and understanding, but only in censorship and morals. Weren't the newspapers full of the recent spate of suicides among schoolchildren? No, she wasn't going to allow the little innocents to be routinely poisoned. 'Your schools are prisons,' she exclaimed with the expression of a fanatical preacher, 'I'd rather be drawn and quartered than condemn my children to a convict existence like that.' *My* children! Ganna, Ganna! My house, my husband, my children: that was all that counted, with 'your' lying on the ground like a dead dog.

What did she have in mind? Ferry was almost ten, his case was becoming urgent, he couldn't go on being kept apart from his contemporaries like a prince; nor could Elisabeth. They were living in a hothouse as it was. They needed to burst through the glass walls. It seemed to me I was fighting an undeclared war with Ganna over the souls of the children. It wasn't love and affection that had started it, but what I term the atmospheric effect of a human being, the silent and pervasive influence of a protective presence. No one has yet established how the blood of father and mother become mingled to inheritance and destiny; nor was it even certain that parentage counted for more than principles. Ganna's cosseting of the children was a serious threat to their welfare. But was I sufficiently different to be able to decide? It's impossible to give a young human enough love, I would sometimes weakly say, as though love can be a universal remedy against unhappiness and suffering; as if I didn't know perfectly well that we feel the cold much more when our warm coat is taken away from us than if we had never had it.

One fine day Ganna dawdles with her usual demonstrative slowness through the narrow lanes of our part of town and comes across a fenced-off meadow, a waving piece of green ground, like a flag, going uphill. She stops. An idea comes to her: this is where the children will go to school. A visionary moment. She sees it all unfold before her: pretty wooden buildings, long verandas, airy dormitories for boarders, assembly room, library, tennis courts, gymnasium; all of it palpably there, within reach. Why shouldn't she build such an ideal establishment by her own plans? Who could get in the way? In the end, it's only a question of money.

Within the next few minutes the following thoughts come to her fertile mind, as she stands there rooted to the spot, smitten with the meadow. She will be able to borrow money, that's what financiers are there for. They will get a share of the business; repayment depends on how profitable the idea ultimately turns out to be. It will be set up as a joint-stock company. An educational company. Such a lovely meadow in such a lovely location must be worth a fortune. Perhaps it will be possible to acquire it for not very much. In a few years it will have appreciated so much that she will run the entire business off it, in the unlikely event that it doesn't pay for itself anyway. Pupils will come flocking there from all over Austria and Germany. They will advertise. They will acquire charitable status – what does she have so many connections for? It will be a gold mine. She will reserve the meadow for herself. It will remain her personal property. Assuming it costs 60,000 or 70,000 crowns, then in ten years' time, when the district comes to be developed, it will be worth half a million at least. With half a million, she will be able to secure independence for me and an old age free from worries. And in the meantime it will be just heaven for the children.

There is no problem anywhere that Ganna can see.

Isn't it just like the character in the fairy tale who builds castles in the air, converting a cartload of pottery into fabulous riches, till an unfortunate accident leaves everything a heap of shards?

It's a psychological puzzle how people like Ganna are favoured by circumstances for so long till the tension between dream and reality bursts with a catastrophic bang. On closer inspection, the weakness of their construction is shown from the beginning by their divided motivation: there's a doubleness of purpose, a having-your-cake-and-eating-it. They want to insure themselves both against failure and against the prickings of conscience by taking the declared purpose and beefing it up, reinforcing it with a remoter one, more impersonal. Instead of thus strengthening the purpose, which is their intention, they divide it, and as they try to keep their options open to all sides, they wreck them both. This was exactly Ganna's case, when with her irresistible energy she set about not only designing an educational paradise for her children from scratch, but at the same time sought, with a grand speculative coup, to assure the future of her beloved husband against any threat from destiny. In the end, both projects failed, and both became mad.

## The founding of the school and everything that is involved with it

Let's accompany her on her next steps, which are as bold as they are technically adroit. She finds out that the meadow belongs to a Frau Nussberger, a little old lady, the widow of a vintner. She pays a call on the little old lady and tests the water. Her hope has not deceived her, the meadow can be bought. The price: 120,000. Ganna pretends she is acting on behalf of an interested consortium and begins to negotiate. She feels there is little to be done, but since the property has a 40,000 mortgage on it, the sum she needs to raise is reduced by 40,000. That same day she goes to her friend and admirer, the lawyer Dr Pauli, one of the most sought-after lawyers in the city and a very influential fellow. She pitches him her project. He is very favourably impressed and promises to help. First question: how to get hold of the meadow? One thing Ganna knows: old Frau Nussberger needs money. Further conversations with the friendly old lady leave Ganna persuaded that she would be prepared to sell the property for a moderate down payment, so long as the balance was secured. Ganna applies her full charm and force of argument to keep the down payment as low as possible. Relatives turn up, daughters, grandchildren, sons-in-law, the whole Nussberger clan – they all need money, there's endless back and forth. Finally Ganna manages to get the down payment to just 2,000 crowns. Only where is she going to get them from? From the bank account? Not possible. It's our iron reserve. A source of funding must be found, some people who are willing to accept the risks for the sake of the enterprise as a whole. One is found. Dr Pauli has persuaded a few of his acquaintances to form a board interested in founding a school. One of their number is talked into putting up the advance. How Ganna manages to get the meadow in her name, and not that of the association, is a masterstroke. She tried once to explain it to me, but I couldn't understand it, these things are too complicated for me. I was astounded that Ganna could manage them so well; she must have a native aptitude for them, I concluded.

Things now start to move. The number of shareholders grows every day. They are all wealthy people. I am amazed at the number of parents there are who want to save their children the trials of a conventional education and offer them freedom, an unorthodox syllabus and modern principles. They must know a thing or two about life, and to them a modest parental contribution that can smooth the way for their unacademic heirs is a reasonable investment.

Much greater, though, is my amazement at Ganna's indefatigable zeal and evident proficiency. Next to the meadow is a villa with a spacious garden. From the very beginning Ganna has had her tactician's eye on it. It's for rent; she rents it; later she means to acquire it for the school. In combination with the meadow, it will provide plenty of scope for the school, especially for boarders. Exciting negotiations are held. Usually in our house. I feel like a man who comes upon some kerfuffle on the street and anxiously asks what it's all about. Ganna's announcements are becoming harder and harder to follow. She doesn't have time for a quiet conversation. Early in the morning she dashes off into the city, and late in the afternoon she turns up exhausted, out of breath, half-starved. Then the writing begins. She writes letters, dozens at a time, and brochures for the printer. Articles for newspapers, pedagogical essays, press releases on behalf of the school board, appeals to the Education Ministry, teaching plans, syllabuses, budgets. I am astounded by her stamina, her mastery, her versatility. Her room has turned into an office. The servants are left to their own devices. The children run wild. By day I flee the house. When I come home at night, the rooms are full of people I've never seen before. Lawyers, civil servants, teachers, journalists, enthusiastic ladies, chancers sniffing a job, all of them crammed into our three rooms, munching sandwiches, drinking vast quantities of beer, wine, schnapps and tea, engaged in loud debates and browsing nosily in my books and manuscripts. The telephone is continually manned, usually by Ganna herself. Telegrams rain in, windy pronouncements are read out, and a charter is drawn up for the civil servants to get to work on.

The school board is convened, the share capital is subscribed; and then the first rebellion breaks out. Ganna has exceeded her authority, or so at least it is claimed. She has violated agreements, apparently, meddled in other people's areas, put the wrong people in important jobs – for instance appointing a nice-looking young man by the name of Borngräber as headmaster on the strength of a few vacuous recommendations and his own smooth manners. And then it transpires that the fellow is intriguing against her and is making a stink. I try and investigate but fail to get to the bottom of the thing. I am perforce left with Ganna's version. With one of her typical unabashed clichés, she says: 'I have given suck to a viper.' But he's not the only one to come out of the shrubbery. Every day there are fresh opponents, distractions, false reports, betrayals, conspiracies. Borngräber is forming a cabal. Ganna forms one of her own. Not the best thing for a school being founded. What's the matter, I think, Ganna wouldn't harm a fly, why is it that all these people are up in arms against her? I hear all sorts of complaints and accusations. I'm not sure what's going on, and ask Ganna what this thing or the other is about. Ganna describes the events as if she were the victim of malice and envy, as if people were trying to twist the reins out of her hands. She asks me to get involved. If I put my foot down, she assures me, then no one will dare to rebel against her.

Now, I don't exactly believe in my authority, but I'll do anything to try and help her, because I too have the sense that she's confronted by a wild rabble. She's unhappy. She has sacrificed herself for a great idea and this is her recompense. It's easy to see the female Don Quixote again, against the background of hostility. Something needs to happen. I talk to the teachers, to the perfidious Borngräber, to Dr Pauli, to a respectable Court Councillor who is the titular chairman of the board and Ganna's confidant. I get nowhere. I no longer know what's what in all this turmoil. An embittered confusion of voices surrounds me. I'm not cut out to be a peacemaker, I can't arbitrate between the warring parties. I am told that Ganna has misinformed me on certain significant matters. When Ganna senses my wavering, she flies off the handle. 'What am I supposed to do, Ganna,' I say desperately, 'it's like being set upon by a swarm of wasps.' I visit the non-executive chairman, Imperial Councillor Schönpflug is his name. 'Frau Herzog's actions are not quite transparent,' says this otherwise sympathetic man. I reply bluntly that I couldn't permit the least doubt of the integrity of my wife. I tell her. She asks me to set down my views in a short memorandum to the board: that will gag her enemies. I can't deny her this, I wouldn't get any peace. On the other hand, I am in danger of myself being exposed, and perhaps even, who knows, perpetrating a lie; Ganna is terribly prone to self-deception – it may be that she is less innocent than she thinks she is. I write my deposition, convincingly affirming the integrity of her character and the ethical goodness of her actions. Then I run away, and spend a few weeks in peace in Ebenweiler.

## The tragedy of the male

Before I relate how the ever uglier and more distressing business of the school went on and finally ended, I want to talk about my own experiences in the years before the war, and in the first years of the war – two in particular that, each in their own way, had a profound effect on the future. The one was the birth of my daughter Doris, the other the gift of a house – a whole fully furnished house, with grounds – the kind gift of a young couple I had been close friends with for some time. I had told them about my domestic trouble, the difficulty of finding peace and concentration in a rented apartment, and the resulting tendency to fritter away the day and do my work at night. Then, on a generous impulse, they offered me the money to buy a house in the country. I was so stunned I could hardly breathe. I didn't dare turn it down, but felt I couldn't accept it either. It was extraordinary; I asked myself if I had any right to avail myself of this favourable smile of fortune, it almost seemed to me it would be betraying my friends to do so. How can you deserve such a sacrifice – albeit those making it don't see it as such – how thank them, when thanks you can't give will end up burdening you? I had none of the greedy self-certainty of those geniuses (I didn't think I was one in any case) who accept support and help from their admirers as a perfectly natural form of tribute. I was too steeped in the bourgeois ethos of deals and contracts. The formulas 'nowt for nowt' and 'you scratch my back, I'll scratch yours' were in my blood. It wasn't easy for me to see myself in any way as (in some higher sense) 'deserving' the generosity of these friends.

Ganna, however, had no such scruples. She thought it was absolutely to be expected that people would seek to spoil me a little. They were only giving me back what they had already had from me in plenty, she said, with eyes wide. 'Come off it,' I said, petulantly, 'there must be a couple of thousand like me. Ninety per cent of us will probably die in a ditch. You're doing pretty well if you have enough to eat and a bed to sleep in at night. What's so special about me? What have I done to deserve a luxury villa? We have no right to such security, it seems to me.' Ganna vehemently disagreed. She was too obviously the child of a well-provided and self-righteous era where mind and work had their value just as stocks and shares did. It raised my worth immeasurably in her eyes, although she seemed not to be aware of the fact that it was her husband who had been given the house. Nothing like this had happened since the days of the Medicis. She trumpeted her and my good fortune to all and sundry, and when I asked her to be a little discreet, she looked at me uncomprehendingly. But it gave us a neutral territory where our shared interests could get to work on a common project. Ganna needed to be kept busy, she was like a stove needing fuel. She could do twenty things at once, and each of them with verve and enthusiasm. And when we discussed the house together, looked for a piece of land, spoke to the architect, studied the plans, bought furniture and lamps and other things, the besetting passivity I fell into whenever I was with her left me, and I could at least be dragged along. And, so that she didn't see I was only allowing myself to be dragged along, I would stroke her tiny hand which was feeding me sugar lumps, so that I for my part wouldn't notice how she was dragging me along. Marriage offers the weaker party plenty of opportunity to show no character.

It took no particular cleverness or endeavour on Ganna's part to induce me to have my new possession – this house, the workplace and refuge intended for me personally – registered in her name as well. One day we went along to the land registry office and Ganna was legally made co-owner of the villa. I gave the matter no thought whatsoever. I didn't think that I was thereby relinquishing the one and only thing that was entirely mine. I didn't reflect that I was establishing Ganna in a feeling of owner-ship and entitlement that – beyond the actual name on the deeds – signified in some magical sense a transfer of body and soul.

But I was only superficially engaged with all this. In hind-sight, these years came to seem like a trek along a dark, over-hung path, with rare moments of rest or looking up. I could sense that tremendous things were imminent. The black cloud, still invisible below the horizon, was already projecting electric waves, and I was continually nervous, like a bird before a storm. There was an awful magic being wrought over the land and over the people, I felt ill at ease when I walked at night, as I often had occasion to, through the streets of German cities; I suffered from my second sight like a sleeper dreaming his house is on fire. It seemed to me another world was claiming me than the one in which I had thus far been content to be. What I had achieved seemed negligible, inadequate; it spoke to too few people, it existed in outmoded forms. I had a sense of others, waiting, but I didn't know anything about them. I was still far from my limits, and far from myself; if I failed to break through my crust, then I would find myself crushed by it.

My senses too were aflame. Ravenous appetite alternated with satiety. No woman was enough for me; none gave me what I was dimly seeking: a sense of who I was, some final easement of the blood. I went from one to another, and it was often as though I had to break them open like a husk or shell with unknown contents, peeling them like a fruit which I then discarded. It wasn't Don Juan-ishness, nor was it sheer lechery either. There might have been something in it of the misunderstanding that takes the living being and half-angrily, half-playfully exchanges it for an imaginary one, and contents itself with that because it can't perfect the other. Perhaps it was something to do with the tragedy of the male who sets off towards the glacial region of symbols and en route forgets himself with warm-blooded nymphs.

By the time the baby was born, we were already living in our new house.

## The truth begins to dawn

Only then did events with the school board take on the shape of the catastrophe that deeply affected both Ganna's life and mine. The main cause of the trouble was that Ganna stubbornly refused to make over the meadow to the company. The stockholders described it as intolerable that the extensive land for the project, on which the newly built school was standing, should remain in separate ownership, and that the owner, herself a member of the board, should charge a substantial rent for it. In the course of stormy meetings, Ganna was upbraided for the immoral and unbusinesslike nature of the situation. It made her look bad, it was said, that she laid claim both to the idealism of the project and the lion's share of the profits. That is very much the way of it: people who have disappointed expectations of money are extremely hard on those who, while on the side of the angels, also want to turn a profit. That's wrong, they say, there are businessmen and there are priests, you can't be both at once. The other side's lawyers even contested Ganna's title. Their claim was that Ganna had managed to acquire the title by some underhand method, and they sought to expose it.

Ganna is left reeling. The world is darkening on her. She swears sacred oaths that she would rather die than give up her meadow; she won't give up a square foot of it, no, not so much as a blade of grass. Inevitably, the children, for whose sake this venture was started, become aware of their mother's unpopularity. The advantage that Ganna sought to gain for them is lost. But neither can I find that they are disadvantaged and emotionally damaged by all this, as Ganna weepingly claims. They needed to learn to take the rough with the smooth, I opine with a calmness that drives Ganna into a fury. 'How can you stick up for those criminals?' she hisses at me. 'That just shows what a weakling you are. The whole world knows that you abandon your wife at the earliest opportunity. Well, God will punish you for it.' Those speeches! I really haven't abandoned her, and why is she coming with her divine punishment? What does she know of God, she who only ever uses His name in vain. Her god is Ganna Herzog's special constable, who will launch his thunderbolts the moment his dear Ganna is hurt by a bad person.

She goes up to the teachers and gives them all a piece of her mind. It fails to improve matters. Ferry goes on strike; we've reached the stage where the children are paying for Ganna's misdeeds. The quality of the teaching, which Ganna once praised to the skies, is suddenly wretched. The same teachers who only recently were paragons, so many Fröbels and Pestalozzis, are now held in contempt. She sticks at nothing in her campaign against the headmaster Borngräber, with whom she was certainly once half in love. She conspires with handymen and charwomen. Day after day she hangs around with people in whom the name Herzog inspires no respect. She tussles with them. Like anyone with a political mission, she is surrounded by provocateurs and flatterers. I worry that she won't come out of this smelling of roses.

The establishment is crumbling. She comes home in the evening shattered from her campaigns. She gulps down the warmed-up leftovers of lunch, not tasting anything, not knowing what she's eating. She runs into the nursery, where she opens the floodgates of her dammed-up tenderness, because, with her maternal care limited to this brief interval, she tries to make up for constancy by intensity of feeling, and remains sternly unaware of anything that might show her idols in any other light than in her immediate passion. But then all it needs is for one of the children to test her patience, or not play along with her latest whim, and she starts to yell crazily at the shocked – a moment ago babied – creature, and if I try and intervene (it's one of Ganna's abiding characteristics that she can't stand any contradiction, not from anyone, in any matter), then she will foam with rage. If the telephone shrills she shuffles out into the corridor in her down-at-heel slippers, and I hear her dull 'Hallo-o' which drives me wild with nervousness, ten times an evening, twenty – a real huntsman's sound, it sounds like the jungle with its grim long-drawn-out 'o-o'. It's very evident if the person at the other end is someone who wants something from her, or if it's someone she wants something from; if it's the former her voice is cutting, mordant, bossy, and if it's the latter it's sweet, beseeching, submissive. After her supper she comes into my room and combs her hair, an activity that seems to take her for ever, during which she dreams and builds castles in the air, and chews over old wrongs she's suffered. The comb drives crackling through her chestnut hair, her wide-open blue eyes stare fixedly into space. What they're so fixed on is anyone's guess, not even she herself knows; but the bottomless pain etched into her features moves me. And when I think she's on her way to bed, so that her tortured soul will finally have some peace, she will remember something and hurry across to the desk, to compose some long screed or epistle which the next day will turn out to be perfectly meaningless and superfluous.

It's in the nature of hell that it affords ever deeper degrees of torment and dread; you think it can't get any worse, but you're only in some antechamber of limbo, some zone of moderate awfulness; and that was my position when Ferry and Elisabeth were removed from the school and put in an ordinary state school instead. Whether it was punishment or a voluntary withdrawal wasn't vouchsafed to me. Ganna claimed it was an act of revenge and I had to believe her; I had no desire to go looking for the truth, I didn't want to create yet more conflict. The heads of the state schools had little good to say about the private school, and Ganna's bewilderment was great when the various gymnasiums refused mid-semester to admit Ferry; and her shock was even greater when it was put down to the insufficient preparedness of the boy. Anxiety darkened my mood. I felt accountable for my son, but how could I stand up for him at the court of destiny, when his mother robbed me of all responsibility and remonstrated passionately with the judge against whose verdict there was no appeal? The thing she had tried to save him from now came to pass, with a vengeance: intellectual insecurity, academic caprice. I didn't have the time to win back from her what she claimed from me and the world as hers of right. No, I didn't have either the time or the energy to fight with her and persuade her to change course. I thought – maybe foolishly, maybe vaingloriously – that God had given me my days for some other purpose than that anyway. Ganna's world was a world of limitless freedom, and for her to help herself from it equally limitlessly was the only way to happiness that she knew, even though whatever happiness resulted wasn't what she wanted. I can remember hours when I argued with her as though my soul's salvation depended on it, tried to break her rigid purpose, tried to make her milder, gentler, more insightful. But it was like trying to draw a face on a sheet of water. Once, in a strange fit of contrition, she said to me: 'For you I would have to be a saint, but I can't become holy without a mortal sin.' I have never been able to forget those painful and terrible words. An abyss opened, at the bottom of which I glimpsed a Ganna fighting with ghostly shadows.

And what about me? What was I? A man being crushed in the fist of destiny. The war was tearing at me, tearing me in two the way a storm breaks a sheet of ice on a frozen lake; it broke me and I flooded and flooded, and the quiet dreamer and worker, the hibernal dreamer, the frozen dreamer, became a waker with the experiences of many, the sufferings of many in his bosom. Sleep and peace fled from me, and I stepped out of my rocky fastness; I tried to help, I tried to serve, I was looking for a soul, and if I hadn't happened to find it finally in Bettina Merck, then despair would have choked me.

Ganna remained oblivious to all this. There was never a conversation about these things, no chance of a serious debate, as she was completely taken up with her business. There was something eerie about the way the global catastrophe seemed not to touch her. Her involvement in the events that shook all five continents was that of a little girl who was surprised to see the sky reddened by distant fires. She didn't quite believe that the news that reached her ears was based on actual events. Her shock had something feigned, it was as though there was some conspirative agreement between people who didn't concern her; all the while the true, the palpable, the Ganna world, the Ganna nursery world had nothing to do with these bruited, alleged doings.

I had volunteered in the first few weeks of the war. No man of heart and upstanding character at that time gave any thought to the rights and wrongs of the war, nor did anyone know what war actually was, or what it meant. We were parts of a whole and the whole was, or appeared to be, a living organism, a people, a fatherland, a place of being and becoming. I made up an excuse to Ganna, travelled into Vienna overnight and went to the consulate. The Consul, who knew me, initially wanted to pack me off home because they were so overrun with volunteers, but I insisted on being examined. The doctor found a cardiac neurosis. I went home desperately disappointed to Ebenweiler and told Ganna what I'd done. She was aghast with shock.

'What are you playing at, Alexander,' she cried, 'a father of young children, a family to support, you're not serious?'

Then it was my turn to be shocked; I think it was on that day that it occurred to me that the female Don Quixote was only a decoy.

'And what's the matter with your heart?' she moaned, when I told her what the doctor had said. 'You see, it's because you don't look after yourself. You smoke too much, you don't sleep enough, you should listen to me.'

'Oh no, Ganna,' I said, 'it's not that. Living means using up your heart. That's the point. I will have got too upset about too many things. Has it never occurred to you that getting upset is worse for me than smoking and not sleeping?'

That hurt her. She wanted to know what had upset me, as though it could be anything I might put my finger on. I was unable to give her a detailed instance; what difference would it have made if I had, she would have tried to talk it away and another argument would have started. Still, she kept boring in on me, and finally she asked me if I thought she was a good wife to me.

'Have you got any grounds for complaint? Tell me, aren't I a good wife to you?'

'Yes, Ganna, you are,' I said, 'you're a good wife to me.'

Then she wanted me to swear that I really meant it.

'What's the point of that, Ganna, don't be childish,' I replied, and more than ever I had the sense of her hopeless trusting in forms of words, believing in hollowed-out notions and being in love with an image of herself that bore no relation to the living being.

## Ganna makes her will

By now, things have got to the point where the consortium or board or whatever the group of directors called themselves have started to demand the meadow back from Ganna. She can name a price for it, she is told, but within reason. It's not easy for Ganna to think of a number, seeing as the exploitation of the meadow is the subject of all her dreams, and she wants to make me happy by it (though I don't seem very happy about it). With a strange unaccountable tenderness she clings onto the piece of property in her mind; 'my little meadow' she says, and smiles just as blissfully as when giving our little Doris her breast. How can such a thing be, what makes someone like that tick? I can't explain it to myself.

The pressure on her from all sides is too much; she loses her nerve. Tossed back and forth between opposition and weakness, tenacity and fear, bitterness and speculative greed, she is unable to make her mind up. She asks everyone who crosses her path for an opinion – her sisters, her brothers-in-law, the servants, the suppliers, the gardener. But if one doesn't coincide with her own secret wishes she becomes unpleasant, and launches into lengthy discussions of her view and praise of the meadow.

She calls a general meeting. People talk, quarrel, shout, and at the end Ganna promises to make her decision public the next day. The next day she communicates the price to the board in writing. No sooner has she posted the registered letter than she takes fright and asks for it back. 'They'd be laughing all the way to the bank,' she says to me, 'I should ask for three times as much, they're all well-off people and I mustn't allow them to bully me.' I warn her. I don't know what's going on, but this seems to me to be playing a dangerous game. More negotiations, more ranting and screaming, followed by an abrupt walk-out. The brothers-in-law are with me in exhorting her to moderation. Dr Pauli describes the offer made to her as decent and acceptable; she resists it with all her might, claims she is being cheated. The inappropriateness of her demand is proved to her; she seems to accept it, only an hour later to be back with her old standpoint. She runs from pillar to post, scolds those who disagree with her, wastes people's time, describes the intrigues being used to intimidate her, comes up with vast sums she is being cheated of by the pressure of the antagonists, asks every Tom, Dick and Harry: 'Should I do it, should I not, at this price, at that price, on this condition, on that condition? Will I regret it, won't I regret it? Is it not a crime against my husband and my children if I let that gang walk away with my lovely meadow?' She thinks about nothing else. She lives like a fugitive. She neglects herself, her domestic duties, me, the children. She no longer appears at mealtimes. Sometimes she can be found sitting on a bench in the public park, eating an apple. Sometimes having a nap in an Automat, listening to a scratchy gramophone record all dewy-eyed as if it were the Philharmonic.

Her indecisiveness, her anger, her restlessness, her wheeling and dealing, her tangled arguments, all the trash of a commercial dispute fought out with repulsive methods – she brings them all to me and dumps them on my lap. I am to 'have the last word'. I decline; the last word would only be the penultimate one anyway. Every evening till far into the night the same song with the same exhausting refrain that it was all for my sake, that this whole struggle was all for me and only for me. 'If you accept that, then I'll stop,' she says. 'Do you accept that, do you accept that?' Echolalia and nothing but. What am I to say? She won't stop anyway, never mind how much I accept.

I can't stand the endless rhetoric of it any more; the canny lawyerly presentations; the suspicions of people who are either acting in good faith, or who have nothing more dastardly in mind than Ganna herself, namely to make some money. I am nauseated by the disagreeable mixing of profit motive and high-mindedness. The story of the meadow is already making waves. To know that my name is being used in connection with it pains me. Old Councillor Schönpflug approaches me once in the club and begs me to keep Ganna from further folly, which might end up in a court case and not just a civil one at that. It's horrible, it's humiliating, I must try and bring it to an end.

One morning, dressed and ready to go out, I walk into Ganna's bedroom to say goodbye to her. She is just coming out of the bathroom, swathed in a red and white chequered dressing-gown. No sooner does she catch sight of me than she launches into the usual daily litany. There is to be a meeting at Dr Pauli's at twelve o'clock, could I not perhaps attend. It would help her a lot. She would be forever grateful to me (or rather, I think to myself, she would never forgive me if I refused).

Of late, I haven't shown her much in the way of friendliness. It cost me too much. I can't be friendly if I don't have it in me to be so. I have become increasingly cold and laconic and irritable. I am angry with myself for my lovelessness. But my heart is blocked. I can't find a kind word. Not now either. I shrug. The thought of more talks at the lawyer's office gives me the willies. I couldn't, I'm afraid, I say. Straight away Ganna turns aggressive. If only I could leave her to rage and walk off. But her tirades are like glue, and I'm stuck fast. When she calls it pathetic, my refusal to support her, the man for whom she is sacrificing herself, I remind her I hadn't demanded or wished for any such sacrifice, and she was more use to me as a housewife and mother of our children. That earns me a salvo of derision from Ganna's mouth.

'That's the thanks I get! I bleed myself dry for such a man, such a monster, more like! What thanks!'

'There's nothing to thank you for,' I remark with a degree of calm that should have given Ganna pause, but it washes off her, 'just as I never counted on a life like the one you're making me.'

Ganna laughs hollowly. 'What do you mean by that? What life? How do you propose to live? Do you want to starve till you get white hair? Where would you be without me anyway? Ask yourself that.'

'I don't know where I'd be without you, all I know is that I can no longer go on *with* you. Either you put an end to the business with the meadow and just sell it, or I'm going to leave you and get a divorce.'

No sooner has the word fallen than Ganna's features are contorted. The word is not one that has been spoken before between us. She never thought she would hear it. She feels as sure of me as if I were a part of her, an arm or a leg. She is fundamentally secure, rootedly secure. Perhaps the dread word lies in some buried depths of her unconscious, like an explosive charge in a cellar. She gives a scream. The scream, which is awful, shrill and guttural, lasts fully fifteen or twenty seconds, and while she is screaming she is running around the room like a madwoman. She is certainly oblivious. She is certainly not in possession of her senses. Even so, I have the feeling that the utter loss of self-control is giving her pleasure, the pleasure of abdication, of psychic degeneration, that epileptics are said to have during a fit. While she rips the dressing-gown off with furious movements, she hurls a torrent of abuse at me. In every register of which her voice is capable she shouts the dread word at me: divorce. Inquiring, shouting, squawking, howling, gasping, with fingers hooked like claws and blue flashing eyes. And as I suffer the ghastly outburst showing me a wholly new, unsuspected Ganna in silence, she runs over to the window, stark naked as she is, and leans over the metal rail with her upper body, as though to plummet down the next moment. I am instantly reminded of the scene sixteen years ago, on the balcony by the Mondsee. Basically, she always does the same thing, I think to myself sadly, reaches for the same trick to get the other person in her power, the same words, the same gestures; only I always forget, and I always fall for it. In spite of my tormenting fury I remain relatively cool. I know she won't do it; anyway there's not much danger, the window's about ten or twelve feet over the garden, which at that point is lawn – at the most she could break one or two ribs. But my certainty that she won't throw herself over gives the situation something darkly ridiculous. At the same time, the rage that has been gathering inside me suddenly bursts out like a jet of boiling steam; it's years and years since I last felt anything like it; with a single bound I am behind her, I grab her by the bare shoulders, fling her onto the bed and start blindly punching her. I still can't imagine how it came over me. I'm laying into her like a drunk in a bar fight. Like a drayman. I, Alexander Herzog, am punching a woman. And Ganna is completely quiet. Curious, because she's so quiet I stop hitting her and rush up to my room, lock the door behind me, drop into my chair, and sit perfectly still and brood about my misfortune.

And what did Ganna do in the meantime? I found out later, by chance. I found a sealed envelope on her desk, inscribed with her big accusing capital letters: My Will and Testament. When I asked her in amazement when and why she composed her will, she tells me with tear-stained face that it was just after I had hit her. I begged her not to bring it up again. But she told me about her despair and how she had sworn to herself to sell the meadow that very day. One day I would surely understand what I had done to her, what I had done to myself . . . From that moment on, we each had our own private stab-in-the-back story. Ganna never let go of the version that I had gone for her at the very moment she was in the process of making me millions. This figment was Ganna's prop through all the later blows of fortune she suffered. In that way, she was like all conquered peoples and power-hungry parties; without a scapegoat she had no chance of confronting reality. And scapegoats are everywhere to be found, since without divided responsibility there is no practical action.

Burdened with this moral debt, whose interest payments I with my usual willingness took upon myself, I emerged into a new phase of my life – the one for the sake of which I have set down these confessions.

*The Age of Dissolution*

Every beast is driven to pasture by a blow.
Heraclitus

## My acquaintance with Bettina

I first met Bettina Merck in the house of a young couple by the name of Waldbauer, friends of mine, very dear people; he was an art historian. At the time Bettina was just twenty-five – seventeen years younger than I. She had been married for seven years and had two children, both girls. Her husband, who was the same age as she, was the director of a large porcelain factory which he had taken over following the death of his father, in spite of his youth. Bettina's father had been a popular composer and band leader, hence her musical gift. A friend of Kainz's and Mahler's, he was still remembered with fondness, and accounted one of the last in the old Austrian tradition. Some of his melodies had the status of folk songs and lived on long after their creator. I had known him. I distinctly remembered this fine, sensitive man. He had a particular sort of lovable mockery about him; lovableness was one of his prime characteristics. When I talked about him, Bettina's eyes lit up. She adored her father more than anything.

Something I noticed about her that very first evening was a kind of laughing cheerfulness. Oddly, I reacted to it with hostility, as though I thought it was somehow improper to be so blithe and cheerful, in contradiction to the age and the world. Just like her father, I crabbed at her in thought, always light, always in waltz time. Every passing jest caused her to laugh her pearly laugh. At times the whole room rang with her laugh, which infected the others and spread a sort of sheen. That bothered me as well. I wonder why? As a child I had been prone to fits of gloom, when I saw some other boy eating a piece of bread and butter and I myself was without. When I gradually loosened up and responded to her levity, as much as I could, it was still with the grim reserve of a schoolmaster, anxiously intent on preserving his dignity when confronted with some prize pupil.

A couple of days later I ran into her on the tram, and we fell into conversation right away. Again I took her lively cheerfulness as a sort of challenge, because it was in such contrast to me and the people I was used to. I had the absurd feeling she wanted to catch me off guard. It really was an absurd feeling: there was nothing of the sort in her mind. I can remember watching in astonishment when her stop came, and she said goodbye, and I saw her cross the street. It was her dancing walk that caused me to be astonished. Is it lawful to walk like that, I thought, and I wrapped myself in my sour mood as in a fur wrap I had merely cast aside for a few moments, because it was warm.

I don't remember how it was that shortly afterwards we started meeting and going for walks together. I think I must have suggested it; perhaps I telephoned her. But I can't say what prompted me to do so. It's often the way that the origins of earth-shaking developments remain so obscurely trivial that they can't even be identified afterwards. It was a tone of voice, a look, a movement of the hand, a smile, a casual word; I can't remember. Nor can I remember if it happened after we had known each other for a short time or for longer, that I gave her the proof of my new novel to read – the book that represented my breakthrough. It was a novel about a town, a provincial town in the middle of Germany, all of a piece, balladesque where the characters were concerned, and, like most of what I have written, sombre in its mood but with plenty of popular touches, which explains its subsequent success. It was my dues to my German background, a sort of physical tribute to the German people – a war book in a certain sense, since I wasn't permitted to bear arms myself.

As I say, I am unable to recall the circumstances in which I presented it to Bettina, but I have a pretty good recall of what she said about it once she'd read it – not least because it was not at all what I'd expected her to say. I had hoped she would be enthusiastic. With my naive author's vanity I hadn't doubted she would be, knowing as I did that she had followed my output to date and openly declared herself to be part of my devoted readership. That had helped overcome my initial resistance to her, I may as well admit, even though it doesn't say much for my objectivity. Now, though, instead of the enthusiastic endorsement I had hoped for, I encountered a disconcerting dryness. I had yet to meet a woman with such high standards. Accustomed as I was to Ganna's unbounded admiration, forever expressed in superlatives, I found myself unhappily impressed by Bettina's brave reservations. She didn't deny that parts of the book moved her, some of the characters convinced her, but overall it was too heavy for her – not intellectually, but in its feeling and construction, too heavy and – the word gave me pause – too barbaric even. There was of course no comeback to that, but a man wants to justify himself, to explain; and I can still see the strangely firm and alert expression of her blue eyes when I told her what I had intended. She understood me straight away, her intellect really was extraordinary; and what most struck me was her intuitive grasp of rhythm, of the subtlest nuances and harmonies. But she would not be reconciled to the petty bourgeois world I laid out; it was too involved, too full of masks and ghosts, not elevated enough, too fusty in its eroticism, too befogged, too straitened. It was at this time that she came to speak of the opposition between the Austrian and what was now held up as German, and what to her and her friends was neo-German, also of the condescension and criticism with which the Prussians responded to Austrian form, lightness, softness and urbanity: that was more than she could stand. I listened to her, I looked at her, I said to myself: not only is this woman the daughter of an artist, she is an artist in her own right. Yes, she was, through and through, in every fibre of her being, in every breath, with a force and a consequence I had yet to find in a woman. No wonder she soon became my confidante and friend. Our relationship was based on nature and on my spiritual situation.

Now I have something odd to say. For a long time I remained ignorant of the nature of my understanding with Bettina. I couldn't even have said if I liked her as a woman or not. When I very gradually, in my obtuse way, discovered that I loved her, I saw to my astonishment that I as yet felt no trace of passion for her. And when my love finally took me over, body and soul, heart and spirit, I still believed in some sort of sublime comradeship, without consequences for the future, without entailing any commitment. How could such a thing be? It had never happened to me before. Perhaps it was because there was nothing darkly grasping in her, nothing that wanted to conquer and possess, nothing that insisted on vows and promises; she simply left me in my freedom, and waited calmly and patiently for whatever might be. Perhaps because she wasn't cramped and addicted and greedy and purposeful, consumed by some splendid notion of what it was that would make and keep her happy. It was this, the lightness and cheerfulness, which I had initially rejected so grimly, that now entered my life, changing all its stresses and emphases. There was always something about the others that hadn't been right – their corporality or their views or their characters or their preferences or their sense of life – and I had always ended up feeling beached and washed up. Here, not only was everything right, but with each new day it made more sense. It was like finally looking up after decades under a louring grey sky and seeing blue overhead, an almost cloudless blue. Sometimes I would reflect in alarm: will things stay the way they are? Can they? Won't she absorb the poison of my darkness into herself?

## One November evening

For a long time Bettina refused to come to our house. Since there were people who refused to see anything in me except a man who breakfasted on young virgins, at first it was her self-respect that kept her from running to me dutifully like a little dog that comes when called. That was how she put it mockingly, later, once. Also, I had neglected to ask her husband as well when I invited her, and she took against me for that. Then we had a proper soirée once at which Paul Merck, and the Waldbauers, and some other friends turned up. They only thawed out a little once Ganna, who didn't feel easy among such people, had withdrawn.

Bettina didn't like our house. She didn't talk about it, but I could sense she didn't. She shivered when she set foot in it. Sometimes I would ask her why, but she would only shake her head. The fact that the rooms didn't appeal to her, that there was something extravagant about the layout – that seemed clear, in the light of her conservative tastes; but I was afraid that it might be the lady of the house with whom she couldn't get along. And so it was, she was unable to keep it hidden from me for long: Ganna was for her the strangest creature under the sun, and when I tried to explain to her what great moral and spiritual qualities Ganna in my view had, she would hear me out in silence with a curious, patient expression in her eyes, but without once demurring. She would never have permitted herself to take such a liberty.

And yet I knew her to be an exceptionally acute observer – to the degree that I was sometimes left gawping like a small boy at the speed and certainty of her judgements when she explained some sequence of events, with details of which I had registered precisely none. Nor was she one of those people who dine out on such a gift. She was able to keep her silence until speech became a matter of urgency. Also, she saw and heard many things that she had decided, for one reason or another, not to hear or see. From the choice of what she observed or didn't observe, registered or allowed to pass, it would be possible to construct a pretty detailed description of her character. For example she knew, as everyone knew, that Ganna didn't just allow me to deceive her (Bettina called it 'deceive', even though there was really no question of deception, in view of my modus vivendi with Ganna), but even used to brag about my adventures, as a way of indicating to anyone who cared to hear that all other women were nothing but provisionally favoured courtesans compared to her. Bettina knew this, and simultaneously tuned it out in her awareness. She did so, as it were, in the name of all women who were offended thus, including even Ganna. It was her view that it was too humiliating to people not simply to ignore the way they chose to lower themselves. I, with the rotten attitude of a libertine I affected at that time, shrugged my shoulders and thought Ganna's attitude had something to be said for it.

Unluckily (unluckily for me, because I was anxiously set on keeping Ganna high in Bettina's esteem), the following once happened in Bettina's presence. Ganna had dinned it into the maid to check that Elisabeth's piano teacher didn't end a lesson early, as she had reason to fear she might. When she was told the young lady had left the room eight minutes before the set time, she hurried out into the corridor where Bettina was just slipping into her coat and confronted the trembling piano teacher. 'I insist on proper time-keeping,' she barked. 'I pay you to come on time and leave on time. If that's too much for you, then you can save yourself the bother.' I have to say, it was like water off a duck's back to me, I was much too inured to such scenes. A man deadens; I had heard it too often. But Bettina went pale. 'I pay you': to say those words to a fellow human being! She felt giddy. Much, much later, when she recalled the scene to me, she confessed that she felt like seizing Ganna by the wrist and calling: 'Woman, woman, get a grip on yourself! That's no way to behave!' I didn't really get it. For me it was an outburst, nothing more. Ganna's just like that, I would comfort myself and others; you have to take the rough with the smooth. And so I failed to see, wouldn't see, what was brewing.

I say that, and yet I knew all the time that the situation was radically changed from what it had been before. From a certain point on, I could no longer show Ganna the sort of openness that during the worst times of our marriage had kept alive the illusion of an indestructible union, and had preserved Ganna in the faith that she was the presiding female presence in my life. I kept out of her way. I lowered my eyes. I was hurtful and cold. And above all: I neglected my marital obligations entirely. That had never happened before. There had always been some left-over scraps for Ganna: an hour of comfort, a little bribe of affection. Now it was no longer possible. Bettina made it impossible. Not that she had demanded or expected such a thing; not a bit. But her whole being was against it, a way of being in honesty and truth. A way of being that flowed into me as what was right for me and shaped me.

One November evening is caught in my memory like a scene of dread.

It's late when I get home. I have experienced something

wonderful. Bettina has played for me on her violin, the first time in the seven months I've known her. An entire Bach suite, ending with the chaconne. It wasn't masterful; the ultimate per cents of the maestro were lacking; but how much song, how much sweetness, how much force and fire; and how secretly altered my pulse beat and my heart, as though I myself had been playing and had invented the rhythms. An unforgettable hour, which had shown me another Bettina hidden behind the cheerful child of the world.

And now the whitewashed walls of our hall, which is at the same time our dining room, stare at me soberly and the grotesque lamps threaten me with their outraged arms. Quickly in to see little Doris, to cast an eye on the little sleeper, quickly choke down a few bites of something, then on to work. But at the other side of the table sits Ganna, her eyes shining with reproach, her lips quivering, her arms folded, the whole woman a single mute accusation and indignity.

I ought to go. I ought to say goodnight to her and disappear up into my eyrie. My loitering just makes the q. and a. unavoidable.

'Why are you so late? Where have you been?'

Of course she knows where I've been.

'What's the matter with you, Alexander? Have you forgotten me? Do I not mean anything to you any more?'

Then more urgent, pleading: 'You spend all your time with that woman now. You're practically inseparable, you and her. Complete strangers are talking about it.'

Still I don't say anything. I stalk around and stare into the corners. Ganna continues:

'You know I've nothing against you satisfying your urges? Have I ever shown myself ungenerous? But just because I am, I'm now being tortured to death.'

My silence provokes her. She wrings her hands.

'Alexander, how can you! A man like you! That woman can do what she likes with you. Have you no pity?'

Another evening's going to go to waste, I think; if I go out now and say a friendly goodnight, then she'll be content, she has such an oddly selective memory. But I can't. I can't walk out and abort the brewing scene before it can get properly started. What stops me is fear. Naked fear. Let me explain, as best I can. Ganna has the frightful gift of unsettling my imagination. No one else has such an effect on me. That explains her hold on me, which, far from weakening, is getting ever stronger. She knows it too. She knows I'm incapable of leaving her alone to brood in solitude. If I am within hailing distance then it's still possible that, in spite of the 'selective memory', she will manage to produce a catastrophe. That's what the voice inside me tells me, even if I can't say what manner of catastrophe it will be. After all, it would be enough if she smashes a mirror and wakes the maids in the attic with her shouting; it's not out of the question that she will do herself a mischief. Everything is possible. From one instant to the next she will quite deliberately turn off her consciousness – it's really quite extraordinary – and then be responsible for nothing she does. Once, in Ebenweiler, she ran out into a storm following an argument, up the mountain, and I had to get up a search party of hunters and farmers. Once something like that happens, it means the end of any chance of working for several weeks; the ability to do work is always somehow the first to go. That's what I dread. What I'm thinking is this: hold things together at all costs, until the work in progress is done; after that my hands will be free and we can sort it out. Of course I'm deluding myself here. Because seeing as I plunge from book to book, like someone swimming for his life in the ocean, from wave to wave, it's impossible to see when I could be able to 'sort it out'. Still, this is how the notion came to be established in my brain that my presence is the only thing that will prevent Ganna from mounting a successful coup against my existence. (In a certain sense, this notion turned out to be perfectly correct.) At the same time, I know that my mere presence is sufficient to give Ganna the courage to go wild. What's the way out of this dilemma? What reasonable man would leave a woman alone at a painful juncture, when he knows that her life feels dire and she will collapse into a bundle of misery? And so I turn myself into the object, the victim, of her emotional excesses. To avoid the theoretical worst, I accept what is truly unbearable. It's like a sulphur cloud. Ganna pours out wild tirades against Bettina. I lose my calm. I shout at her. Which is exactly what she wants, to wrest me out of my equanimity – that's her satisfaction and vengeance. The words fly back and forth like so many poison darts. The door opens silently. Elisabeth, startled awake, is standing in the doorway in her nightdress. In deep, half-asleep confusion she looks at her father and mother. The look of those child's eyes! It condemns me for ever. I pick her up and carry her back to bed, with silent caressings. When I return to Ganna she is sitting there in tears. She at least is able to cry. I cannot.

## Ganna defends the fortress by mounting an attack

There's no mistaking it: a beaten dog doesn't suffer worse than Ganna. Her world is askew. Her world is me. She can't understand what's happened. It's as though the heart has slowly been cut out of her breast. At night she lies there sleepless, thinking about everything, her tear-dimmed eyes are incapable of seeing anything. She is pondering what she may have done wrong. Because, try as she may, she can see no fault in herself. She has always done her duty, she thinks, her intentions were always of the best. She thinks, if life is too much for two weak arms like hers, then one should have pity on her. My supposed 'pitiless-ness' skews her take on everything. An evil charm has taken me over, otherwise I could not have been able to forget her love and the fact that there is no other woman in the world who is so endlessly obedient to me. It remains her unshakeable conviction that I will never leave her – after all, haven't I said so often enough, in so many words – she tells me with an alarming flar-ing of her eyes, but then why do I not take her by the hand and lead her out of the labyrinth of her great sorrow? And she builds herself a little hope. I am just setting a test for her, she thinks; I am testing her craft for buoyancy. Surely it doesn't need such an extreme test, not such a heartbreaking one, she says with the charmingly innocent smile that her face still, on rare occasions, breaks into; I need only indicate to her now and again that she would be my Ganna again, once she has passed the test, take her for a walk again as she yearns to be taken, say something sweet and affectionate to her, as in former times. She is continually perplexed at the wrong-headedness of men. They could have it so easy with women, but they go about it so badly. But this philosophical musing about 'men's' foolishness does nothing to alter the fact that her breast is burning with woe, and I am standing there like St Sebastian, shot full of arrows . . .

Then why this sudden agitation, this panic, this dread of los-ing me, after so many years of benign indifference to my infi-delities, as she termed them? It hasn't escaped her attention that everything is different with other women. So she finds herself confronted by a conundrum. What can be so special about this Bettina Merck, she asks herself – sometimes she asks me as well. She studies her. She wants to be fair to her. But she fails to see the attraction. To her, Bettina is neither beautiful nor intelli-gent. If only she were at least intelligent. Nor is she even in the first flush of her youth. Evidently (thus Ganna full of woe) she avails herself of cunning amatory arts; I in my simplicity and straightforwardness fail to see through them; she is endlessly subtle; subtlety is the thing; I wish I could learn to be it, but I am too honest for that; besides, she's an unscrupulous man-chaser who doesn't care what the world thinks of her. Or she bores, like this: she's the lucky one, a wealthy background; husband away at work all day; nothing to worry about except how to do herself up, and what instructions to give her cosmetician and her hairdresser; whereas I, worked to the bone, with no time to think of myself. Didn't I always say so: I should be hard, unscrupulous, stop at nothing, deny the heart or soul in my body – with a man hungry for experience and sensation it never fails . . .

I repeat these litanies of thought because I heard them not only in occasional remarks and suggestions, but because they were familiar to me from the deepest insights one can have into human nature. The interesting thing about them is the perpetual division, the sharp alternations between light and shade, understanding and doltishness, fear and loathing, foolishness and impetuosity, suspicion and self-doubt. If her thinking had been less scatty, her emotion less erratic, then it would never have knocked her over. But her inner distractedness extended even to her pain, so at disconnected moments that were drifting like pieces of cork on an agitated sea, she was capable of being good and cheerful. Admittedly, the intervals when she was permitted to sit there half-extinguished and dream, and paint herself a rosy future, grew ever fewer and further between. Blow after blow was delivered to her psyche; life bared its teeth at her. It cut her to the quick when she learned that I had read part of my new work to Bettina and her friends. The fact that I hadn't asked her to come, even once, aroused the bitterest envy she had ever felt, worse than any physical jealousy. She felt rejected and snubbed. But it was unfortunately the case with me that I didn't want Ganna as an audience, because my friends didn't want her. Ganna was unbelievably alien to them. She didn't follow the rules, she didn't know the routine, she was jarring. Nothing was said, but it was abundantly clear to me. I suffered for Ganna, with Ganna. There was nothing to be done. And then Ganna and Bettina in the same room, and me in the middle, even only as a voice – that would have been a lethal discord. To ease Ganna if only a little bit, I took refuge in a lie: her reactions and her judgement were so important to me, I claimed, that I had to be alone with her, I needed the immediate and undisturbed connection. Even though she didn't altogether believe me, she did half-believe me, and maybe that got her over the worst, for a little while at least. But since it could only be for a while, in a deeper sense my lie was more cruel and traitorous than the most unsparing truth could have been.

If Ganna had been only a very little more sensible, if she had known a little more restraint and self-discipline, then it would not have been quite so hard for me to inculcate my friends with a little understanding for her baroque, volatile and unconventional ways; though there were other, more destructive traits of hers I was still in awkward denial of myself. But Ganna will do everything to make herself detested or, more, feared. Such tiny hands, and what is there they can't uproot; such tiny feet, and what can't they trample! One day she dashes over to the telephone, asks to be put through to Paul Merck, and tells him she has heard his two daughters have chickenpox and that in these circumstances our doctor thought any association between our respective families was unadvisable. And she closed with these incredible words: 'Mr Merck, kindly keep your wife from seeing my husband until there is no longer any risk of infection.' Paul Merck, who was a gentleman, couldn't believe what he was hearing. 'Forgive me,' he stammered back, 'I'm not in the way of telling my wife what she can and can't do.' He put aside the earpiece like something red-hot, so Bettina told me later, picked

up a thick periodical and in his rage tore it into little scraps –
something an athlete would have had trouble doing.

Cold shivers ran down my spine when I got to hear about this,
and the next time I was with Paul Merck I went to great lengths
to come up with some extenuating circumstances for Ganna.
Indeed, I went further; I spoke about Ganna's eccentricity, her
feminine genius, her rare spiritual and human depth, and talked myself into such a lather that both Paul Merck and Bettina were
reduced to looking at me in silent astonishment. In the end,
Merck was unable to suppress a sceptically amused smile, but that
only heightened my advocatory zeal. In Bettina's face not a mus-
cle moved, there was no trace of doubt, or curiosity or sympathy.
I might have been talking about some woman in New Zealand.

In the meantime, Ganna had decided to approach Bettina
directly. She's a sensible woman, was Ganna's thought; perhaps
she'll understand my position. It did feel like going straight into
the lion's den but, convinced as she was of her superiority, she
thought success was pretty certain, and so she had herself
announced one day at Bettina's house. Bettina approached the
meeting with trepidation but gave no sign of it, greeting Ganna
with the politeness with which she received any visitors to her
house. She told me about the conversation later, but it was
many months before she included certain details she wanted to
spare me, under the depressing first impression.

A daintily laid table, tea prepared in accordance with a tested
recipe, a plate of freshly cut sandwiches – the times would have
allowed or expected nothing less, but in Ganna's eyes it is a feast.
She is starving. She looks wretched, tired and tormented. Her
dress is at least three years old and fits her badly. Bettina feels a
profound sympathy for her, prevails on her to have something
to eat, keeps refilling her cup. Ganna eats and drinks. Her eyes
scan the room. She appraises the tasteful furnishings with a
woebegone demeanour.

'Yes, you have good taste all right,' she says sadly to herself, 'there's no denying that. But it all takes time.'

Gently Bettina indicates that she doesn't think it's a mistake to have time, or to take time.

'No, but it leads one to have too strong a sense of one's own interests,' Ganna delivers the pedantic and well-prepared counter.

That depended on the nature of those interests, Bettina observes coolly. Ganna laughs, a little shrilly.

'Well, as far as yours are concerned, I would imagine they are largely confined to your person,' she says. Bettina is astounded to be offered so much insight into her nature so quickly.

'I can see from Alexander how easy it is to fall for such frippery,' Ganna continues; 'ever since he met you, he's become terribly pernickety; he used to be so modest, now all of a sudden he knows where to go and buy ties and he demands – it's hysterical, really – that his trousers are pressed every week. I could die laughing.'

Bettina doesn't understand quite why it should be funny, but is agreeable enough to chime in with Ganna's rather forced laughter. Ganna thinks the moment has come to cut to the chase.

'Frau Merck,' she says, and her voice has a palpable edge to it, 'please don't suppose you can capture my husband with such blandishments. Oh, no. Better women than you have tried. Please understand – I'm telling you this out of niceness, to put you in the picture, in case you don't know – my marriage to Alexander is a *rocher de bronze*. Alexander will never divorce me, not under any circumstances. My mind is perfectly at ease on that score. Don't deceive yourself. I am not at all worried. All I want is to prevent you from entertaining false hopes.'

Bettina needs a little time to collect herself. Such a thundershower of horrors has never, in all the time she can remember, fallen on her. Once again she has the sense she needs to call out: 'Woman, watch your mouth! Stop and think. You can't talk to people like that.' She forces a smile and replies as one might to a raving child:

'I'm sure you're right, Ganna. But there's no need to tell me that. No one intends to take Alexander away.'

Ganna emits a sound like a menacing gurgle. 'I don't advise it either,' she says coarsely, concludingly, and gets to her feet.

Bettina walks her out into the hall and helps her into her coat. She sends her regards to the children. Ganna is moved. She departs with gushing thanks. She has no idea how badly she has behaved. She carries her head high and takes pleasure in her victory. Once she's alone, Bettina has a fit of vertigo. She pulls open the windows. Her feet are ice-cold, her nails are blue. She is chilled to the marrow. She goes into the bedroom, gets undressed and falls into bed. She feels a deadly wretchedness all day. She tries to forget the awful events. She has to get rid of them. She won't keep them. When she told me about the visit a week later, she was still shaking, trembling, a-chill.


### Circe

Since all my previous relationships fizzled out after a year, two at the most, Ganna – though at a greater level of upset than at other times – still waited with reasonable confidence for this one to end too. When the end refused to come, she was completely unhinged. Grim old superstitions awoke in her. Sometimes she expressed, perfectly seriously, the suspicion that Bettina must have slipped me a magic potion. Anyway, the danger of a lasting bond seemed so great to her that she thought of ways and means of freeing me from Bettina's toils. This was the basis of one of the most durable Ganna fictions, to which she resorted to keep herself afloat a little longer: that in her view I was trapped in a most reluctantly borne erotic dependency in which I was tormented by the longing to free myself from the bands of this heartless Circe, and sink back into the much more dearly beloved Ganna. Only my cruel seductress wouldn't submit, she made me dozy with her sex potion and robbed me of my manhood to the extent that I even slandered my Ganna to her, which was all the easier as Circe of course had contrived to reinterpret all Ganna's virtues as vices. But this relatively bland fantasy wasn't enough for Ganna. By and by she became convinced that Bettina had had a hand in the forced sale of the meadow; and not her alone, but the whole of the 'Waldbauer set' had been involved, given that the sole desire of these people and their hangers-on was to slander Ganna and take me away from her, and utterly to destroy her.

This farrago of evident nonsense was proof against all arguments; no evidence, no straightforward appearance of things, no amount of pleading or imploring or head-shaking helped; it grew and grew, linked itself to other conspiracy theories, turning the air I breathed into a dirty soup and blackening the sky over my head.

## Bettina's and my culpability

I ought really to write far more about Bettina than I have so far, but it's not easy. My every picture of her straight away moves into such intense close-up that I am unable to make out any outline and am confined to listing, step by step, what changed in me and in my life through her entry into it. I hope that may give a clearer impression of her nature than if I were to cover pages with her qualities, her looks, or her various moods. The actual person with whom you live is bound to be, in a curious way, invisible, in just the same way as you yourself are invisible; all you can do is sense their presence, feel them within you, and in turn expand in them. The word love, compared to that, has little meaning.

It's clear that, from the very beginning, Bettina's marriage gave me much to ponder. Without our ever expressly talking about it, it seemed clear to me, and accepted, that in this matter she would not lower herself to half-measures and dishonesties. By and by I was able to make out how things stood between her and Paul. Basically, it was all very straightforward. They had fallen for one another when they were very young, and had got married, almost on a trial basis. They hadn't fared too badly. Early on there had been a few blameless contretemps, and then they had sealed a compact and were now living harmoniously with and alongside each other. For a little while now, both had had the feeling their relationship was nearing a new status and clarity. They often discussed it, amiably enough, neither wanting to make trouble for the other. Bettina had no money: 'I went into marriage like a church mouse,' she once told me, 'and if I have to, I'll leave it in exactly the same way.' Another time she said: 'Marriage isn't a form of public welfare: you decide what to do about the children – for their sake, if nothing else – and apart from that, why should I be concerned with the man who doesn't want me any more, or I him?' To be light-footed and free, that was all that mattered. Some friends who watched as she span her thread were inclined to describe her as trusting to providence. But that was probably a highfalutin way of putting it. She was, quite simply, not one to feel sorry for herself. She wasn't afraid of life. She didn't need a man with money to pay her way. She scorned the idea of security.

Those months in the city were hard for both of us. It was the time the carnage of the Great War was getting going. The belief that people were suffering for a just cause was being eroded from every side, and was soon to collapse altogether. Men dear to me, who had gone out with enthusiasm, returned wrecks in body and soul, useless for any occupation. At the Somme a half-brother of mine died, whom I had loved dearly in his youth. No letter, no farewell, just a silent death. Inflammatory lies from above and below and beyond the frontiers ground up my heart. The rich with their plenty, their bacchanalian orgies, offered a contrast not to be outdone in its brazenness. While they danced and whored the nights away, armies of mothers stood outside the bakers' and butchers' shops, patient files of lemurs. Many a time, Bettina and I would find ourselves wandering through unlit suburban streets; we were numbed by the extraordinary weight of misery. Once again, by letter and in person, I asked to be taken into the army; my petition was settled when I fell victim to a chronic gall-bladder colic. But for Bettina's close participation in my life and work, I wouldn't have known what to do with myself. 'Is it permitted for two people to live for each other like us?' I asked her anxiously. 'Isn't it tempting fate? Two wretched humans seeking to put off the end by a moment or two of snatched happiness; as if that were the point, and waking wouldn't be the worse for it . . . ' Bettina didn't bite. In her humility, she didn't bite. There was a bird of ill omen that used to scream at night in the garden behind her house; she had called him Giglaio, in imitation of his cry, and when she heard him her every drop of blood would freeze. Luckily she had the blessed gift of forgetting bad and ugly things, that was the obverse of her courage; and when the first green shoots would show above the ground, and the sun rose above a certain gable, she would be desperate for spring and slowly climb out of winter, and the darkness and sickness associated with it. Evidently she had her own darkness in her as well. So-called cheerful people often have much darker hours to endure than self-proclaimed pessimists.

At the beginning of summer we were able to free ourselves from our melancholy existence in the city. It had become a regular thing with us that we would spend the weeks from early June to mid-September in Ebenweiler. Ganna would arrive with the children in July, after the end of the school year, but the weeks Bettina and I had the place to ourselves were the happiest of the year. There, in the valley that had become home to us, we were allowed to forget the world in flames. We weren't mocking the war; rather it became subsumed in nature. When the guns' thunder boomed up to us out of the south, it sounded like God's anger about a humanity that vandalized His creation; the glaciated peaks were like bolted green gates at which human dying stopped. Everything belonged to the two of us, the forests, the lakes, the bridges, the white footpaths. There were starlit evenings when the trembling firmament sprinkled golden flakes on the bed of our love, and rainy nights that seemed they must quench all the flaring hatred of the world. I wandered back and forth, between Bettina's house and mine, at all hours of night and day, in the evening when the cows were watered, in the morning when the farmer sharpened his sickle; the day was called Bettina, the night was called Bettina, Bettina was the whole of life.

But when Ganna is there, that all needs to be paid for. She arrives with endless boxes and cases, bags and bundles; each child has to have its own personal toys, she packs books for any whim she may have, there is enough there for five years of solitary confinement. I reproach her for bringing so much clobber, for the inundation. But that has the opposite effect: why should she have to do without, she asks feistily; where are her ballgowns and her hats and her fourteen pairs of shoes, would I have the kindness to point them out to her? Is she to do without her deckchair? Her Schopenhauer? Behold the man set on putting his wife on the equivalent of bread and water!

I had often beseeched her to stay away from Ebenweiler. Didn't she have her lovely house on the edge of the city, couldn't she just send me the children on their own, with their governess? She dismissed the idea haughtily. She refused to be displaced. She was the lawful wife. 'Do you want me to make it even easier for you and your mistress,' she hissed, 'so that people might think I'd given you over? No, I'm not going to do that person such a kindness. What you are doing to me cries out to high heaven in any case!'

That first summer, Bettina had taken a farmer's cottage a quarter of an hour away. It had been poorly thought out, taking somewhere within such easy range for Ganna. But she fell in love with the place, and not until the fourth summer did she decide to move to another house at the far end of the valley. For too long we failed to see our mistake in choosing as a refuge a place where I had had many years of business connections and was so to speak a public figure. But the landscape was more precious to me than any other; I owed it, in addition to my physical base, everything that nature in the form of atmosphere, water, stone and vegetation can give a sensitive and creative man; I could think of no other refuge and, had I done so, Ganna would have followed us there anyway. It was here, if anywhere, on the basis of my acquaintance with the locals, that we could hope to escape the otherwise unavoidable anathema and be a free couple.

Ganna accepted the advantage that was offered her. The fact that Bettina and I were flouting the bourgeois order represented a triumph for her. Her martyred expression appealed to the sympathy of others. If she had been a little less assiduous in creating a following, a Ganna party, then she would have had even more followers. Inevitably, there were circles in which Bettina was vilified. Cold glances brushed her; tongues wagged behind her turned back; slanders flung up in the air like rubbish when a wind strikes it. Every second or third day some bossy missive of Ganna's, some peremptory note, was delivered to her. She ignored them. She refused to dignify them with her attention. With hasty stride she walked on, her ankle spattered by a little filth. What did it matter? The local ladies didn't invite her to their *jours* and cut her when they meet; doesn't bother her. She barely notices. Sometimes she feels a little jab; a person has their pride, they know who they are, but it's soon overcome. The sight of a flower bed, half an hour on the violin are enough to cause her to forget it altogether. She is not the sort to lower her eyes in front of people. She has no comprehension of meanness, no ear for gossip. A timid acquaintance feels obliged to counsel her to be careful; surely there was no need for her to appear in public with me so much. She replies: 'Why not? How else are we going to get people used to us?'

It remained the place where we were vulnerable. We should have been more discreet, more considerate, more thoughtful. We shouldn't have rubbed Ganna's nose in our happiness. That only stung and provoked her. We made ourselves guilty, incurred an obligation that in later years was called in, in full, and with usurious rates of interest. If Ganna still had any sense then of womanly dignity, we choked it mindlessly, and in the intoxication of being-there-for-each-other we didn't listen to the voice of reason. Of course, I had long since despaired of Ganna, thoroughly and comprehensively despaired, I should long ago have given up the idea of making her any sort of helpmeet; isn't that how things had been for fifteen, sixteen, seventeen years now; and shouldn't I, either by determination or by kindness, with every conceivable sacrifice have cleared things up instead of – through weakness and timidity and a conscientiousness born of cowardice – dragging myself along at the side of a woman to whom I had nothing more to give – or she me – or to become. And Bettina in her loftiness, her aversion to everything murky, divided, difficult or grim, shut her eyes and walked wilfully past. Yes, it took boldness, it took strength, there was a noble stubbornness to it, but it accomplished nothing and didn't help. It merely sowed more destruction.

The way individuals live together. The truth of each individual is only the truth of his own narrow perspective. The entirety of mankind and of human qualities is always seen through a prism, where its colours are broken. Observation is so utterly different from experience; there is no hope of fusing their contradictions, as the I and the not-I have been foes from the world's beginning.


## The case of Klothilde Haar

No question, it was the Klothilde Haar episode that finally killed off whatever hope there was of my achieving peace with Ganna. The months leading up to summer 1919 that I spent with her were sheer nightmare.

While the Dual Monarchy was collapsing and being torn to shreds; while Germany was racked by revolutions and contorting itself into cramps; while the charnel smell wafting over from the battlefields was poisoning the cities and the influenza epidemic seemed set to mow down whatever was left of youth and life; while hunger drove desperate men to crime and disappointment turned former willing sacrifices to bandits; while a new world came into being in the east and the old one killed itself off in the west with paper deals: while all these other things were going on elsewhere, Ganna in her little domestic state was turning things on their heads, piling discord upon discord, and making the lives of her loved ones into a private inferno, for the sole reason that she had the crazy obsession that Klothilde Haar was my and Bettina's creature, paid and instructed to supplant her, Ganna, in every way.

Mlle Haar had joined our household shortly after Doris's birth. She was a woman in her mid-thirties, a chilly, morose creature, neither very industrious nor especially trustworthy. But at the outset, Ganna had been unable to find sufficient praise for her qualities, mainly because Mlle Haar absolutely doted on the baby. I have to say such passions are not unusual among carers; it doesn't mean they have a scrap of affection for any living being.

Circumstances forced me to take a hand in the household; the difficulties were such that Ganna could not deal with them on her own. I had made the mistake of ignoring Ganna's objections and according certain freedoms to Mlle Haar. For instance I had given her the keys to the larder and negotiated with her over the supplies of flour, sugar, rice and fat that she had purchased on my instructions. I could no longer stand to see the children going without proper sustenance; Ganna seemed to be quite incapable of laying in provisions – the acquisition of a kilo of butter was entirely beyond her in her unworldliness.

Once it turned out that Mlle Haar had connections to the black market, and offered to use them on our behalf, I grasped the opportunity with both hands and paid the asking price. This was enough to enrage Ganna because to her, in her lack of wants verging on asceticism, any expenditure on food and drink that went beyond the satisfying of basic hunger and thirst struck her as superfluous, if not criminal. In addition, the man who liaised between Mlle Haar and the black marketeers was himself her lover, a fellow by the name of Wüst, who had been in a reserve posting for every day of the war until it ended and now, like so many others, was looking to make a living. In the evening, under cover of darkness, he would lug into the house whatever he had managed to wangle in the course of the day; and then Mlle Haar would present me with the bill, an inflated one to be sure, barely sweetened by her unpleasant crooked smile.

The intercession and covert wheeling and dealing of Wüst had a poisonous effect on Ganna. She hurled foul accusations at Haar. Who for her part was not short of a word or two in reply. In the end, she threatened to sue Ganna for defamation. I told Ganna: 'You mustn't allow that to happen.' She replied that a common thief like that would hardly go to law; why would she anyway, and lose out on the fat spoils I had, with my typical spinelessness, let her get away with. Haar, who always listened at every door, took sadistic pleasure in such scenes. She had conceived such a ferocious hatred for Ganna that it gave her another reason to cling onto her job, so as to relish the torments of her enemy. I in turn could not bring myself to send her packing, because at that time of the cessation of all idea of service I would have had no easy job in finding another nanny to look after the baby, whatever the rest of her qualities were. In addition, I was thrilled to have someone in the house who cooked properly and kept the household ticking over on a reasonable basis.

Distressing rows between Ganna and Haar became more frequent. Even at night they would suddenly begin; the screeching reached as far as my desk, forcing me to plug my ears with cotton wool. When Herr Wüst slunk into the house in the gloaming, heavily laden, Ganna would be lurking in wait for him and welcome him with insults. One day, when I was out of the house, the fellow had the nerve to lay hands on her; Ferry rushed over in defence of his mother; he was very strong; he knocked him over, tightened his hands round the man's throat, they rolled around on the floor, and in the meantime Ganna called the police. Mlle Haar refused to leave the house without a written declaration of honour from Ganna. Ganna claimed

Mlle Haar had stolen a crate of eggs. Mlle Haar complained to me; I told Ganna that, to the best of my recall, the eggs had been eaten. Ganna foamed with rage. Never in the history of the world had there been anything like this, she wailed, her own husband in alliance with the servants and their pimps – this was worse than anything I normally and daily did to her. But she knew, anyway, the heart of the conspiracy was Lady Merck, who had expressly taken on Haar and her fancy man to wreck her, Ganna's, life; it was clear as day, the sparrows were shouting it from the rooftops. 'Ganna,' I appealed, shaking her. 'Ganna!' I drew her next door. 'Ganna! Wake up! You can't be serious!' She looked at me blankly and replied: no, no, she was quite serious, she had evidence. 'Evidence? What kind of evidence? Evidence for nonsense like that?' She stayed mute and truculent.

The Haar business had got around the neighbourhood. One night a stone was thrown through Ganna's window; another time the front door was smeared with excrement. Once, I was passing through a cluster of men; when I was past them, a high voice called out: 'Chuck it in her face, the bitch!' I locked the door behind me and the cry seemed to fill the hall, the stairway, the rooms; and when I sat down at my desk I saw it written on an empty sheet of white paper: 'Chuck it in her face, the bitch!'

## Poetry

I didn't mention any of this to Bettina. I couldn't bring myself to. Shame sealed my lips. To condemn Ganna was tantamount to condemning myself. But nor can I claim that Bettina knew nothing about it. What did she need gossip for? My silence was as transparent to her as tissue paper. I'm not the sort of man who can keep a secret. My moods, my experiences, even my thoughts are in plain view. Friends have often made fun of my futile attempts at discretion. And Bettina sensed what was happening in my life before I had even crossed the threshold. She didn't need to ask me any questions. There was no point. What she wanted was to help me get over my depression and anxiety. It wasn't her view that two people who love each other should spend all their time wailing and moaning. Better to ease it away. At that time, nothing so terrible could happen to her that it quite clouded over her sky; there was always a ray of sunshine somewhere. If you pulled yourself together, remained true to your better nature, didn't give yourself airs, then the powers could be reconciled. With violin in hand, it might even be possible to secure some improvements from them; enough to live by for a while to come.

I can't express how much it meant to me, this belief in a way out, in destiny, in the victory of goodwill over life's glooms and travails. I watched her in astonishment and not a little envy. Everywhere were people who were well disposed to her and others whom she did everything to help: a poor seamstress for whom she found work; a friend who had returned from the war ill and infirm, and whom she tended and fed. She was always on her way somewhere or other to do something helpful and purposeful – not like a do-gooder, that wasn't her at all, but more like someone who sees it as a challenge, almost a game, quietly to iron out some of the little kinks in fate. And for all that, I know no one who was as regularly and maliciously misunderstood, with her bonny blitheness and her honesty. It often gave me pause. Perhaps it was because she was too quick with words, too certain of her judgement and fearlessly coming forth with her own brave truths. Of course that was bound to upset a lot of people. It's a good thing to have someone you can think about without being at loggerheads with them. An inexhaustible wealth of perspectives, when she would talk to me about her day, material for conversations deep into the night.

At that time I wrote a whole string of sonnets for her.

## The decision

And then, in the autumn, the great convulsion in my life began.

It was a mild day in October. We were returning from a hike in the mountains and sat down on a bench not far from the main village street, glad of the isolation that, along with the autumn, had returned to our beloved valley. We spent a long time gazing silently across the meadows, where the evening fogs were boiling up, when Bettina asked me whether I had given any thought to what would come of us during the winter ahead. I looked at her in consternation. It wasn't immediately clear to me what she meant. 'Well, what should be any different?' I asked. She lowered her eyes. She said if that was my answer, then I might as well forget her question. I realized then that this wasn't a trivial question popped at a peradventure, and now I did know what she was getting at. I had a bad conscience. I stammered a few scraps of phrases: I could understand . . . I'd often thought about it, of late . . . Then I fell silent. Bettina felt her way cautiously forward. Did I think it was right for us to carry on living with blindfolded eyes? . . . Was it proper that I went back to Ganna again, as I had every previous year?

'Do you think it's good? I'm not sure,' she said.

'What? What aren't you sure of, Bettina?'

She plucked up all her courage. 'I'm not sure I can do it. I'm afraid I can't go on,' she whispered.

I stared at the ground. My lips formed the words that were even now unthinkable:

'Leave Ganna? Is that what you mean?'

Bettina had never explicitly raised the issue, but over the past few days I had had a sense that she was waiting for some initiative from me to relieve her. Only she couldn't force herself to prompt me. Even now the yearning, the inner necessity for a decision were contained only in her agitated features, her expressive eyes. I had the feeling: now of all times, I mustn't fail, everything is at stake.

'What about the children?' I asked. She laid her hand on mine.

'The children, yes. It's hard, I know. But I can tell myself, you've seen two grow up under your care . . .'

'Doris needs me, Bettina.'

'Of course she does. Well, you won't lose her, will you? I'm sure she'll want to spend as much time with us as possible.'

I heard only half of what she was saying, and that half with trepidation. I reproached myself for having let the children down. What is there more destructive than the presence of a mother taut as a wire, harassed, contradictory, at war with herself and mankind, ignorant of people? All the inner alarms are tripped, tenderness becomes a burden, punishment arbitrary, self-will fails to encounter the opposition it secretly hoped for, the kernel of the personality shrivels and, with some dim sense of its imperilment, conceals itself behind protective layers that don't allow it to develop, but merely indurate it. And now I'm to leave them altogether, when the only thing shielding them from the worst was my presence?

Bettina said softly:

'I'm sure you know what you're doing. I'm just making a suggestion. The past four years have helped both of us to mature. It no longer feels right to me, to have our relationship as a sort of open secret. It's no longer true and it's no longer defensible.'

'Of course I agree with you, Bettina. But Ganna will never agree to a divorce, never.'

'This isn't about a divorce,' Bettina replied gently, 'it's about an act of cleansing, my darling. At least, for now.'

'What?' I asked in astonishment, 'you could . . . you would agree . . . in front of everyone . . . ?'

She smiled. The cat was out of the bag.

'Even if I stop short of the official legal step,' I insisted, 'do you have any idea of what we're letting ourselves in for?'

She nodded. She knew.

'And where would we live? There? Not possible. She would . . . No, you don't really have any idea . . . '

She had thought about it all. She detailed her plan to me. We would stay in Ebenweiler. We would keep out of sight. There was an old Court Councillor, Wrabetz, who owned a spacious and comfortable villa which she would let out to us for an affordable rent for the winter months. In spring, admittedly, we would have to move out to a farmhouse, and in autumn return to the villa. She explained it all to me with calm certainty, the way you lead a child's thinking, while all the time indicating to me that she knew herself to be led entirely by me.

My glance erred between two visions, the one blissful, the other hopelessly grim. I felt paralysed. My years came over me to warn me. Forty-six years and the whole of my life; to turn them upside down, I said to myself, so radically that not one stone would be left on another. Instinctively I looked for counter arguments. I pointed out to her shyly that she wasn't at liberty either. She made one of her astonishing gestures that made all speech unnecessary; in this case, it meant I will be free on the day I have to be free for you. That slayed me. I said I would write to Ganna, this very day. She seemed to approve, but I could tell right away that she didn't approve. I asked her what objections she might have to such a course. She said her objection was obvious: I needed to speak to Ganna. Definitely, I conceded, but it was better if she was prepared; that would take the edge off her shock. Above all, she needed to see it in black and white that divorce was at issue. Bettina didn't understand my anxiety.

'Aren't you in charge of your own life?' she asked. 'Who has a stronger claim than you?'

'All the same. It'll be ghastly.'

Bettina said it was wrong – yes, positively dangerous – to awaken any false hopes in Ganna; I mustn't make any more promises. She kept saying 'in my view' when she was talking of the solution to a problem, but I had long since discovered that this view of hers was almost invariably the correct one to take, and in fact the only solution. If for no other reason than that I would have to see Ganna, to prepare the needful next steps in my house, she enjoined me (and with that it was also settled where I would stay during my time in the city) to stay not in a hotel but with a mutual friend, for the sake of appearances. This plunged me into a new round of terrors. It was so brusque, so precipitate and final in its consequences. (As if it could have been anything other than final!) If a true Alexander-Bettina axis was to be created, then it wasn't possible for me to return to my former home, to resume living there as Ganna's husband. Otherwise Ganna would never have believed that I was serious. I said:

'You're right, Bettina. You're completely right. There's no more putting this off.'

In spite of that, I continued to fight the idea privately. I didn't have the courage to follow her advice and beard Ganna without a preparatory letter. I was in favour of a gradual approach. I was no Gordian like my namesake. What Bettina had in mind was something terribly simple: to make me happy, to be happy with me, to take some of the weight off my shoulders. Strangely, though, I felt wrong-footed. I had never seriously contemplated detaching my life from Ganna's. It didn't matter that it had felt to me like a failed life for some time now, and that I even understood it to be such. It must have been my innate antipathy to action that kept me from taking a clear decision. There are two types of human beings, the doers and the procrastinators, and I am a typical case of the latter. Associated with that is a certain phlegmatism that, while it isn't absolutely identical with spinelessness, does tend to be associated with certain other negative qualities, such as attachment to comfort and habit. Novelty has an alarming quality for us. Please, no changes, no new battles in my day-to-day life, we say to ourselves, the old ones are bad enough. A philistine loyalty to things can also play a part; the house that has become a haven; the bed one has become attached to; the old brown desk with its ink-spattered green baize and its dozen or so familiar knick-knacks. Some relationships that are even stronger. Take my daughter, little Doris, who was so attached to me that her whole world seemed to revolve around me. How to break it to the four-year-old that her father was moving to a different house to be with a different woman? Might it not cost me the love of my little princess? Might she not forget all about me? Wouldn't it become a trauma for her?

But such thoughts, gloomy as they were, were only clustered in the waiting room; within was my fear of Ganna. And that fear darkened my spirits so much that I didn't dare confess it openly to Bettina. Ganna oppressed me, like an Alp on my chest. All-present, she filled my days and nights. Maybe what I took to be duty, and even now – even now – 'mystical union' was really based on habit, habitual tussling and bickering, dragging loads and paying off debts? Adventurous flight plans shot through my head, how I might get from one woman to the other. Bettina's demand, that cleansing either-or, in my confusion struck me as a coarse intervention in my life. If she hadn't been the dearest person in the world to me, to be without whom was something I could no longer imagine, I would probably have mutinied during the early days of my inner schism and, albeit crushed and broken, would have slunk back into my Ganna hell. Yes, if Ganna had been a rational woman, I thought, persuadable, changeable, if she had some access to the world, or the world to her – how wonderful it would be then to live with Bettina, how lightsome and glad one might be, serenity and joy at last. But the mere prospect of having to talk to Ganna was like a burning dread.

Still, I had made up my mind. Once the procrastinator has finally decided to act he tends to move with a somnambulistic clank in the chain of events, so that even a misstep can assist him. And since any author will tend to favour his written word, since a letter makes for a certain soothing of agitated nerves and needs fear no interruption, I sat down and wrote Ganna a long letter. First the contents. The impossibility of letting things go on like this. My emotional condition these past several years, the need for me to get out of my bleakness. Urgent plea to Ganna to help me, and not set her face in opposition. I closed with the solemn assurance that neither Bettina nor I was thinking in terms of a divorce, and that all we purposed was to link ourselves in a free association. This disingenuous attempt at calming Ganna was, as Bettina had predicted, a bad mistake, and the cornerstone of all the wretchedness and horror to come.

A few days later I went to Vienna. As agreed, I stayed with a friend of Bettina's, Baroness Hebestreit, a young war widow. It wasn't easy for me to be a guest in the city where my home and my children were. To Ganna, though, it was a kick in the slats.

## Unending

She didn't believe it. Yes, she'd read the letter, two times, five times, ten times, but what is a letter. She needed presence. A letter wasn't presence. A letter is subject to recall or revision. A letter may be written under the influence of others, even under duress (and her certainty about this influence, this duress, turned into an incontrovertible fact in her brain which made it, again, the basis of the coming catastrophe). I had told her in a postscript that I would see her on Tuesday at noon; I was coming down on Monday. Announcing my visit seemed to her nonsensical. What was it supposed to mean? I was going to visit myself in my own house? Absurd. On Monday evening I telephoned her and let her know where I was staying. Now she had her presence: she knew I wasn't with her. Her last illusions went crashing to the ground.

Once she had got over the initial shock she thought about what to say to her acquaintances, her in-laws, her sisters, her mother, the children, the servants. It was more than a calamity for her; it was a black spot. She had no idea how she could show herself to people, disgraced as she was. Although she comforted herself by saying it would only be for a matter of days, the staggering thing had happened: I had sought shelter for myself with strangers. The strangers would talk about it with other strangers, and with that she was doomed to dishonour.

In order to steal a march on the gossips, she had herself put through on the telephone to various men and women who were all very surprised to learn from her that I had returned from the country sooner than expected and, because of urgent and unforeseen repairs to the house, had gone to stay with Baroness von Hebestreit. Even though she was canny enough to slip in this fact with some other snippet of information, or some question she was asking, as if it were a casual matter, of course the very casualness put her interlocutors on guard. She followed the same method of correcting fate and eliminating reality with the children. They didn't believe her either. When they heard that I was staying somewhere else in town they looked half-stricken.

Probably they had been expecting something of the kind.

In all these undertakings and endeavours I can picture her in front of me, padding round the house in her felt slippers and speaking with lisping voice; how the knowing Ganna hid herself from the imperturbable Ganna, the one heartsore, the other burning with impatience; how she darted, eyes staring, to the telephone whenever it rang; how, after a given time, she paced back and forth in my study incessantly, magicked me back to my desk, drilled through me with her reproachful glances and under her breath muttered her tawdry imprecations that I'd heard so often – that woman . . . May God punish her . . . He will punish her children . . . I'll destroy her . . . But there was yet another Ganna, who didn't indulge herself in such shrewish speeches; her eyes ran with tears, and she wiped them away with her clenched fist. When I opened the door and stepped inside, she threw herself against me with a choked cry.

It's not possible to record all the discussions I had with Ganna, not even to list them. Among the locations were: the library, the terrace, the garden, Ganna's bedroom, the street; among the times were: morning, noon, evening and night. All together, they would make up an uninterrupted conversation going over many days. Put on record, they would represent the exhausting and perspectiveless efforts of two people to get something from one another that it wasn't in the other's power to give. One seeks to tear a band; the other, seeing belatedly how cracked and holey it is, wants to patch it. One wants to leave the cold hearth; the other claims the fire is still burning, a holy flame, to extinguish which were an act of godlessness. One is coming to terms with the past; the other won't accept the reckoning and is whimpering for more credit. Conversations as old as the world, as sterile as pebbles, as agonizing as toothache. Here, they were given a new point and terrible amplitude by Ganna's character and methods.

I had come to her with the best of intentions. In order to persuade her to willingly relinquish our union, I offered all the kindness of which I was capable. I spoke of the nineteen years of our living together and the obligations those years imposed on her; that she must on no account lightly destroy the memory of those years. Ganna agreed, but wondered why I should not be equally bound by such an obligation. I appealed to her understanding of my writing, my work. Indeed, Ganna countered, that was why she must hold me back from a step that would cause my intellectual ruin. 'How can you say that?' I burst out. 'Aren't you ashamed to be so presumptuous?' She could trust her feelings, she replied gnomically; never had she erred when it was a matter of my welfare and the course of my life.

She didn't understand. She didn't want to understand. We got nowhere.

Never would I take away from her my friendship, I declared, if she showed herself equal to this hour of destiny. She was shaken. She howled. It was so hard, she said, so terribly hard. Of course it was hard, I put in, but she mustn't deprive me of my right to manage my own life; she must have learned and read enough of me to understand that a man's ordained path couldn't be diverted by wantonly digging it up. She agreed, sobbing, but in the same breath reached for the argument that she had to fight for her children. To which I said they were my children too. Then she said: 'But you don't care about them when you're blinded by passion.' However insulting that was, I mastered myself and replied that the children weren't going to be taken away from her any more than I was going away from them myself; if only for their sake she had to behave with dignity and humanity – they had already witnessed far too much in the way of quarrels and strife.

'You're to blame, it's your fault!' she cried.

'Maybe so,' I allowed, 'even though there's no single responsibility in these things.'

I put it to her that I wouldn't easily get over my disappointment with her if she stuck to her unworthy perspective; surely
she had the potential for good- and great-heartedness in her, she
had read the poets, loved painting, loved philosophy; I believed
in her, had always believed in her, but what had come of all that?
She blinked in despair. She was so all alone in the world, she
lamented, as she wrung her tiny, wizened, always-old-looking
hands, she didn't have a soul she could rely on. Solitude would
strengthen her, I offered her Jesuitically; I needed her; I had a
mission for her; distance would take the edge off the shadows
and gild her sufferings. She was moved. She gave me her hand
and promised with trembling voice to do all that I said; I didn't
know her; I had no idea of what sacrifices I would find her capable. I kissed her brow with gratitude. What I failed to notice was
that my great effort at persuasion succeeded only in persuading
her that she must not leave a man who addressed her in such
lofty, deeply felt language. 'What shall I do? Just tell me what to
do,' she whimpered. I: there could surely be no doubt about
that. She: she would willingly pour out her heart's blood for me,
but there was one thing that in the name of God I must never
ask of her: a divorce. I: she need only to relax her grip, bear the
new condition with dignity and not burden me with a responsibility that was strictly speaking hers.

This last thing I should not have said; with that I gave her a
recipe by which she slowly poisoned me. She had always been a
loyal friend to me, she said, beginning again; there was nothing
petty about her, not a bone in her body; others were, she wasn't;
and that other woman who made her suffer for no reason –

'For no reason, Ganna? Now you're tearing down everything
we've just laboriously built up!'

'Because you're thinking of a divorce,' she breathed, 'and
divorce would be the death of me.'

I caught her burning eye. In my foolishness, I thought the

moment had come for me to remind her of the oath she had sworn to me on the lakeshore nineteen years before.

'You swore by God to let me go if I asked; don't you remember, Ganna?'

'Of course, of course I do,' she said, gulping.

'Well, then, was that a meaningless vow?'

She cast her eyes down. She knew perfectly well that a vow given by an inexperienced girl couldn't really matter, but at the same time she understood that, morally, it couldn't be denied.

'If you're fair, you'll have to admit that I kept my word,' she said at last, with her martyr's upward look (she had avoided the word 'vow' I noted), 'or have you any complaints about the freedom you've been given, you Don Juan, you.' And stroked my hand in a motherly sort of way.

It was unending. Ganna couldn't get enough of the dispute. It was pleasure, pain, spur, hope. She talked the lungs out of her body. To secure an extension of the debate, she would appear to give ground at crucial moments only, an hour later, to take back all her concessions. When I left she would accompany me, often for long distances, tried to keep pace with me, to disarm my old complaint that she was too slow, and breathlessly blabbed out her reasons, false reasons, promises, complaints and litanies of my sins in ever new versions. She couldn't understand what I saw in Bettina. Bettina was just a woman, and – quite honestly – no better than Ganna. Couldn't I tell her what it was about her that had turned my head; perhaps she might be able to offer me the same thing; maybe there was some trick to it; she would try and learn it; she was willing to take instruction. Every night I fell into bed like a dead man.

## *The counter-image*

Bettina had gone back to the city a week after me, to wind up her household. One evening I called on her in her apartment and found her in the half-cleared dining room in her furs. The weather had turned cold, and she had run out of wood and coal. Her children were already in Ebenweiler in the Wrabetz villa. I kept my own coat on. There was no need to tell her what was currently going on in my life. She knew it anyway. She could tell from looking at me. I asked after Paul. She said he had left. 'Where to?' I asked. 'To the factory,' she replied. I noted a brittleness in her, like an over-wound violin string, jingling. She had accompanied him to the station, she added; the train had left at half past five. Then she abruptly asked if I was cold. 'Yes, I am,' I said. She ran out of the room and came back with four pairs of cobbler's lasts, which she took out of already packed pairs of boots. Kneeling down, she set light to a small pile of paper and put the lasts on it. Since they were made of hard wood they produced some heat after a while, and I praised Bettina for her skill. 'Once we burn the table and chairs it'll be quite cosy in here,' I said. She smiled vaguely. I eyed her uncertainly. I wondered if she had had a falling-out with her husband and asked her how things stood with him.

'How things stand? They don't,' she said.

'How do you mean, they don't? What did he say?'

She didn't reply immediately; she got out a whole lot of empty boxes and crates, and fed them to the failing fire. Suddenly she said, with a strangely squeaky treble:

'As of twelve o'clock today we are divorced.'

Bright tears sprang from her eyes and ran down towards her mouth. I stared at her. So, it is possible, I thought, real people can do it.

'What about the children?' I asked.

'He left them with me. Of course.'

I stared at her and shook my head in wonderment and envy.


## *The succession of fictions and phantasms*

One sleepless night, Ganna had a saving idea. Early the next morning she sent a messenger with a note to me where I was staying. She told me to come right away; she had something to tell me that would remove all our difficulties at a stroke. What was it? I couldn't believe my ears. A *ménage à trois*. She meant it. She was besotted with the idea.

'Oh, come on, Ganna,' I said glumly, 'that's childish. What world are you living in? That's not a serious suggestion.'

She was offended and perplexed.

'Why not?' she retorted. 'Think of Count von Gleichen.'

References to fairy tales wouldn't get us anywhere, I interrupted her in annoyance.

'Fairy tales? I don't see that at all. It's just an example. Aren't we modern people?'

'If by that you mean an unappetizing combination of feelings and a ridiculous situation, then: no.'

Bitterly, she called me a bourgeois who didn't have the courage to try out in his life what he was happy to promulgate in his books. I couldn't remember exactly having set Count von Gleichen up on a pedestal, but that's what Ganna seemed to think.

She persisted with her plan. While she stalked up and down excitedly, still unmade-up, in a grey woollen jacket whose sleeves went down to her knuckles, she talked wildly into space:

'With goodwill, everything is possible; everyone has to make concessions in a case like ours; why should one person get everything he wants? My rights antedate hers; Bettina needs to learn to suppress her egoism; we have enough room in the house, God knows.'

I didn't speak, picked up a book, flicked through its pages, and didn't speak.

'Let me talk to her about it,' she went on enthusiastically, 'if she's not completely lost her head, she'll surely see it my way.'

She had it figured like this: Bettina would take on external, representative functions that accorded with her ambition, while she herself kept the reins on the household; in the case of conflicts – but of course there wouldn't be any, she had the firm resolve to be wise and considerate – in the case of conflicts, then it would be up to me to decide.

Even today I don't know whether Ganna actually believed in that Gleichen idyll or not. There's no point in racking my brains over it either, since there is no line to be drawn between her dreams and her doings; her special kind of imagination does without even that dream logic that the most garbled dreams have. Her dream world was perfectly autonomous. The events she moved among were products of waking deliriums. Each day afresh she started out on the fantasy of the *ménage à trois*, and with the subtlest arguments sought to present its advantages to me. In my impatient refusal she saw the effect of Bettina's malicious whisperings. As if I'd so much as breathed a syllable of any of this, as if I wouldn't have prayed for the earth to swallow me up if she ever got to hear of it; as if I hadn't kept making superhuman efforts to conceal from Bettina what Ganna looked to me to do, so as not to betray the woman I had lived with to the woman I wanted to live with.

Once Ganna finally accepted the hopelessness of her endeavours, she presented things as though her noblest intentions had been undercut. Her logic went: if the two refuse the solution that she, Ganna, so selflessly offered, they must have compelling reasons, reasons that involve hurting Ganna, ruining Ganna. What could be more plausible than the suspicion that Bettina Merck had it in mind to acquire ownership of her house? She had already had that in view when she launched the Klothilde Haar conspiracy. I, so endlessly obliging, was the cat's-paw in this, because that sophisticated Circe could wrap me round her little finger. Then Bettina will play the sole, exclusive mistress, will lead the life of a princess and send the vanquished Ganna packing. Yes, that's the way things will be unless she takes timely counter-measures. So clearly could Ganna see the picture of a triumphantly enthroned Bettina in her, or Alexander Herzog's, house that she would sometimes groan out loud and grind her teeth. When she heard that Bettina had quietly obtained a divorce, this (far from giving her pause as an example that might be followed) only confirmed her in her grim suspicion and she was filled with dread. Reality had slipped away from under her, but then again she didn't really need it: everything was the way she imagined it in her free-floating fantasy. The house was in danger – the house, a concept that swelled in her mind to dream proportions, the concept of ownership, of rootedness, of security cast in stone.

And commensurately, so her readiness to share her dearest goods, man and house with her blood and ancestral enemy grew in her eyes to heroic proportions; and when she saw how curtly her offers were rebuffed, that gave her a stamp of nobility for all time.

Everything in Ganna's mind marched to the beat of Ganna's imagination. It wouldn't permit any doubts: she was a model wife, an embodiment of kindness, punctuality and good order. Though wreathed in such qualities, she was slandered in my ears, and her 'enemies' have dug and dug until I could only think of breaking with her. Those same people who paid Klothilde

Haar. Those same people who were able to foil her scheme to make me a millionaire with the meadow. Further, the conviction takes root in Ganna that for the past nineteen years we have lived together like two lovebirds and that no cloud has ever spotted the sky of our bliss. This conviction settles into a myth in her, like certain historical 'events' in history books. But since something seems to have happened in this lovebird existence for which Ganna isn't to blame, someone else must be the guilty party. Hence continual poking around for guilt, questions to establish guilt, investigations of guilt, and no end. Phantasms and fictions come out of thin air. Ancient sayings, ancient deeds are produced in unrecognizable versions. Opinions are distorted, statements twisted, things a million miles apart are forced into a false pattern. An army of the envious, the malicious, the ill-disposed, the liars and intriguers appears over the decades, and surrounded by them a Ganna, like a seraph in the golden ether, keeping watch over her Alexander.

This was unrolled before me day after day, and day after day I was to account for myself, supply proofs, offer evidence. I wonder why I didn't just go. Why did I not tie up my bundle, and up and leave? Hard to explain. I think there's something wrong in my make-up. I am not capable of leaving emotional devastation in my wake. Either from softness, or from pity. After all, I have my fair share of selfishness. I am not an easy tolerator, no particularly eager helper, not a good giver; and before I decide on some act of kindness outside the area of my work, I have to get through every possible stage of caution and inertia. What operates here is different. It's not a singular phenomenon, but present in accretions. First, there's my sense of the simultaneity of actions, which has its seat in the nerves. The high degree of emotional vulnerability associated with this leads me to relocate myself in different times, in other rooms and beings in my imagination. And in such a way that I can see, hear, taste, touch, smell them, which necessitates further protective measures, which cost me more effort and more thought than any amount of real-life difficulties. At times, at my most desperate times, I remind myself of a surgeon who dithers and dithers over an operation and finally, madly, instead of anaesthetizing his patient, administers the morphine to himself.

But there's another factor as well: there was an ethical imperative in me after all, a higher voice that refused to be silenced. There was this woman; whether she was inadequate or not, whether she had made her own bed or not, whether I, whether Bettina, whether the world as a whole approved of her way of doing things or not – it remained the case that I was tied to her. I had sworn vows to her; I was responsible for her in spite of all my words to the contrary; I had given her three children; she was an unstable, pathless, directionless woman who without me was lost. Could I really just quit her like that and go and start a new life (a new life – that most mindless of all expressions), without tidying up the old one after me? Not least hacking back that tangle of phantasms and fictions? It seemed possible to me. I didn't know at the time that they had their own terrible autonomy and proliferation, these phantasms and fictions; that gradually, like the djinn in the Arabian story, they would grow to fill up the whole of the sky. I couldn't get free. I wasn't cold-blooded enough, not brutal enough. I wanted to save a piece of Ganna for myself. A memory, a stirring of gratitude, a sense of respect.

## On joy

Week after week passed. For all my heart-constricting effort, an amicable solution was no nearer. I decided I'd had enough and would go to Ebenweiler, where Bettina had been waiting for me every day. I pack up my books, manuscripts, clothes, linen. Ganna watches me in distress; the children ask me barely audible questions. Then the hour of parting comes; Ganna accompanies me to the station. What to say to curtail, to abbreviate the pain of sundering? Ganna talks and talks, her throat is hoarse and dry, her words stumble over each other, she's worried I may catch cold, afraid of a train crash, everything is so uncertain nowadays; she gives me dietary advice, she talks till the very second the train moves off. I look past her. She breaks into a trot alongside the carriage and waves. I never forgot the scene. It had something of Ganna's whole being in it.

Seventeen hours in the train. In those days all transport was difficult. The carriage is filthy; it jolts and clatters like a post coach, the windows are boarded up, the rain comes in through the roof, the lights don't work. I stare out into the gloaming; Ganna is running alongside and waving. And at night she's standing outside the door of the compartment, begging to be let in, in her hoarse, floury voice.

Then Ebenweiler in the sparkling snow. The familiar scene has a new aspect. Its loveliness has turned to majesty. Bettina meets me at the station, her cheeks flushed with cold, her glaucous eyes shining with inexpressible happiness. We ride the sleigh to the house, buried in snow up to its doorknobs. The whole world feels like Christmas.

It had never occurred to me that a peaceable home and its well-ordered running could have something so intoxicatingly pleasant about it. I had never experienced such a thing. With this winter a long period of intensive work began for me, in spite of all the horrors I shall have to report on. In a certain sense, I was sheltered. Partly by the landscape, which struck me in light of a modest genius, always soothing, never arousing; but above all by Bettina's careful, silent and apparently completely effortless attention to my welfare and my tranquillity. With her and in her company I felt as sheltered as if I'd been inside the mountain on whose flank we were perched. The end of the world and the Ganna war were a thousand years ago. In the intoxication of those early months, it seemed to me we had fused into that coupledom of which I had dreamed for so long as a kind of higher actualization.

Bettina's two little girls initially kept their reserve towards the new head of household. The way children judge us grown-ups is among the most mysterious things there are anyway. Half-suspicious, half-reserved, they waited to see what would develop. My inexhaustible need for tranquillity, my sensitivity to all noise of voices and forms of disturbance were to them much like what leash and muzzle are to playful puppies. They could surely have held it against me that I was permanently out to curb their exuberance. They did not hold it against me. They also took me reasonably seriously; at any rate I found myself the subject of serious conversations which they had between themselves before going to sleep.

It was a bitter experience for me: in spite of the change in my outer life, I did not feel any more joyful. Or perhaps it would be better to say, joy was unable to reach me. When she came calling, I let her know that I was unavailable. No matter how long she stood outside my door, I didn't let her in. This proved a disappointment for Bettina, the first in our new life together, and it grew from month to month. Naturally, Bettina asked herself what was the point of her if she couldn't lift me off the surface of the earth, rootling vole that I was in her eyes. She had hoped to take flight with me. But how can you lift off with someone who does everything in his power to make himself heavy, nothing to lighten himself? She had imagined she might be my lamp, but how can you be a lamp when the one you are to light keeps insidiously blowing you out, because his element is the dark? It was moving to observe: when I was cheerful, when I happened to laugh, then her whole day was rescued; a smile from me and her heart would leap with delight.

But the times I was able to laugh and to smile grew more and more infrequent. Just as well that Bettina had so much of her own amusements, even though her supply occasionally threatened to run out. In a setting where all sued for my favour and begged me for a friendly glance, I became a remote and introspective hermit. And that was the only danger that Bettina had to fear for herself and her life, the lack of light, the absence of blue sky, the chain of days without laughter, without a smile. Then her violin could be nothing to her either, or music; no tunes came into her head and her whole world went silent. In one confidential hour, she told me about it. Not without apprehension. Her clear eyes couldn't hide their fear. The very fact that I should have needed her to admit this to me shows my extraordinary obtuseness. I saw what it was about. I understood that I must not allow Bettina to wither. That at any price, I had to achieve the capacity for joy. And since it was Ganna who stood between me and joy, whose fault it was that I could no longer laugh or smile, so Ganna would have to be induced to restore to me my cheerfulness, my insouciance, my undaunted courage, whatever the price – because if not, then everything was wasted and I would lose Bettina.

But when a man is sitting on a powder keg, with a burning fuse leading up to its bung, then it's not such an easy matter to laugh or to smile.

## Various alarums

First of all, there were the letters. Six, eight, ten pages in length. I can only say that a hail of molten lava would have been a refreshing spring shower by comparison. Ganna stretched out her arms 200 miles to reclaim her errant husband. Her words boomed out 200 miles away, demanding support, advice, comfort, in the name of the children, in the name of justice, in the name of undying love. Whatever wasn't written down screeched, rampaged and wailed between the lines, behind the jagged, foolish, plangent letters. Lamentations, how sad it feels, living in a house from where the man has gone. Did it have to be this way, Alexander? Did I deserve to be thus kicked and trampled underfoot? That Doris was inconsolable without her father. That she was having trouble with Ferry and Elisabeth; how it was impossible for her to control two grown-up children on her own; how could I justify it to my conscience to leave her at such a critical time in her life, and with circumstances so brutal? Dreams, presentiments, horror stories. Little pinpricks: how so-and-so expressed surprise at the behaviour of a man whom he (or she) had hitherto deeply respected; how nice her sisters were being to her, how much sympathy she encountered, how much friendship was extended to her from every side . . .

Then the house, our lovely house, began to play up. The water mains burst, flooding the hall. The septic tank needs to be moved, the local council refused to connect the house to mains sewerage, the atmosphere was endangering the children's health. During a storm one of the chimneys had blown over. A stove needs to be installed in Doris's room, the heating system is inadequate and it's not possible to get enough coke to burn in it. The builder presented a bill which she can't possibly pay out of her monthly allowance. Nor can she keep up with the other bills, the deliverymen are driving her to distraction with their demands; what is she going to say to those people? My husband has gone away, she says, he'll be back soon; but those people refuse to believe her, and sometimes they are downright insolent.

And with that I have come to the question of Ganna's economy, her whole way with money, which was far and away the most striking aspect of her life and character. As we happened to be living in the middle of the Inflation, that ghostly phenomenon appeared right away in full force.

Indescribable, her rigid horror when the gigantic numbers turned up in her housekeeping book: 200 crowns for a kilo of butter; 50 for a dozen eggs; 500 for a pair of shoes; 2,000 in wages for tutors and domestics. Ganna in the battle with money that was ceasing to be real money, that melted away between her fingers, all the while there seemed to be more and more of it, that thumbed its nose at her with a number and sent her staggering with the lack of value of the number – all that instilled a nameless confusion in her, a total relocation of concepts and a growing panic in her calculations. Another week and the hundreds have become thousands, the thousands have become hundred thousands, and the hundred thousands are millions. When a chicken cost 80,000 crowns, a telegram to me 10,000, the monthly butcher's bill was more than one and a half million, she broke down under the weight of the figures. It was for her the triumph of bedlam. For her, to whom money and the value of money were holy fixities, solid and etched in bronze, the experience resembled what it must be like for a believer to be given incontrovertible proof (could such exist) that there was no God. She dangled in space. The laws of nature had been suspended. One must imagine that a trauma developed out of this, which partially explains the catastrophic developments that unfolded. First, the view took root in her that such a collapse of all values could never have happened if I had not left her. That gave her a completely delusory satisfaction that my faithlessness, my so-called betrayal of her, was connected with the calamity of the nation and the catastrophe of capitalism.

It shone through in every one of her letters. Each one came

larded with figures and statistics. No sum of money could ever be enough. Others managed to look after themselves, kept reserves, stuck to their budgets; Ganna was always knocked flat by the exigencies of the moment. She had no sense of time, only of the moment. It was her mystery, the way she didn't live from moment to moment but in an unbroken chain of milliseconds without soul and sense, which was why behind her breathless busyness and industry there was something like a continual tragic fade into nothingness.

Under the pressure of desperation, the old faith in magic awoke in her. She knew a few bank managers and paid calls on them. Bank managers, in her eyes, were magicians; they did magic with money. They were bound to know, too, about a witches' sabbath. She got tips from them. She sent me hieroglyphic dispatches with the names of bonds and certificates I was supposed to buy. She then had the illusion of having given me some decisive help, and was convinced I was raking in millions thanks to her. To that came the next, perfectly unshakeable conviction that Bettina and I were enjoying 'the high life' while she, the spurned Ganna-Genoveva, was condemned to a life of penury.

The confusion of numbers in Ganna's letters buzzed round me like a swarm of horseflies. I would have thrown money at her, if only I'd had it to throw. What did I care about money; what did Bettina care about money; even less. I did what I could. I fitted the sums to the situation. By now, the collapse of the German currency had turned my earnings into ridiculous elephantine sums with tiny real purchasing power. I could hardly count all the zeroes, but the net income was far less than the average of the past few years. Without a few sums from abroad, I would have been unable to pay our way. Of the shadow money, I transferred as much as I was able to Ganna. Meanwhile, what yesterday was still sufficient, was insufficient today. When inflation finally ground to a halt, such great holes had been torn in her finances that Ganna was unable to plug them. Her shrill cries for help rang out in the silence of my study. I scraped together everything I could possibly spare. I wasn't counting; I stopped thinking about my actual household. But no sum was enough for Ganna. She crossed every line that was drawn in front of her. Every instruction struck her as wicked. She swore I was accruing fortunes and was keeping them from her, to live it up with Bettina. Whenever she got a biggish sum in her hands, a stupid optimism straight away came over her, as though she couldn't possibly get through it; then, when it was gone, and much sooner than expected, she didn't know what to do; she sat miserably in front of her red book, checking through the receipts, going through all her pockets and desk drawers, insisting she had been robbed; and the upshot of everything was another screed to me.

Her engagement with these vast figures, once she had grown used to them a little, gave her a strange, exciting pastime like solving puzzles or doing jigsaws. The millions and billions gave her morbidly speculative mind the satisfactions of infinity for which it was always athirst. They suggested astrology and magic. What did the true value matter; the *appearance* was there with its sweet alchemy of name and number. While prices climbed into the unaffordable, and figures into the unsayable, the hope sprang up in her that (even though in another part of her dream world I was a secret Croesus) I couldn't continue to afford to pay for two women and two households, and would therefore be compelled to return to the bosom of my family. This wasn't a wish or an occasional fantasy, but a solid conviction; she would talk about my return as of a fixed event, and as though the time of ordeals, of abandonment and disgrace would then be for ever at an end.

## *Intellectual morass*

She didn't accept fate. The core of her being was rebellion. It was reported to me how, shortly before the death of her mother, which happened at this time, she had had an altercation with the eighty-year-old woman in which Ganna had been extremely forceful, because her mother had upbraided her for her want of humility: 'Humility,' she is reported to have come back, 'where does humility get you in this world? Where did your humility get you, Mother?' With the death of her mother, Ganna broke with the last memories of breeding and restraint. She was just forty-four.

One day she said to herself: I don't want to be financially dependent on this heartless man any more (she meant me). Since the whole world was plunging into enterprises of one sort or another, and the crazy money seemed to be lying around on the street, she looked around, had discussions with all sorts of seeming friends and experienced chancers and decided to start a film review. The cinema was at the centre of interest, and as far as its intellect was concerned, there was an evident match between Ganna's being and the silver screen. Both, if you will, were in the business of dazzling. Ganna was always drawn to anything that sparkled, all sorts of hocus-pocus, star-gazing, Mazdaznan, chiromancy. They afforded her a rich field for self-promotion and self-abnegation; the whole of creation was a cheat pleasing to the eye of the Lord.

A financier was once again soon found. He was a man with a printing press. People wanted to get rid of the phoney money so as later to exchange it for real, at extortionate rates of interest, and everyone welcomed opportunities to do so. The fact that Ganna had contributed quite a bit of her own money – which is to say, of mine – was also kept concealed from me. The exploiters and schemers in her set could comfortably pluck her any time they chose. Being quite incapable of seeing through them, she thought of them as selfless philanthropists. More and more she inclined to the opinion that in order to succeed in literature, one had to use one's connections; and so she took to pestering various important figures, including some who were close to me, and was extremely angry when she was fobbed off with polite evasions. Extreme in everything as she was, her admiration straight away curdled into contempt; and the distinguished man was a louse who a split second before had been held in high esteem. She was editor, proofreader, publisher and manager all rolled into one. She wrote till her fingers were sore, and she walked her legs off. The morning the magazine appeared she hurried from kiosk to kiosk, asked after the sales, exhorted the sellers to greater efforts and suggested ways of enthusing the reading public. If an astonished or pitying glance struck her, reminding her who she was, she quickly blotted it out.

Very well, then, film review: there was nothing really improper or contemptible about that. Get busy, I thought to myself, get it out of your system, see what happens. But first there were the opaque financial manipulations and transactions which I found very alarming, and which had a sort of whiff of wheeler-dealing and 'you scratch my back, I'll scratch yours' about them. I had a notion of money-laundering and extortion-ate obligations entered into behind my back, shady deals and corrupt relationships; from time to time I would catch a short-lived rumour; from time to time the ghost of a warning; in a word, it was as though repulsive things were going on behind a thin partition; you listen to it tense and excited, though you don't fully understand what's happening.

What was much worse, though, was the actual publication itself. First there were Ganna's personal contributions, dashed-down news items and stories of a teeth-grating vulgarity and stupidity; among other things, the maliciously distorted portrait of a woman widely known for her charitable works, for whom – God knows why – Ganna had conceived a personal antagonism. Then there were the wretched, sometimes even scandalous products of the pens of various other male and female scribblers whom Ganna favoured, and to whom she was happy to offer a literary playground and royalties; and finally there were the advertisements, by means of which the whole enterprise was to pay its way, those announcings and toutings familiar from other such periodicals. And all of this appearing under the name of Herzog, by which Ganna was pleased to go – my name. All over the house unsold copies lay around in stacks, and whenever little Doris was bored she would pick one up like a picture book and turn its pages. I saw this myself one day. I ripped it out of her hands. A lead weight lay on my skull; I could feel the slurry splash up to my knees.

## Ganna and language

That first winter already I had Doris to stay, as affectionate as ever, full of love and deeply rooted trust. It had taken complicated negotiations with Ganna to obtain this concession, and subsequently whenever I sought to have Doris to stay in the summer and winter holidays, Ganna made difficulties each time. She said it was a risk. She demanded guarantees and set conditions. She tried to persuade me and herself that the little girl would only prosper and remain healthy if she was with her, that there was no substitute for Gannacare, Gannaprotection, Gannalove. At the most, she might allow that I had good intentions; she denied that I had the moral ability. Because I was under the influence of a woman whom Ganna had every reason to distrust. She assured everyone who cared to listen that she couldn't leave her precious darling, the apple of her eye, to a person living with me in an immoral relationship. The fact that this 'unethical relationship' was one she, by her doing, insisted on, she readily forgot. The outcome was constant argy-bargy over the girl; can you understand the shame I felt?

If Doris happened to be lying in bed with a sniffle, Ganna would announce a grave streptococcal infection with a temperature intended to terrify me 200 miles away. Her intention was to alarm me, to awaken my sluggish conscience so that I didn't forget about my family while living with the hated woman. I shouldn't be surprised the children were continually ill, she wrote to me, seeing as I was refusing to give their mother the means to keep them safe. I sat down and demonstrated to her, black on white, that even in the worst months of the Inflation she had enjoyed a respectable middle-class income; I converted the sums into Swiss francs to prove it. Her reply was the righteous flaring-up of a duped woman since, in her version, she had been duped of everything that my life with Bettina was costing me. She wrote that there was no justification in keeping her short, she was aware of no guilt in her, her claims would stand before God and Man.

She had no control over words. What transpired in her was a strange alchemy, an inflammation remote from thought. Associations were thrown up randomly in her limitless self-indulgence. I saw Ganna over the years growing, and with her grew and swelled the word, the self-indulgent and random word. She didn't discriminate between good and evil, she couldn't tell the difference between a bridge and an abyss. Lyrical paean and toxic brew, plea and threat, truth and contrivance, emotion and business, affection and embitterment – it was all one hopeless inextricable tangle. Overheated style, ice-cold calculation. In a typical run of four consecutive sentences, the first one would be self-pity, the second accusation, the third a demand for money and the fourth a declaration of love. While taking the high ground as the representative of an ethical world order, she haggled for a rise in her monthly payments. At the same time as she scribbled enthusiastic lines about my oeuvre, she used the children as pawns and demanded, both directly and indirectly, material compensation for agreeing to let them stay with me; above all, more frequent meetings with me for the purposes of 'friendly discussions' and the repetition of my vow that I wasn't seeking a divorce. It was to such a storm that I had to stand and expose myself. Ganna and Ganna's language kept me breathless like a drunken binge of nocturnal housebreakers.

## A few miniatures along the way

We go out into the star-spangled night, Bettina and I. Below us the lake glitters; the heavens are like a curtain pricked with innumerable needle-holes, with gold and blue fires burning behind it. The Milky Way is a baffling curve of silver grains. Above us lies a delicate veil of mist. The silence is so powerful that it feels like a blissful transmutation of death. Ganna's din, Ganna's language, has gone away, as though a steel gate has been shut on it. We stand there arm in arm, as though lost in prayer . . .

There are mornings when we sleigh downhill over the fresh snow on the slopes, as on a ghostly carpet, surrounded by the dark forests, the crystalline air full of the laughter and chatter of Bettina's daughters, who will soon be off to their father in the city, to school. Then we walk across the frozen lake, which creaks so menacingly at night; now it sighs like a Stone Age creature in its death-throes. Ox-drawn wooden sleighs run silently across the smooth expanse; with a swish like tearing paper, the curling stones of peasants run over the swept surface.

In the first days of spring, it's as though Nature is angrily pulling off a dress that has grown too tight for her. The waters plunge down the stone runnels created over millennia, above avalanches thunder, heather and hepatica peer shyly out among the grass and mosses, everything is an irrepressible growing and burgeoning; March smells differently from February; we hike into the woods, we wander in the neighbouring valleys as though conducting tours of inspection of our realm, and sometimes Bettina seizes my hand and asks, thrusting her face against mine from below: 'Are you happy? Tell me that you're as happy as you can be!' I look at her and nod at her in gratitude. Would the other thing have been bearable, otherwise? Life would have broken apart like a piece of rusty metal . . .

## In cursed circles

For years, divorce loomed at the back of things as the silently desired conclusion; by and by it became a simple necessity. There is a call to order which comes from society, irrespective of personal freedoms. No pretence was permitted, no contrived, lofty standing-above-it-all; I could feel the growing insistence within me of a demand that connected my sense of honour as a man and my responsibility to the community with that other, still more urgent feeling that included my undischarged debt to Bettina, which in introspective hours I thought of as my inner reparations, or the interest payable on joy.

That was what the fight with Ganna was first about. If the loader could be induced to take the harness off the panting beast and unstrap its burden, then it would be able to breathe and walk again. Ganna's first condition was that she could only consent to a divorce if she was certain of my friendship. Very well, I said, all right; that's self-evident really. Albeit, there is one difficulty: how can one be certain of friendship according to Ganna's definition? By signature. By deed and seal. I am to certificate it. I am to commit myself to it solemnly for all time. I am stupid enough to try and talk her out of it. Instead of saying yes and amen to all and signing on the dotted line – which would have the automatic effect that she would drop this demand and insist on something else, harder to give – I make an honest attempt to persuade her of the foolishness of a documentarily attested friendship, to teach her that friendship needed to be earned and worked for, and couldn't be signed like a lease agreement. She doesn't see it. All she hears is my refusal, which she takes as proof of my bad attitude. She was being softened up; this was a tactic for softening her up. 'You'll drive me over the edge with your tactics,' she fulminates, shaking with rage. She refers me to my solemn promise of October 1919. I admit I wrote that unsympathetic letter. Then bitterness wells up in her and she screams that I would never have set my knife to her breast in this way were it not that I was under the instructions of my hypnotic mistress. I have to smile when I hear of Bettina and her 'instructions'. Ganna misunderstands my smile and claims I swore to Bettina that I would get a divorce; what Bettina was doing for me in return was of course something no one knew; but she would show Lady Merck that she had miscalculated and would bite her teeth out in granite.

But it wasn't Ganna's intention to fob me off with any final 'no'. She wanted to deal. She wanted to keep everything in play. That was her way of compelling my attendance. Of course, to be fair, as deeply fair as only God can be, one would have to ask oneself whether love wasn't part of what was driving her to this – a frightening love admittedly, dipped in darkness, but still love, whichever way one wanted to define it, however damaged the loving heart might be. I, naturally, could feel only the terror and the darkness; but she was suffering as much as I was, or at least at the time I still believed that, and I was indulgent and patient with her because suffering does disarm the beholder. She was still victim to the delusion that I was angry on her account when I got angry; and when I shoved her away she took it the other way; as a sign that she was still in play, was still a partner. And so she ran rings round me with her promises, she repudiated our agreements of the day before, and took things I had said a thousand times and made them appear nonsensical. If she wired me – come over, we can sort everything out together – and our talks once again went nowhere, then it wasn't sabotage on her part but lack of goodwill on mine. 'I'm not quite ready,' she said to me in August, 'can you give me another three months?' So I gave her three months more. In November it was: 'I can't commit myself. No one nowadays can commit themselves to anything. Circumstances are just too volatile. In March I'll do whatever you want; I give you my word.' Then in March:

'I want to test your proposal seriously. But there's one thing I can tell you right now: you can't keep two women on what you earn. It's my duty to save you from financial ruin.'

'No excuses, Ganna. We can, we must find some basis of agreement.'

'I have been deceived too often. You can't force me to commit a crime against my children!'

'I'm not about to leave my children in the lurch. You ought to know that.'

'Maybe you wouldn't, but what about your mistress? I'd need to have commitments of a completely different order from those you are able to offer me now.'

'What commitments are you after, Ganna? What more can I do than mortgage myself to you body and soul?'

In vain. With tenacity and fury Ganna clings onto her promised seventy kilos of live weight. Whatever new thing she brings up is a hallucination. Behind hallucination and mirage a sober and brazen legal mind points and gesticulates. I don't want to know, I'm not supposed to know about her. All I see is the burbling sleepwalker, the unhappily entrammelled one, the tormented tormentrix, the endlessly isolated woman, Ganna whom I must buy off, whom I must compensate for my offence against morality. Ganna the frightened mother, the disappointed consort, the abused bride, the failure in the face of reality – that Ganna is obscured from me by the raving Ganna, by Ganna the legal eagle. I'm starting to hallucinate as well. I'm going round in cursed circles.

## M'learned friends take a hand

My friends advised me to get a lawyer. They were worried for me. They noticed my irritability. I was past fifty; possibly I was no longer equal to the strain. One Dr Chmelius was recommended. I knew him from various social occasions and I remembered him as an affable fellow. It turned out he was the man who had got Bettina's divorce put through so quickly. Bettina had never talked about him, never so much as mentioned his name. She didn't like lawyers. She didn't think they could ever do anything worthwhile. In the course of my life to date, I had never yet had dealings with a lawyer. That was about to change.

Initially, Dr Chmelius was supposed to be Ganna's financial adviser, and supervise her money arrangements, since her demands and expenses were growing exponentially and I was unable to influence them. Ganna, though, declined to accept Dr Chmelius as an adviser; she found out that Bettina had been his client four years previously and quickly put a conspiratorial construction on the plan. She claimed he was working for Bettina and acting under psychological pressure from her. Dr Chmelius was a subtle jurist and a gentleman, and perhaps therefore overly hesitant. Even so, each one of his polite and respectful letters drove Ganna to white heat. What was the man playing at? Telling her, Ganna, what to do; giving her, Ganna, advice; daring even to speak and write of divorce; outrageous!

Immediately she set up her own man, Dr Pauli, in opposition to him. Pauli was fond of her and wanted to defend her rights; but he had far too much on his hands and, for all his admiration for her energy, her initiative, her resourcefulness, he found conferences with her too taxing for him. He couldn't meet her and listen to her, as she demanded, twice a day, and he got upset when she completely changed her instructions to him from one meeting to the next. Therefore he passed the file on to a friend and colleague, one Dr Grieshacker. He in turn soon found himself under attack from Ganna and passed the thing on to his partner, one Dr Schönlein. The result was that the case of Ganna Herzog was being pursued, steered and trundled back and forth – putting on weight as it went – by all three men at once.

It put on weight, nothing else. No one knew what Ganna actually wanted. She herself least of all. Did she want a divorce? No. Did she not want a divorce? Everything indicated that, but she was loath to say so. What are we going to so much trouble for, the lawyers asked themselves. Ganna acted more or less like the owner of a farm that has been threatened with nocturnal attack, who has posted security guards round the premises. Dr Pauli wanted her not to be served the standard running bills; he knew the strain she was under and was able to persuade his colleagues to exercise forbearance too. A noble gesture; what he didn't anticipate was that it was also a ruinous one. Because of it, Ganna got into the habit of spending time with her lawyers and changing them the way a man might change his socks. Since she had no understanding of work, and no respect for it, she looked to everyone she had entrusted with her affairs to be exclusively busy with them and treated them all like insubordinate juniors if her unique prerogative was denied her. And however pleased she was that her financial predicament received consideration, so, equally, she was unable to rid herself of the secret suspicion that anyone who was working for her for little or nothing was doing bad work. Caught in this schism, she was ever more dissatisfied, excitable, disputatious, confused, bewildered. Humanity, where she was concerned, was divided into two camps: there were her supporters and her opponents. And in the middle stood those lightsome guides to fortune and triumph, the lawyers. Of course that was only true of those lawyers she had taken on; those of the other side were the dregs of mankind.

She lived on the telephone and with her warbled throaty 'Hallo-o' talked to the various lawyers, including Dr Chmelius. He was not able to refuse her pleas for money any longer. The conversation was always the same. 'But Madam, I transferred a substantial sum only last week.' To which Ganna, with breathtaking argumentation: she had had some unanticipated expenses, some '*imprévus*', a term she very much favoured, given that her whole life was in the sign of the unexpected, and she refused to allow him to meddle in her finances. But each time she was really stuck she would pack her housekeeping book under her arm and drive in to Chmelius in the city, to show him column by column how carefully and modestly she was keeping house. Like all writing, it was sacrosanct for her, founded in her fetishistic faith in words and figures. The accounts in her book were just as unassailable to her as her passbook with the Reichsbank.

In the same manner, she treated every one of her missives as a Papal Bull. 'Did you not get my conciliatory letter of the 16th?' she might write. 'I'm waiting for your decision on my very modest proposals. It seems to me, my letters aren't reaching you. Please wire back to confirm that you have received and read the letter in question.' And so we had the myth of Bettina intercepting letters. It was a charge that could not be defended. Dr Chmelius was a plant. She could never forgive me for having turned that man into her beadle, she said; that had thoroughly opened her eyes. I mustn't count on a divorce any more; practically it was impossible and morally it was unhuman. Only if I sent Dr Chmelius packing could there be a chance of resuming negotiations. If I continued to knuckle under to those parties terrorizing me, I had wrecked things with her. My hopes had, in any case, gone down to nil. If Jesus Christ in person had turned up to represent Bettina and me, he wouldn't have stood a chance.

There was no peace for her anywhere; not in any house, any room, with any person, in any book, in any bed. She had problems with her gall bladder, her heart, her breathing; she consulted specialists and quacks, used ointments and teas, scooted off to Karlsbad, to the Adriatic, to her sister Traude in Berlin; spent the whole of one day on her feet, claimed to be dying the next; but that illness was another fiction, it was refuge from her ghastly restlessness.

In the chaos of her affairs, the failure of the film review barely showed. The printer had sued for his outlay. Presumably she had taken on more debt in the effort to partly buy him off. She told Dr Chmelius she hadn't. But where would all that money have gone? A black hole. Did she have secret acquaintances she spent it on, leeches who sucked it out of her? Was it just the sinister will-to-destruction compounded of things hard to itemize: various impulses of love, hate, jealousy, self-assertion, self-destruction and wish-fulfilment? Dr Chmelius told me he had done the sums and informed her that in the past year more than half my income had gone to her; whereupon she had hissed at him and talked of deception and cheating – she knew from reliable sources that I had earned five times what I claimed. I said:

'I know, I've heard that sort of talk, but how can I convince her that she's wrong? How do you ever persuade someone that you don't own something when they believe you do?'

Dr Chmelius replied gloomily: 'I'm afraid you can't persuade the lady of anything at all. Except by jumping back into bed with her. Not otherwise.'

And so the conversations Ganna, seeming willingly, agreed to were all without exception shadow-boxing. In her endless nights of scheming and pondering she came up with three stipulations whose impossibility she surely couldn't for one moment doubt but which she needed so as to play the innocent afterwards, once the meetings had failed, so that she could say to herself: I have done everything with the best will in the world – the tricksters and the double-crossers are you lot.

Since these three points are in a certain sense unique 'sanctions', let me list them. First, I am to renounce parental authority over my younger daughter. A legal innovation of Ganna's; no jurisdiction on earth would have ever recognized such a renunciation. Second, for each daughter I had to deposit a substantial sum for a dowry. I had no idea where I was to take such a sum from. The kraal decided it. The kraal's imperative was: provide for your brood, man; first and foremost your brood, we don't give a hoot about what happens to you; let the deserter work himself to the bone; let him fail to come to his senses; let him and his mistress fail ever to free themselves from the shackles. Hence: provide, provide until your dying day. And third: Bettina was to sign a fully notarized agreement that she would never stand in the way of my spending part of each year with Ganna. Ganna saw such an arrangement not only as legally binding, and as practicable; she also saw in it a way of dragging her rival into the courts whenever she chose. When Dr Chmelius was presented with these three textbook instances of Ganna's garrotting methods, he cried out: 'I've never seen anything like this in all the years I've practised, and I've seen some things.'

## Ate

In the course of the proceedings which the printer of the film review had brought against Ganna, there was a falling-out between her and Dr Schönlein. I never found out the exact cause; I only learned that certain scenes had taken place in Schönlein's office, and that one day the lawyer threw in his power of attorney. She complained bitterly to Dr Pauli, who sought to calm her and, seeing as Dr Grieshacker had long since given up representing her, suggested she take her case to Dr Stanger-Goldenthal, a known tiger at the Bar and a specialist in divorce cases. This was exactly the man for Ganna. Thus far, if I may so put it, she had not yet found the lawyer of her dreams. Now, Dr Stanger-Goldenthal filled the vacancy to a nicety. He knew at a glance what Ganna wanted from him. He sniffed a great cause. It is in the nature of the law that it keeps those who have recourse to it in suspense, until they have lost their fortune, their life and their belief in right and justice. All this, admittedly, applies more to me than to Ganna. She had already shown herself to be insensitive to evil; whatever she had had by way of mind, dignity, pride and heart had already drowned in that circle. 'Just leave it to me, Madam,' said Dr Stanger-Goldenthal, once he had read the file, 'we'll get everything to come out nicely.' From his expressions Ganna saw that she had nothing to fear. She sensed a twin soul. A great weight fell from her bosom. The reverence with which she used to speak about this man in the early days had something cultish about it.

Dr Chmelius was dismayed by her choice. He made no secret of his worry from me; he had had a few brushes with Herr Stanger-Goldenthal himself. He even tried to warn Ganna against employing him. But Ganna smiled slyly, in the manner of someone who has the philosopher's stone and is being told that its possession will cost them dearly. Dr Chmelius went as far as he could; he went to Dr Pauli to discuss the case with him. Since he put a written record of their conversation in the file, I am able to reproduce it in its essentials.

'It will not have escaped you,' he began, 'that Madam Ganna by her inscrutable and unpredictable behaviour is tormenting my client, is harming his ability to work and thereby, as the saying goes, is killing the hen that lays the golden eggs.'

'And yet the only person who can secure a divorce from Ganna Herzog is Alexander Herzog,' replied Dr Pauli.

'Maybe in two or three years,' Dr Chmelius quipped back, 'maybe . . .'

'The mistake is,' Dr Pauli replied, 'that the other side claims it wasn't a happy marriage. That upsets and provokes the wife.'

'Why would Herr Herzog wish to end a happy marriage?'

'External influences. It's perfectly clear.'

'My dear colleague; I do hope you haven't allowed yourself to be influenced by a fanatic.'

'And what if I have? Isn't a fanatic an ideal match for a poet? Madam Ganna has shown me countless letters of his. Love letters. The genuine article. She has shown me printed and hand-written dedications in his books that pay honest tribute to her qualities as a companion and colleague. I don't think you have a leg to stand on.'

'Is it for us to judge the moral positions of our clients, Herr

Pauli? You know as well as I do that the past can be tricked up to look more seductive than it was.'

'But there can be no doubt that the Herzogs' marriage would not have been set at risk without the intervention of Frau Merck.'

'Of course not. That's just the way things happen in this world. It's destiny. Let's face facts.'

'Ganna's hurt and loyalty are facts as well. They demand respect, especially if your name happens to be Alexander Herzog.'

'Very good. So what should he do?'

'Go back to her.'

'Back to prison? Back to his cell?'

'Oh, come. We're all of us prisoners and convicts. Aren't you?'

'And the woman he loves?'

'At his age, you don't put your name and reputation and the future of three children at risk over an affair.'

'I don't see what his reputation has to do with it.'

'A man like Alexander Herzog has another reputation, in addition to his bourgeois one. Doesn't he know the meaning of dishonour? Does he mean to explode bourgeois order, and tread on the toes of the *Weltgeist*?'

Dr Pauli paced back and forth in agitation and laughed a little nervous laugh. Dr Chmelius was at a loss for words. He had tried to come to an understanding with a fellow lawyer and left speechless and baffled, leaving a man who had agreed to represent the other party, and whom he basically couldn't understand. At that point the grizzled old sceptic remembered something, and he smirked to himself when he told me that Dr Pauli's own marriage had been singularly unhappy and that his wife, whom he still loved, had left him for another man. The position he took towards me, therefore, for all his professionalism, was nothing but a perfidious act of gender retaliation.

A week later, Dr Pauli suffered a stroke and died. He was sincerely mourned by many people. Ganna was stunned by the death of her friend. She lay in bed for three days straight. It was during these days of grief that she found the time and opportunity to write a lengthy memorandum, incorporating all the unsettled questions between us. She sent it to Dr Stanger-Goldenthal for him to rephrase in legalese, which Ganna at that stage had not mastered, as she would later. It was nevertheless a piece of writing of considerable lawyerly and argumentative skill. Her lawyer congratulated her on it. When he had finished polishing it up, giving it the requisite qualities of ambiguity and opacity, it was ready for Dr Chmelius and me to bite our teeth out on.

Not a single chink of light. A hopeless tangle of proposals, measures, discussions, euphemisms, accusations, conjectures, cunning distortions, coarseness and hair-splitting. The lawyers inundate each other with letters, inundate their clients with letters, inundate each other with more letters. Typewriters clatter, telegraphs click, telephones bleat, messengers run – each of the parties involved is raking it in, all except the one that has to pay for such endeavour, the costs of the materials and the nervous strain with his own dearly acquired money, his tranquillity, his blood and his life, and who gets nothing in return except – more paper.

And always at the back of everything – Ganna, unmoved, immovable and brazen, the deceptive Perhaps always on her lips, the rigid No in her heart, the goddess of discord like the grim Ate, misconceived daughter of Zeus. Undaunted and indefatigable, she shores up her mad world, which has so surprisingly many points of contact with the real world and at the same time bears the stigma of doom.

## Little Caspar Hauser

I am now coming to a phase of my life that, externally, bore all the hallmarks of success and fulfilment, but within it concealed all the more the seeds of destruction. I just managed to stagger through it for a long time in my dazzlement. In 1923, the Buchegger manor in Ebenweiler dropped into my lap – almost literally into my lap, because not even in my dreams had I contemplated the acquisition of such a manor. Each time I walked past it, as I had now for over a quarter of a century, I had felt a yearning for it as for a fairy-tale palace; this would be a good place, I thought, here I could do good work. The estate was (or I suppose I should say: is) situated on the lakefront, the spacious house in the middle of a large parkland. The last Count Buchegger had sold it following the end of the Monarchy to a Dutch gentleman who no longer had any use for it, seeing as he hadn't managed to settle in the area; and when he learned that I had been looking for permanent accommodation for years now, he offered it to me, in some patron's access of generosity, for half what he had paid for it.

The continual toing and froing with all our things between the Wrabetz villa and a nearby farmhouse, and then back again, had become rather wearing. It gave our lives a quality of vagabondage. But how was I to raise even the generously reduced sum the Dutchman wanted? Further, a permanent base that kept the severe winters at bay would entail considerable rebuilding. Luckily, there was a superabundance of furniture, silver, linens and all sorts of household items, which by themselves were worth half the purchase price; but even though the Dutch gentleman was happy with a modest down payment, the estimate for upgrading the house was beyond anything I could contemplate. I had no savings. I lived, as I had always done, from hand to mouth. We had substantial outgoings; to cover them I needed considerable earnings. Thus far, I had been lucky. But how things were going to go on – that remained unclear from month to month. It was rather an adventurous existence, not one based on solid facts.

It seems that certain events recur in some lives. While I was hesitating between desire and sensible refusal, a friend who had come into money offered to help. When I doubtfully set the thing out before him, and showed him the house, he was mad keen on the acquisition and in a handsome gesture offered me the capital for down payment and building work. The repayment rates were so easy and the time so generous that I saw no grounds for any worry, only occasion for thanks. Once again, as years previously, the kindness and nobility of a friend had afforded me shelter.

A German architect appeared on the scene and assembled a team of masons, carpenters, roofers, electricians, glaziers, heating engineers and painters. Materials and tools arrived by the wagonload; for four months walls were knocked down, others set up, windows were put in, balconies erected, traverses and pipes laid; there was hammering, digging, clearing, plastering, varnishing, painting; and by the time October came round, and Bettina and I moved into our new house, like a couple of children who are allowed to go up on a stage where a fairy play is about to be performed, Bettina was in her fourth month.

I mustn't keep back the fact that Bettina was rather apprehensive as regards our new circumstances. Such an expansive life made her uneasy. She warned me. Her sense of the world didn't permit her to be taken in by appearances. She kept presenting me with the problems: in addition to existing burdens, further indebtedness for many decades; the help that was needed to run such a house; the upkeep of the fabric of the building; modernizing it. She was afraid that in the long run I wouldn't be able to afford it. One had to plan for bad times; there were always lean years after the fat. I mustn't make myself into a wage-labourer, nor enslave myself to property.

I laughed at her. I was all too sure of my resources. Once I had been out of the Ganna tempest for a while, I felt certain destiny couldn't touch me. Bettina was set at ease by my unshakeable self-confidence, even though she still worried about the future. She was often depressed, and then she would flee to me, the way an animal might seek out its nest at the approach of a foe.

'I'll manage it,' I said; 'after all, if the worst comes to the worst, we can always flog the place.'

I added that to me it was a comforting idea that she and the child she was expecting would have a refuge and a piece of property in the event of my death. Bettina smiled.

'If we're talking about your death,' she replied, 'do you really think . . . Can you see me as a chatelaine? Look at my fingers.'

In surprise I looked down at her hand, which she held out to me.

'These fingers are no good at keeping hold of things,' she said. 'Once it was prophesied that I would never be in debt, but nor would I have anything to call my own either.'

For all her fears, it was a happy thought for her that our baby would have a place it wouldn't have to leave at six-monthly intervals. A fortress sure, in a world out for aggression. She herself didn't need any fortress. She could look after herself. But the little person who was on the way (she was convinced from the outset that it would be a boy) would need to be given shelter, like a little Caspar Hauser. And if – as Ganna wished – it were his lot to grow up without his father's name, then there was a double need to put some protective space between him and Ganna's world bristling with laws. Suddenly, she was no longer afraid. Early on in her pregnancy she had sometimes –

most unusual for her – cried with fear. That was when she wrote her 'Song of an Unborn Child', one of her loveliest composi-tions; when she played it to me the first time I still had no idea of her condition.

That same evening, she was lying in bed, I was sitting reading by the lamp; she called me over and asked me to sit with her. She took my hand and broke the news to me. Hesitantly, half-audibly; she couldn't predict, after all, how I would react to news of such a disruption.

I was shocked. Straight away I realized a new situation had been created in which I must show no weakness. Our little Cas-par Hauser wanted his place in the world. Our eyes met, and we gazed at each other deeply and earnestly. I clearly saw the flecks of grey in Bettina's blue irises. I knelt down beside the bed and kissed her hands, first one, then the other, many times . . .


## Interval of being different

I can only guess what Ganna felt when she heard about the pur-chase of the Buchegger estate. What later transpired suggests such a confused mixture of rage, bitterness, agitation, sympa-thy and murky hope that any attempt to describe it would be doomed from the start. At first she felt humiliated and duped. Her agents had run to her with the information that I had paid half the purchase price, or perhaps more, in cash; and since every rumour that circulated about me, even the least well founded, not only turned into an axiom with her, but by and by passed through every form of exaggeration and distortion, to the point of the nonsensical – yes, the ridiculous – so the sum I was said to have shelled out, not batting an eyelid, swelled into the fantastical. Naturally she will have said to herself: he saves and economizes on me, but he has a fortune to lavish on 'that woman'. That it was Bettina who wanted the palatial house for herself, and that I had been driven to buy it for her by her subtle tricks – that was an established fact from the start, which only the malicious unbeliever would dare to question.

At the same time, she wrote me a letter in which she expressed her pleasure at the splendid acquisition in the most gushing terms. If there was the least drop of wormwood in her joy, then it was over the fact that she had been told the wonderful news by strangers and had asked herself sadly what she could have done to lose my trust. What had made her especially glad was the fact that I had got together such a huge sum of money; that allowed her to conclude that I was in more than easy circumstances, and the laments and fears I had brought to her, thank God, lacked any real cause. But she wasn't upset with me about this little dishonesty on my part; all she cared about was that I should be happy and flourishing.

I made haste to correct Ganna's misunderstanding. She didn't believe me. I referred her to the property register, to put an end to the malicious false reports on the purchase. She didn't believe what she saw there. She preferred her fantasies of my vast wealth and a rosy fog of money hocus-pocus. The fact of my wealth gave her claims such an air of entitlement that she fell for her own golden mania, like a woodworm in the hole it has itself tunnelled.

But I didn't really care if she took me for a successful gold-digger who was cheating her of her just deserts. Enough of the scheming, the cards held to the chest, the black arts of lawyers. She must be made to understand the inevitability of what was happening. It was make or break time, I said to myself, as I sat down in the train on my way to see her.

My news that Bettina was expecting hit her like a bolt from the blue. She looked at me in utter disbelief.

'A baby,' she whispered, 'she's having your baby! I can't quite believe it yet. I promise to look after it as if it were one of my own. I promise. Do you believe me?'

She wept with emotion. I indicated that her looking after it didn't really come into things.

'You know what this means,' I said.

She nodded enthusiastically. She assured me she would go to see Dr Stanger-Goldenthal this very day; she would call him immediately; then we would sit down together and talk everything over amicably and in peace, no terror, no duress; she would prove to me that she was still the old Ganna ... What would I say to a nice bowl of soup in the meantime? No, I said, please not, please no soup ...

Her large blue eyes were humid with tears; she was overcome by the notion of herself as devoted self-sacrificial spouse and friend; stripping away all reality, she fled into the sweet interval of being different. And I believed her.


## Stanger-Goldenthal

She kept her impulsively given word, inasmuch as she went to see Dr Stanger-Goldenthal that same day, to inform him of the new development. But it wasn't, as she had promised me, to instruct him to prepare for the divorce. Hardly. Her showing me goodwill was enough. The idea that 'goodwill' needed to be followed by action was baffling and a little repugnant to her.

I told Dr Chmelius:

'Thank God, Ganna has changed her mind. I think you can go ahead and prepare for the next stage.'

Dr Chmelius, no little surprised, made report of this to Dr Stanger.

'That's the first I've heard of it,' Stanger replied to the still greater bewilderment of Dr Chmelius. 'Your client must have misinformed you.'

'I'm afraid you took her at her word again,' Chmelius said to me.

I went to see Ganna.

'Your lawyer insists you haven't given him any new instructions.'

'That's a wicked lie,' yelled Ganna. 'I talked and talked to him till he promised me – and we shook hands on it. Everything will be sorted out in three days.'

I believed her. Obviously, it was Dr Stanger who was responsible for the delay. I asked Dr Chmelius for leave to write to Dr Stanger myself. He had no objection. I sat down and wrote Dr Stanger-Goldenthal one of the most straightforward letters that can ever have been written, a letter of a kind that you write to a human being, not to a lawyer for the other side. It was a minor epic, the story – filling many pages – of my marriage, and the presentation of the grounds that made it impossible for me to remain with Ganna.

His reply was highly ironic. 'Let us assume for the moment,' he wrote, 'that the complaints you level at your wife are justified. This begs the question: were you really lord and master in this union, as the law and the wider organization of society expects? I leave the yea or nay to your conscience. Your exquisitely written, logically constructed memorandum I view not as a legal weapon but as a human document. [That finally proved to me that the two were utterly antithetical.] The weight of the moral responsibility for the discord in your marriage is yours. If my client expressly requests a divorce, I will execute her wish. If she decides against a divorce, then I will support her to the best of my ability in the legal battle that may be expected to ensue.'

I was in consternation. What was the fellow on about? Ganna

said she was in agreement. It couldn't be that, at this vital juncture, she would slip back into her old duplicitousness. I read her
the passage in Dr Stanger's letter, where he said everything had
been left up to her. She was clearly embarrassed, gabbled a bit,
played the doe-eyed innocent; but inside she was shaking with
fury and later she went on to make a ghastly scene with Dr
Stanger, in which she set things out as though he had gone over
her head and given me a binding agreement. That was bound to
rile the man up against me, and he wrote to me crudely: 'Sir, it
is not right that you tell my client things about me that are half-
truths at best. Such things confuse my client. She thinks I am in
favour of a divorce. I am against a divorce. She must have the
freedom to act. She must not feel any pressure, not even, or
especially not, from her legal adviser.'

Now nothing made sense to me any more. The walls and the
buildings were spinning around me. I conferred again with Dr
Chmelius and reached the acme of folly when I expressed to
him the wish to meet Dr Stanger-Goldenthal in person in his
office; a personal conversation, I blethered, would clear up all
the misunderstandings. I believed in talking and in clearing the
air; I believed there had been a misunderstanding. I believed in
the effectiveness of my person and its truth; it's as if someone
being mugged made great play of the fact that he has studied
Greek. Dr Chmelius shrugged his shoulders and said: 'Try it. It
can't hurt.' Seeing me so put upon, he wanted to leave every
avenue open, even the least likely; he himself was out of ideas.

Dr Stanger let me know it would be an honour to receive me.
Our conversation went on for an hour and a half. The man wore
an invisible gown. He was berobed in the full dignity of a cham-
pion of the ethical idea of marriage. A consummate actor. I had
the sense I was stepping on air and speaking clouds. For the
most part it was he who did the talking. With emphasis, dignity
and from the elevation of his legal pedestal. I felt giddy, and then

a little sick. When he saw me out, with many assurances of esteem, I knew that I had suffered a defeat and a humiliation.

Dr Chmelius now thought it right to inquire politely of Ganna whether she had come to a decision and, if so, what it was. We got back the twining phrases of Ganna: the assurance she had given me remained in force, but she couldn't permit herself to be cajoled or bullied, as there were a series of upcoming birthdays in the family and her family piety forbade her from taking on anything so distressing as the modalities of a separation; moreover, her heart was giving her trouble and on doctor's orders she was to avoid excitement. I, for whom time was breaking up into shards because I was so impatient, was smoothly put off until January. It was now September. She gave me her 'sacred' word of honour that by January she and Dr Stanger-Goldenthal would have drawn up the final deed; at that time I must allow myself four weeks to talk everything through with her lovingly; if I managed to fulfil that essential condition, then all obstacles would have been overcome. The daily attrition of those meaningless and perspectiveless conversations with Ganna and the lawyers had exhausted my strength; I wanted to go home to Bettina; what was I supposed to do, give Ganna a new heart? Myself a better head? I returned to Ebenweiler with a head like a beehive and nothing accomplished, and duly told my apparently credulous and not terribly interested consort that Ganna would agree to a divorce in January.

Then, when I appeared on the battlefield in January, Dr Chmelius really did hand me the Stanger-Goldenthal-composed, Ganna-inspired 'final' deed. Without a word of commentary. With face set in grim expressionlessness. I read the document carefully, folded it up and returned it to the lawyer without a word. I had the feeling I had landed among horse thieves.

Must I really list what that piece of paper looked to me for? I'm afraid it's beyond me. My pen jibs. Before long I will have to talk, in any case, about the thumbscrews and leg-irons which were applied to me when I resolved to make an end to this disgraceful process, whatever the cost, and which (in my psychologically easily understandable blindness) struck me as acceptable and even comparatively humane – certainly compared to the murderous sequence of paragraphs that Dr Stanger and his obstinate amanuensis caused to march before my staring eyes. For the first time I could see my situation with complete clarity and received such a horrifying picture of Ganna's true being that for a while I felt turned to stone, like those individuals in mythology who behold the face of the Gorgon. But no, that wasn't it; there was no true being and no false being, there was only an illusory zone in between, something abyssal and cloven, shadowy and derelict, and in its proposed coherence arbitrary and illogical. Hence no Gorgon either. The Gorgon may be harsh and severe, but she is infinitely preferable. She offers solid outlines and fixed positions, not the ghastly unpredictability that gives the outstretched hand a sensation of dipping into some slimy brown primal soup.

'Tell me,' I said, turning to Dr Chmelius, 'what am I supposed to live on if I manage to pay off this mountain of obligations in their entirety? How does she think I can do it?'

'I have no idea,' replied Chmelius drily, 'let's ask her.'

'The way things are,' I resumed, 'she confiscates not only all my goods and chattels, but beyond that she asks for gifts that bleed me dry. It's as if you knock someone out, and chop him up and eat the pieces. Have you ever known anything like it?'

'Would you care to see my files?' Chmelius asked me mockingly.

'But I have to get to the end, I have to!'

'Very well. Then in God's name sign this Treaty of Versailles. But count me out.'

'Is there no judge, no law, no mercy that can free me?'

'Only in your dreams.'
I left, feeling utterly distraught.


## What is Bettina waiting for?

The remaining two years it took while the divorce was finalized were a grisly, sickening tussle. It was about money and money and more money, and about files and deals, and guarantees and security; and when I thought a final settlement must be close, everything turned out to be flim-flam and fake. The peaceful Buchegger estate was no good; Bettina's courage and her mastery of the day-to-day of living, no good; immersion in work achieved nothing; conversations with friends, nothing; even the little new person, Helmut, the son we had prayed for from heaven, born at his allotted time, and solace and balm to our souls from the very first hour, nothing.

My depression remained in place and deepened. My shame at my helplessness was like a canker in my flesh, like prussic acid in my vitals. And Bettina watched and watched. I didn't know what she was going through; there was something, but I didn't know what it was. All I knew was that joy was no longer an issue, nor were laughter and smiles; there was something else, I couldn't say what. She let Ganna's letters rain down, and the writs snowed down, and she watched. They were bad winters in those years . . .

On one occasion, when I was in Berlin, I suffered a breakdown. An organic malady had snuck up on me. The doctor who saw me recommended rest and taking it easy. But how could I rest and take it easy while a raving Ganna ripped through my world, and I was forced to look like a toy in the hands of an evil hobgoblin to my beloved companion, while the innocent eyes of my youngest child gazed up at me and asked: where is my birthright? While those obtained, I could neither rest nor die.

## Hornschuch

For all my liking for Dr Chmelius I could no longer blind myself to the fact that this overburdened man was lacking in dynamism. He could feel it himself; on several occasions he had made the friendly suggestion that I relieve him of his brief, if there was someone else I would prefer. Then a young lawyer was enthusiastically recommended to me, one Hornschuch, who had moved into our area and within a short time had built up a large practice among the local farmers. He had served on the Front for four years and people said he had displayed exemplary courage as an officer. When the war was over, he felt no inclination to return to the city and the circles he had formerly frequented; a passion for solitude unusual in a man in his prime, bursting with energy, had prompted him to go into voluntary exile and live by his own lights and following his own rough-hewn and unconventional methods.

In his service of justice he now displayed exactly the same cheerful positive attitude that he had previously shown in the army. Almost all the cases he took on involved some striking injustice that his clients had suffered. He saw it as his duty to shed light on public maladministration, and to jolly along the snail's pace of bureaucracy by his forthright and occasionally dangerously eccentric campaigns. It was no surprise that he was not the authorities' favourite. But everything I heard about him made sense to me, and so one day I went along to see him. He lived and worked out of a tiny house about an hour away. There was no sign on the door, no office; it was a civilian receiving a visitor. He was a boyish-looking man with Tartar features and a stubborn expression in his blue eyes. Silently and almost impassively he listened to me. Then he said: 'I'll take a look at the papers. Perhaps colleague Chmelius will be kind enough to have them sent to me.'

Which duly happened. For a couple of weeks I didn't hear from Hornschuch; he didn't write, didn't call. Then, one afternoon in late autumn, he had himself announced and the following conversation took place between us:

'Having traded my colleague Chmelius for your humble servant,' he began, 'you should try and see that the other party dispenses with Dr Stanger-Goldenthal. One good turn deserves another.'

'And how am I supposed to do that?'

'Very simple. Who do you think will end up paying for the services of the double-barrelled one?'

'Presumably I will.'

'And do you have much hope that his bill will be moderated by his appreciation of your work?'

'Hardly.'

'Do you want to proceed on that assumption?'

'All right.'

'I would.'

'And then?'

'Then you tell him: I will pay you, but only within reason and not until after the divorce is concluded.'

'Won't he laugh at me?'

'Never mind that. Let him laugh, and I'll see to the rest.'

'You mean, he needs to see that delay isn't in his interest?'

'Exactly. Either he will compel his client to take an irreversible step, or else he will give up representing her.'

'That's a possibility. But then Ganna will just go to someone else, and who knows whether we'll be any better off.'

'You should leave that to me, Sir. Allow me to operate as your brain for a while.'

'So tell me what will happen.'

'Since, as you rightly predict, Mme Ganna will not take the irreversible step, you will ask my colleague at the appropriate time for the bill, while pointing out to him that he will have to talk to his client about the size of the sum. He will not be gentle with her once that's on the table, you may be sure of that. He will take her by the throat and then, if she wants to breathe, she will have to accept a lawyer of our choosing.'

Columbus and the egg. That, more or less, is precisely what happened. I had often appealed to Ganna to give up an adviser who used all his cunning and experience to stir things up between us instead of calming them, to tangle the threads instead of combing them out, but she believed in Dr Stanger-Goldenthal as in the Bible – no, what am I saying, more than she had ever believed in the Bible. When two individuals, whose pleasure and art it is to fish in troubled waters and intone abracadabras, join forces, their relationship will be closer than most real friendships, just as bonds between thieves – 'thick as thieves' – tend to be firmer than those between honest men. But when Ganna was suddenly presented with the bill for her *entente cordiale*, when the vast sum showed her how much she was paying for personal and legal support, that every telephone call was rated as highly as dinner at Sacher's, that a single one of the delightful and stimulating conferences swallowed more money than she spent in a week – she screamed blue murder about villainy and extortion. There was only one comfort that remained to her: that she could tell herself and persuade me that it was all for my sake that she had broken off relations with her star lawyer. There followed a brief interregnum, a time of no lawyers; to her it felt like a time of no drugs to a morphinist. Disturbed and bitter, she wrote to me: 'There, now you've achieved what you wanted to with your tactics, and I'm to be put under pressure of an inadequate lawyer.' And when I brought up Hornschuch, and suggested using him as our mutual counsel, the name sounded like the rumble of thunder from a black storm cloud. An unknown; she didn't know the first thing about him, and yet she already hated him with the consuming hatred of the maniac, whom fear of the unknown drives to the most desperate and dangerous pre-emptive efforts.

## Sixteen to twenty Gannas

At one of my frequent conversations with Hornschuch he gave me to understand that the greatest obstacle to a rapid settlement lay in my continued personal dealings with Ganna. He advised me to stop answering Ganna's letters and not to arrange any more meetings. I told him I had to look after my children, Doris especially.

'In that case, why don't you have the children stay with you if you need to be in the city every four to six weeks anyway?' asked Hornschuch.

'That's not much good. If I call them, it's Ganna I get on the phone.'

Thereupon Hornschuch made a remark that caused me to fold in on myself as if I'd been pricked with a pin. He asked me if I had ever considered how hurtful my continual dealings with Ganna were to Bettina. I denied this most vehemently. That wasn't possible. He was surely mistaken. I wasn't aware of the least sign of that being so. He smiled, in his ironic way.

He wasn't mistaken. When I think about it today, my stupidity or sheer blindness of that time astounds me. If I'd been given the gift of awareness, I should have realized long ago that these regular assignations with Ganna, the regular, repeated visits to her, the meetings in the city and in various places between Ebenweiler and Vienna, must have been mystifying to Bettina.

She had seen that the – to her – repugnant fight she had got involved in against her will was destroying far more in the way of life and happiness than it could ever create. The dubious victor's prize meant nothing to her. She wasn't in the least tempted by the status of certificated bourgeois and wife, that wasn't where her ambition lay, it wasn't even possibly her style; and under no circumstances would she have condescended to bend the knee to Ganna or become indebted to her. It went against her pride, it went against her dignity as a woman. One day she said as much to me quite openly.

'You know, I don't really care whether you get a divorce or not,' she said, 'in fact, I don't give a damn either way.'

I was shocked. 'What about our son?' I countered.

'What about him? What's it got to do with him?'

'Do you want him to grow up without a name, as a bastard?'

'Those are archaic notions,' replied Bettina, glowing with the spirit of the anti-kraal; 'anyway, what do you mean, without a name? He'll have my maiden name, it'll cost a petition as Horn-schuch says; the name of my father, it's no worse than the name Herzog.'

I looked at her in consternation. 'No,' I said, 'no. You're right.'

But nothing changed: in terms of Bettina's sense of things, Ganna might as well have been living under the same roof as her. Ganna's high parrot squawk filled the rooms, the whiff of greed and lust for possessions came in through the doors and windows, and there was no man in the house to keep them out, no master, no strong hand. Maybe in some far corner of my soul I could feel her disappointment, but I know I closed my eyes to it. I had yet to abandon my hope of getting Ganna to see sense, though it was absolute folly. I stopped telling Bettina about my meetings with Ganna. When I went to see her – part of this time, she was staying in a nearby mountain resort – I needed all kinds of get-outs, even resorted to bare-faced lies, and went to her in secret, an absurd parody of the lover slinking off to his beloved. There was something so warped about it. But the meetings with her left their trace in my features. When Bettina saw the leaden shadows under my eyes, she knew. She, who had always slept like a baby, eight or nine hours straight through, now sometimes lay awake until dawn. She was helpless in the face of my suicidal and traitorous doings. She didn't talk to Hornschuch about it either. Ganna, who had wanted to make him see that she and I were one heart and one soul, didn't shrink from writing him the occasional letter, claiming we were well on the way to a peaceful solution; of course, all lies.

I went to Ganna each time with a feeble, half-witted hope and each time left her numbed and bruised. At night I started up out of my demon-haunted sleep, in which bitterness, like a toxin in my blood, had kept me tossing and turning, and sixteen to twenty Gannas stood around my bed to fill my ears till they rang with her glibly stereotypical sentences: 'I will make you a binding offer when you come back.' 'It's mean of you to call me wasteful. I keep a household book with numbered bills in it.' 'I want to do what you say in everything. Just don't make it possible for me to say no.' 'Since it's happening against my wishes, at least let me tell myself that it's not to my disadvantage.' 'You can curse me, you can slander me, I don't care a bit, my conscience is almost oppressively clear.' 'It's all up to you, Alexander. For the sake of your peace and quiet, I'll give you your liberty, but it'll have to be on the correct basis.' 'If the heating pad gives you palpitations, you should try putting a damp flannel underneath.' 'There can't be many women in my position who are concerned with nothing but making their husbands feel even better off.' 'I'm going to walk hand in hand with you under the Lord's arc on Judgement Day.' 'Bettina must understand that if the bond between us breaks, you won't survive it.' 'Your behaviour vis-à-vis me is doing you untold harm . . . ' And so on and on and on. The Cassandra makes way for the flatteress, the greedy market woman for the concerned spouse, prophecies alternate with threats, pleas with violent quarrels; there's one Ganna that has a soulful Madonna face, another has the wild eyes of a witch; one turns up in a dirty chequered wool jacket, the other in the fake kimono, with the stockings bagging down under it like empty sausage skins; one talks with her throat full of flour, the other has a vulgar squawk; one is continually calling out 'Hallo-o' to make herself heard, the other is looking vainly for money, kneeling on the carpet in tears; one has a look that is fixed on the fourth dimension, having failed in the other three, the other scribbles out sentences on pliant paper; and each one insists that I account for myself, to each one of them I have to prove and explain something. Why? Prove what? Explain what? That I am a fool, and ripe for the madhouse?

### Ganna gives me a divorce for my birthday

Hornschuch had quietly and efficiently made his preparations. He was like a hawk, a tiny dot hanging in the upper air, only to swoop down once he was sure of his victim. He was in correspondence with Herr Heckenast, who had taken over Ganna's interests and had stepped forward to speak on behalf of the kraal. He had also got in touch with Ganna's new lawyer, Dr Fingerling. (Ganna had turned down the idea of merging our agendas and leaving them in the hands of Hornschuch; a lawyer, like a husband, was someone you wanted all to yourself.)

Hornschuch appeared not dissatisfied with the choice of Dr Fingerling. It looked as though he had been able to exert some influence on Ganna. Even though Dr Fingerling got his information from Heckenast in Berlin, who in turn referred to the decisions of his sister-in-law Ganna, the fog of dispute seemed to lift slightly and permit a glimpse of a structure that might be an agreement.

No sooner did things approach the stage of possible realization, though, than Ganna was seized by increasing anxiety. Her situation was like that of someone followed by the police, who has changed his abode so often and so long, till one day he finds himself fingered by a cunning detective. She tried everything to give him the slip. For sure, the new deed that had been doing the rounds now for weeks between her, brother-in-law Heckenast and the two lawyers – being added to, cut, critiqued and commented on – included payment demands and other commitments from me that made it difficult to contemplate its signature. But could one be sure? Bettina had only to stamp her little foot. All at once, Ganna felt uneasy. The danger was that she herself was caught in the trap she had festooned with bacon. Also, she didn't know what to do about her debts. Dr Stanger-Goldenthal insisted on payment like some latter-day Shylock, and threatened to have the half of the house that was registered in her name held as surety. She begged Hornschuch to see that Dr Stanger's demands might be at least partly met, and then she would certainly expedite the settlement out of gratitude alone. But Hornschuch came back coolly: no cash before the deal.

In her extremity, Ganna decided to quit the scene for a while and go abroad. Her thinking was primitive: if two people are to be divorced, then they both have to be present; therefore, if I'm away, they won't be able to get my signature. So in a tearing rush she packed her suitcases, scraped together all the money she could and hauled Elisabeth and Doris off to the French

Riviera. Two days prior to going she had told me of her intention; her purpose was quite transparent to me, even though she
had made a play for sympathy by talking of her asthma attacks,
which required nothing less than a trip to the south. I could
hardly keep her from going; I would have had to lock her up.
But I had forbidden her to take Doris. After many unhappy
attempts and trials, a suitable school had at last been found for
the girl, now eleven, in the autumn just past; the one who was
happiest about it was Doris herself. Now, in the middle of term
time, she was going to be plucked out of her setting and taken
to a foreign country. My angry veto was answered by Ganna
with a cheeky message, followed by an express letter, about
how Doris was overstrained and required sea air; the school
was making her unhappy – the poor mite had to get up at six
thirty – so she had had the wonderful idea of putting her in a
dance school in Nice; the little darling's delight was probably
more than I could imagine. I tore up the letter and asked Hornschuch to convey my absolute and categorical opposition to
Ganna. With that I thought the matter was at an end. Later that
same day I had to attend a business meeting in Munich. No
sooner had I gone up to my hotel room than I received a telephone call from Ebenweiler. It was Bettina. She begged me in
pressed tones not on any account to go to Nice. In confusion I
asked her why I should want to go to Nice. She told me a telegram had arrived from Ganna, who was already in Nice with
our daughters, and – how could it be otherwise – was in need
of money. 'But Bettina,' I cried into the telephone, 'why would
I want to go to Nice, I had no idea the woman was going there
. . . So she took Doris . . . well, that takes the biscuit.' When
Hornschuch's voice then proceeded to boom from the earpiece, warning me with uncustomary seriousness not to do
anything rash – because if I did, he couldn't, as he put it, vouch
for Bettina's reaction – I didn't know what to say. What did he

mean? Gradually it dawned on me. Bettina was afraid I would pursue Ganna to rescue Doris and then would get caught up in some further round of negotiations. During the conversation I suddenly had the sense that she didn't believe my assurance that I had no idea of Ganna's whereabouts, and that tipped me into a fit of panic. I went back to Ebenweiler as quickly as I could.

Next, I blocked Ganna's monthly payments. Hornschuch informed her of my step by letter. She protested in a blazing forty-word telegram. A second, even longer telegram went to her brother-in-law Heckenast. He in turn addressed a lordly and insulting telegram to me, and another to Hornschuch. Hornschuch wrote to Dr Fingerling that he was astounded that he, Fingerling, had not only allowed his client to absent herself during a crucial phase of the talks, but had seen fit to send her money abroad. Fingerling wrote a piqued letter on the high-handedness of his client to Heckenast. Heckenast wrote a cross letter to Ganna, summoning her home. Ganna wired back saying she wouldn't think of it; she wasn't going to allow herself to be violated. I was surprised the lines between Nice and Berlin and Nice and Ebenweiler didn't self-combust with her pathetic ranting. In the meantime, she was running out of money. She couldn't pay the hotel bill and was forced to borrow money from strangers. The strangers became suspicious when she didn't keep her repayment date and threatened her with disagreeable steps. She wired, threatening to take legal action against me. Ganna letters and Ganna wires were raining down like shrapnel in a battle. Our little post office had its work cut out.

While this whole crazy fuss was going on, the deed was being worked out. Beset by her lawyer, who in turn was being pressed by Hornschuch, Ganna saw herself forced to quit the Côte d'Azur. Hornschuch travelled to Vienna to meet Heckenast in

Dr Fingerling's office. I was told to keep myself available and be ready to go to Vienna at a moment's notice. The signal came and I went.

The scene: Heckenast's hotel room. Dramatis personae: Heckenast, Hornschuch, Dr Fingerling and I. The burden of the drama: the big haggle. We haggled over every single point. There were so many points that, at the end of three hours, there was still no end in sight. My brother-in-law Heckenast was a man of Prussian laconism. He gave us to feel that by his presence he was dignifying all Austria, which was such a small, poor country. He was as passionless as a paperknife. Although considerably younger than I, he behaved towards me like an uncle swelled with his own moral rectitude, dismissing a naughty nephew from his affections; his bourgeois sensibility was lastingly offended by the reprehensible behaviour of this runaway from the kraal. Cold and impermeable, he placed himself before the rights of his sister-in-law Ganna like a wall. He was utterly objective. Ever allow the implacably objective to come to power, and that will spell the end of compassion and imagination on earth.

Dr Fingerling was a gaunt, red-haired, polite gentleman who would have liked to settle the case to the satisfaction of all. Furthermore, he was anxious to trouser his fee. Ten thousand schillings had been agreed for him, quite a chunk of change. From time to time he beckoned Hornschuch over to whisper something in his ear. He, keen-eyed, alert, brisk in attack and on guard, reminded me of a foil fencer. More like a student than a fully fledged lawyer, it wasn't hard for him to back the rigid Prussian into a corner, though admittedly that had little effect on the toughness of the conditions. Even though he was seeking to secure a deal for me somewhere at the upper limit of what I could bear, I still thought he disastrously overestimated my circumstances and resources. But there was nothing I could do. Things had gone too far. It was like a landslide: if you try to push against it, you'll be crushed.

I stood the whole time leaning against the window and allowed the hail of paragraphs, figures and punitive clauses to pass over me. My thoughts followed one of two tracks. One was remote from this slaughterhouse, in which I was playing the bullock; what is all this to do with me, I thought, this chain-rattle of punishments, what is it to do with me, it's just money, let them have it, I'll chuck it in their faces, let them fight each other over my hide, they won't get my soul, that's for sure. But the other track was black with worry, the question kept coming up: where am I going to get it from, all this money, year after year, welded to a contract that's more like a guillotine than a piece of paper, my whole life a coolie's service, my whole future fenced in with sanctions and reparations, my own personal Versailles; how can I prevent the work of my mind and imagination being diminished to an endless series of instalment payments and personal guarantees for Ganna?

At last there was agreement. The notary was standing by. Heckenast ordered up some brandy, we all formally shook hands and as I walked down the stairs with Hornschuch he said:

'I think congratulations are in order.'

'It's by no means certain that Ganna will sign,' I replied cagily.

Hornschuch said he thought Heckenast didn't look as though he would stand for any more monkey business, while Master Fingerling was pretty hard up. On the pavement he took my hand and said with a strange giggle, because he really was proud of his triumph:

'Pack money in your wallet! Lots of money! Money for Fingerling, money for Goldenthal, money for Ganna's debts, blood money, ransom money . . . Have you got enough? I am at your service.'

'I've scraped together everything I've got,' I said.

This conversation took place at two in the afternoon. At four, as arranged, Ganna came to Fingerling's office with her brother-in-law in tow. The notary had been summoned. One might have supposed the formalities would be over in minutes. In the event it took five hours before Ganna, with floods of tears and sobs, set her name to the document. 'It was like an amputation,' said Dr Fingerling when he told his colleague Hornschuch about the scene. As late as five o'clock, Ganna had shouted that she wouldn't agree under any circumstances. After everyone had talked at her for an hour, she seemed to be on the point of passing out and a cordial was brought. At seven o'clock she demanded a series of changes. Not possible, she was told, they had committed themselves as fiduciaries by handshake and word. She swore on the lives of her children she wouldn't sign any deed that made her the unhappiest woman in the world. She accused her brother-in-law of being bribed by Bettina and me. She threatened to take an overdose. She claimed to be the victim of blackmail. The sweat was beading on Dr Fingerling's brow. For the first time Heckenast lost control, grabbed her by the shoulders and roared that if she didn't see sense he would have her committed. At that she turned very quiet. With shyly fluttering eyelids and lowered head, she sat down at the desk and signed. Then, once she had signed, she heaved up a groan like a dying person from the deepest recesses of her heart, flung herself on the sofa and howled for twenty minutes in such tones that the three men present looked into one another's pale faces and didn't know what to do.

The following day, the day of the court appearance, I turned fifty-three. In the anteroom of the assizes Ganna walked up to me and said in dulcet tones and with the charming innocent smile of her girlhood days: 'I'm giving you a divorce for your birthday, Alexander.'

I was speechless – as speechless as I was an hour later when, with shaking hands, she stashed the many thousands of schillings I had counted out onto a table in front of her into her leather handbag. I stared intently at her ancient, wizened hands. Had they really opened to release me? We shall see.


## A look at the deed

While all this was going on Bettina was sitting in Ebenweiler and waiting. So as not to be completely alone, she had invited Lotte Waldbauer to keep her company. At twelve noon Hornschuch phoned through news of the divorce. When she returned to Lotte in the blue salon, Lotte leaped up because her friend was staggering so. Bettina was indeed on the point of collapse. 'It's too much,' she stammered, 'too dear,' and she lost consciousness. It wasn't money and price that she was referring to with her 'too dear', because she only got to hear of the financial conditions I had been forced to accept the following day, when Hornschuch brought her the divorce agreement.

She read it with her typical attentiveness. Then she remained silent for a while, with head down. Then she softly said: 'But that's awful.' Hornschuch made a disappointed face. He thought he deserved thanks. Feebly Bettina held out her hand to him. 'Don't think I don't appreciate your effort and goodwill,' she said, 'but look at what that man is taking upon himself! How could he set his name to it! A man who lives off his intellect and imagination!' Hornschuch didn't know what to say. He wasn't able, not then and not for a long time afterwards, to question the excellence of his legal edifice. Most men are a little like that. It's the gambler and the player in them all, and in their professions. The gifted and honest ones are dazzled by their idea, the

mean and brutish ones by success and profit. So between them
they rule the world. That's how Bettina saw them. Besides, from
the very beginning she was under no illusion about the situation. She knew with prophetic certainty that the garrotting
agreement, as she called it, hadn't shooed the ghost out of our
house. And she said: 'I'd sooner love in a hut than share a palace
with a ghost.'

However embarrassing and chilling it is, I must still, as briefly
as I can, talk about the conditions imposed upon me in that no-
torious deed. There was, first of all, the payment of Ganna's debts
run up over many years. Then, I was accountable for all the legal
bills; these, including the demands of Dr Stanger-Goldenthal and
the cost of drawing up the deed itself, came to 48,000 schillings.
Ganna's monthly allowance comfortably exceeded the salary of
a government minister. In addition there was a considerable
sum that I had to raise within the next three years, which was
described as Ganna's emergency fund. That I was also responsible for the upkeep of the children was only to be expected and
need not have appeared in the deed as a further compulsory
obligation. But Ganna wanted it there and so, from the look of
things, I was also in hock to my children. A further condition
was clearing the house my friends had given me fourteen years
ago of all mortgage debt and making it over to Ganna unencumbered. Very well; one might very well come to terms with
such clauses. It was a huge material burden; an investor, a bank
director, a captain of industry presumably wouldn't have sought
to oppose it, still greater sums wouldn't have cost them their
sleep; after all, freedom costs money, bourgeois society makes a
business transaction out of divorce and a person's freedom into
an object of trade. Very well. The last two clauses were different: that Ganna was to inherit one-third of all sums realized
from my writings and my possessions after my death; and further, that, as a guarantee for her allowance, a lien on the Bu-

chegger estate to the tune of 100,000 schillings was to be conceded to her. The first clause was tantamount to disinheriting Bettina, since there were four children plus Ganna who had to share the estate; the second devalued the house in Ebenweiler by loading it with debt, which would help make it unsellable.

The gift of the one house, the lien on the other and the claim on a third of my worldly goods all derived from the marriage contract that, if you'll remember, I had signed rather skittishly twenty-five years before. Now at last I learned what the so-called 'revocability' was all about: namely that, in the event of the marriage ending in divorce, I would not only have to return the dowry of 80,000 schillings, but pay it back twice over. And this doubled capital, with inflation, now came to some 200,000 schillings. You will concede that the kraal knew their business. They had succeeded in taking the naif, who with culpable innocence had run into their toils, and wringing him out. Honour and respect the kraal. A little curtsey to the age of security. And so Ganna took no harm from her sortie into the terrain of literature and the 'higher life', while Bettina and Caspar Hauser, beggars both of them for the foreseeable future, will have to look out for themselves. Ganna will sleep peacefully on her securities, as on a pillow of rose petals. Or am I wrong? I know it defies credulity; but all those 'securities' only served to shred their lives and mine with them.


## Money


At first money was a whip, driving me on, without opening any deep visible wounds. My capacity for work multiplied. The experiences of the last few years had ravaged me to such a degree that they seemed to have renewed me intellectually and spiritually, and transformed my picture of the world. All you need is to understand the suffering of a single being, through and through, for him to be the source and focus of everything there is to know about humans. The thing that eats us up inside becomes our fuel, if we are strong enough to keep going. Almost every sickness refines the organism. I no longer allowed myself to be guided by the sweet whims of a spirit loitering in remote imaginings; I heard the call of the now which pierced me more deeply in my solitude than if I'd been in the world's hubbub. Also, fortune had given me the gift of shutting myself away in working hours against worries and pressures, admittedly only – once the bolts were undrawn and I was a human being again among other human beings – for me to succumb to my fears, my existential panic, my gloomy forebodings, all of them exacerbated by my periods of solitude.

The seeming tranquillity that Bettina and I enjoyed early on in our marriage glossed over the oppressive obligations with which it had been bought. In order to meet them, to finance our own lives and the payments to the Dutchman and to my friend who had helped me to acquire the Buchegger estate, not to mention taxes, I had to earn a vast sum every year; and although, by some freak of fortune and a delirium of creative work, I even managed to top that for the first couple of years, it wasn't long before I saw myself under pressure and was forced to take out a considerable loan at extortionate rates of interest.

Since my income at the beginning seemed able to keep step with our outgoings, I got into something of the mood of a gambler, trusting to luck, risking ever higher stakes; or of a man who is so deeply indebted, and has given out so many promissory notes that in his life he will have nothing to do with economy of any kind, remains oblivious to rising consumption and greets each inner prompting to prudence with anger and contempt. So I expanded my lifestyle, I ran a household, added to my library, bought a car and took Bettina abroad. The all-too-evident result was that Ganna, who of course remained minutely informed of all of this, was confirmed in the belief that I was in possession of vast means, that she had been crudely deceived and practically criminally deprived of the possibility of securing her fair share by the divorce agreement.

My relationship to money at the time could perhaps best be described by the paradox 'selfish indifference'. Like anyone who has climbed out of poverty, I was devoted to the pleasures and advantages conferred by money; but not only did I not love money itself, I despised it. Which is to say, I despised it when I had it and couldn't imagine what it must be like not to have it. I had never been avaricious, but neither had I been carefree. Without my being by nature a lover of luxury, a certain dull sensuality in things I had become accustomed to made it exceedingly difficult for me to do without.

With Bettina it was different. She neither loved nor despised money. To her balanced sense, it was a means to satisfy a few basic needs. Sometimes, admittedly, for luxuries as well, inasmuch as they were presented to her in terms of aesthetic value – that classical simplicity that causes more heart-searching and trouble than any pomp. In the years in which I didn't allow her to see into my finances and she – partly so as not to burden me, partly awed by my creative furor – declined to question me or rein me in, she gave herself up with a secret reservation, just as I did, to the illusion of an overflowing horn of plenty. She decorated herself, she decorated our home, decorated the garden and was happy that she could surround herself with beautiful things, which she chose with discernment, because she has the most incorruptible eyes of anyone in the world. To have visitors made her very happy, and for the most part it was old friends whom we had to stay; she was loyal and devoted to them. Never was she immodest, much less rapacious in her wishes. She didn't care about having possessions. To know that the beautiful thing was there, to be communed with and to make her richer inside, not to plume herself with it – that was her style of ownership; and in any case the two things that remained dearest to her were music and our little Caspar Hauser.

Till one day these brilliant dreams of beauty, peace and art burst, and a baleful reality eyed us like a hyena that had crept out from under the bed.

## Ganna in preparation

And Ganna? The severing of the formal bonds between us failed to persuade her that privately, in our hearts, we were now separated as well. The mood in which she returned to her now barren life was glum. It was as though the lights had gone out and all the visitors suddenly disappeared. A hush descended. Suddenly it was dark. She was all alone. Yes, there were the children. But apart from Doris, they were grown up and didn't need their mother, not in the sense Ganna understood: as provider, comforter, protector. They lived in the baffling world of people. They had opinions, experiences, friends and who knew what attachments.

And, like someone clearing out an old flat before moving into a new one, she ransacked wardrobes, boxes and chests of drawers and pulled out all the memories and souvenirs she had of me, old photographs, gifts from the early years of our marriage. She couldn't get enough of these things. She used them to remind herself how happy she had been then, when she received them. In her imagination it was a happiness beyond computation – such as she had never really felt. She leafed through her girlhood diaries and refused to accept that things had turned out so differently from the way she had dreamed they would. She made the upsetting discovery that dreams lie. Admittedly, this only happened in brief little intervals of consciousness, as when a persistent beam of light forces its way through a shuttered window. She hurried to seal it up again.

Her chief resource was the letters I had written to her in those first ten years. Greedily she supped full of them. She put them in chronological order and numbered them. So as to make them even more strongly present to her imagination than by merely reading them, she copied them out by hand, one after the other. When she was finally finished, weeks later, she took the copies to a stenotypist and had the whole collection typed up in several copies. One of which, nicely bound, went to me. I didn't see what I was supposed to do with it. The hidden purpose of the exercise was presumably to tell posterity the truth about the relationship between Ganna and Alexander Herzog. Posterity was a sort of fire insurance firm for her.

Every day was like a holey curtain. Through each hole, a piece of the past peeped through. What could she do, to fill up the dreary days? There were no files, no documents, no nail-biting negotiations any more. Sometimes she took down the books of her favourite poets and philosophers. It was a hollow gesture. A real counter-factual as-if. There is pleasure to be had in as-if. To its devotees it allows a rush of seeming existence after periods of feeling dead. Over the summer she read everything I had written, in sequence; and when we met at the end of that time claimed, half with feigned regret, half with unconstrained satisfaction, that the books I had written while I was living with her were incomparably better than those I wrote since falling in with Bettina. She was on the point of saying: I always knew God would punish you and He has. The old formula. The conversation took place one fine evening in the garden of her house. She was wrapped in numerous blankets when

I arrived, had made herself comfortable on her chaise-longue and looked up into the sky where, one by one, the stars popped out. I asked myself: what is she looking for up there? She was capable of lying there for hours on end, looking up at the sky, almost like a person of faith, all the while foolish and resentful notions crowded her mind. What does she look to the stars for? What was she wanting, craving, overarched by the eternal canopy?

There was one thing she couldn't be reconciled to, and she gnawed at it like a poisonous wound. I had promised her my friendship, had sworn to cherish her, if only she would agree to a divorce. Well, now she was waiting to be cherished. But since I gave no appearance of being ready to do so, an anxious disappointment came up in her. Whatever time I devoted to her, it wasn't enough. I talked about all kinds of things, in her view, only not about friendship. When I got up to go, she asked me with a troubled expression why I didn't spend the whole day with her. When I had spent the whole day with her, she wanted me to keep tomorrow for her as well. Sometimes I had the car parked outside the house. She smiled and passed remarks that were intended to show how free from jealousy she was, but that on the contrary betrayed the fact that she was consumed with regret. She regretted that she had agreed to the divorce, regretted it with every thought she had, day and night; bitterly she gave me to understand that she felt she had been outwitted and ambushed, by Hornschuch and by Bettina. The notion that I was gadding around the world with Bettina, while she sat there in her own four walls, mocked and betrayed to her scorn, almost drove her mad.

I asked her in what form the promised friendship was to be realized, if not in tentative efforts at renewal, as I was honestly attempting, the gradual forgetting and removal of her unhappy past. Forgetting? Unhappy past? She was beside herself. 'How

can you say such a thing, Alexander! How really mean of you!'
Absurd, the idea that I was going to her to find out how to convince her of my friendship. Nothing easier: going to the theatre
together, to a concert, just to demonstrate to the world that a
divorce between two fine characters like her and me didn't
mean anything and didn't change anything; we could go on little spring or autumn jaunts together; I could come and stay
with her when I had to be in the city; she will give teas and
soirées at which I can meet her new friends. That was what she
insisted and insisted on; that was the wonderful thing, the only
thing that could compensate her for her monstrous sacrifice.
Instead of which she was being fobbed off with charity; it was a
disgrace, a disgrace . . .

I couldn't believe what I was hearing. That was it, the ambitious wishing on the stars as they opened. What did she care
about the stars? She was carrying on the great process against
the wrong that had been done her. Many years before, I once
summed her up like this in one of my notebooks: 'A being with
a blind heart, a salamander.' It was just a scribbled jotting. In her
blindness of heart she never was aware of what tied her, of what
was seemly, of what was right. In her salamandrine nature, she
slipped out of time and space and every form of law and instruction. She was like a figure outside of any mathematical order –
what the mathematicians call an unreal number. Something
unthinkable. But in matters of morality and ethics one can
come across the unthinkable readily enough, because to a
human being nothing is impossible.

In the preceding pages I have consistently been at pains to
write a chaotic sort of love into her that broke all bounds and
turned destructively in the end against herself. A psychological
aberration, in short. Don't we handle the term love as though it
were some jemmy or crowbar that could open any lock? Don't
talk to me about love / hate, or the chase or such things, it wasn't

that. 'Amor demens' would be closer to it. But delusion is a mysterious, underexplored element; no mirror has ever caught its reflection, no pen has described it utterly, because it reaches down into the lowest depths of humanity.

Everything that now happened was preformed, prefigured in Ganna. There was no scheme, no fierce unspeakable determination, but it was resolved in her, just as it is resolved that when heat is applied to a boiler steam will seek to escape through the vents. Since she couldn't have me physically, she had to have me every other way. How, you may ask. Meet me. In every sense of the word. Meet me where I was most vulnerable: she felt herself chosen by destiny for that purpose. If she couldn't be by me and with me, then within me – if not for my good, to which she firmly believed she was contributing, then to my ill, to which she really did contribute. Madness can do anything.

## Psyche bleeds

I must take care not to fluff the connections. There is a mixture of triviality and breathtaking audacity informing the events which makes it difficult to set them out in hindsight. The sober truth of things runs smack into the pandemonium they created when the brain that bore them followed them through to the end with fanatical logic.

It began one fine day when she told me that she and a journalist friend of hers had adapted my *Treasure Seekers of Worms* for the cinema. When telling me this, she reminded me of the written permission I had given her to do this eight years before. In the meantime, however, I had sold the book to an American firm. I thought I had told her about this, either verbally or in writing; she claimed I hadn't. I suppose it was just possible that with everything going on I did forget to mention it to her. In alarm, I warned her against trying to place it anywhere; one couldn't sell the same thing twice. She claimed she had a right to make the film sale. The fact that I had neglected to tell her about it (the possibility that I might have suppressed the news had the status of a fully fledged fact for her), was to her proof that I was always out to deceive her about my income. I replied that it was only by such windfalls that I had been able to provide for her and the children during the years of the Inflation. She wasn't interested. She totted up my supposed wealth; the fact that she had benefited from all of it, if not taken the lion's share, was not thought to be worth mentioning. She refused to withdraw the screenplay. She said her co-author, with whom she had a contract, insisted on his share and was even threatening to sue. I remarked in surprise: how can you sign a contract relating to something that doesn't belong to you? She replied that her lawyer saw matters differently. Hence I found out that she once more had a lawyer engaged for her, one Dr Mattern. I was left with no alternative but to assign the conduct of the unwanted case to my own lawyer. Hornschuch was back in business. During the final stages of the dispute, I was abroad with Bettina. I was sent newspaper articles in which the quarrel about the screenplay was vulgarly sensationalized with nasty jabs at myself. At the same time, Ganna was again bombarding me with long telegrams in which she swore blind that she was not to blame for the press attacks, which were the work of people who wanted to damage her in my eyes. 'How does she always know where we are?' asked Bettina, shaking her head. I had to confess I had told her where we were going. After that, Bettina said nothing.

Hornschuch came up with a settlement. I had to pay Ganna's journalist friend a considerable sum to compensate him for work he was neither qualified nor hired to do. Ganna herself finally declined the sum she had first demanded, even though she claimed the state of her finances was not such that she could do so with an easy heart; however, for my sake and that of the peace between us, she would give in. At this time she spoke of literary plans and showed me some of her work, asking me to help to secure its publication; she badly needed to earn money. I didn't understand the urgency, given that she drew an allowance that permitted a person to live comfortably; but I did what I could, if only to be helpful to her, and I did it too against my better judgement, because what she had written struck me as neither entertaining nor useful. I concealed my opinion from her to avoid pointless debates and so as not to disturb her in an occupation that at least kept her from others that might be more destructive.

I was mistaken. It wasn't long before she came to me with a new project. In order to make money from her house, she decided to add another storey to it and rent out the lower part. Not a bad idea, *ceteris paribus*; but to put it into effect was an expensive business and involved drawing on her reserves (in case she still had any at the time), and taking out expensive loans. I thought it my duty to warn her. I pointed out the dangers of falling into debt. With smug superiority she dismissed my concerns. There was a disagreeable tendency in her whereby she would take something she was determined to own but didn't own, and so mortgage it and load it with debt that by the time she did own it, if she was successful, she was left with nothing but the title and the illusion of possession. She resembled a person desperately racing against her shadow, trying and trying to overtake it. Then once the folly of her enterprise struck her, in blind fury she lashed out at the shadow and demanded to be compensated for her effort, her disappointment and the investment of trouble and money. But the shadow was only a stand-in for me, and so it was the living Alexander who had to cough up; there was no getting out of it, he had to pay and pay.

The conversion of the house hadn't, as I'd supposed, got in the way of her other work. From time to time she made mysterious references to me to some sort of book that she was writing, for which she had the loftiest expectations. So far as I could glean from her words what she had in mind was a prose narrative, an account of her life and sufferings, a memoir of spousal love and constancy. Often she said, wide-eyed, that in the conception of the work she'd above all had me in mind, the only thing that mattered to her being to free me from the error I'd committed; once I'd read her book, seriously and attentively, as she stipulated, then there would be no question but that I, shaken by the truthfulness of her account, would return to her forthwith. All this she said in her typical fashion – threatening, flattering, accusing – in which she had such mastery.

Earlier on in these reminiscences I had occasion once to mention the mischief done by literature. The world I was referring to then was decent and harmless, blatant in its deceits, pathetic even in its efforts to use art and intellect as a figleaf for its nakedness. Since then, three decades have passed. The amateurish belletristic Ganna world of that time is as different from today's heady iconoclasm as a water pistol is from a Gatling gun. It used to be that they played with their innocent weapons at literary teas; now they are shooting in deadly earnest. They set word-bombs, they throw word-grenades, they poison the world with printer's ink; every frustrated idiot, every publicity-crazed complainer dumps his revenge complexes from his desk onto the street below; there's no question of any inner calling, or truth and honesty; paper is cheap, the setter willing, the word costs nothing; the call to arms of the epoch is write and howl down all the other misery of humankind, which gradually gurgles its last under a mound of paper.

Hardly surprising then that Ganna too was contaminated by the plague, sought her salvation in the production of printed matter; after all she was born with a pen in her mouth, writing had always been the essence of her being, her most living expression, her emphatic insistence, her refuge and her consolation. And this passion, which was so close to being a vice, in the same way that a good book from the outside may resemble a bad one, grew unstoppably. I think it was the source of all her unhappiness, her disorder, her godlessness, because it replaced the mirror in her heart wherein every soul-endowed creature can recognize itself – itself with death over its shoulder, the way it is shown in old paintings. She didn't think about death, she knew nothing of God and over the mirror of her heart she had stuck a ream of paper, so that she could write and write and write . . .

The slim volume, a novella, had the nauseating title *Psyche Bleeds*. There was already a publisher who had agreed to take it on, probably in the hope of a minor scandal. It didn't pan out; there was a storm in a teacup, nothing more. The letter which Ganna enclosed with her product was a sort of written cringe. Further insistence on her love, further humiliating reference to the need to make money. All in all, the blurting of an uneasy conscience.

I opened the book. I read grotesque absurdities. My first instinctive act was to hide it so that Bettina didn't see it. But once I was alone in my study I would sometimes get it out of the heap of books I had put it in with, in the way that one might look at some obscene pornography after first throwing it away in disgust. What was this thing so palpably on paper! Behind a cloud of emotional gush and saccharine romance I could make out a dirty distortion of Bettina's likeness, the depiction of her ostensible sins and sly contrivances, with the addition of a shameless bed and adultery scene in which the cheated husband is supposed to excite the sympathy of the reader. Bleeding Psyche was – you guessed it – Ganna, the white archangel Ganna, pursued and violated by the tribadic monster of a Bettina.

Friends and acquaintances occasionally came to me to express their sympathy. Here and there, from the holes which lurking enviers and haters had crept into, there was a malignant murmuring. Ganna did publicity for her opus and spurred her journalist chums to praise it in the papers. In the end it was inevitable that I spoke about the book with Bettina, especially as she had heard about it first from Hornschuch, then from divers other sources. I have never witnessed anything finer and nobler than the way she disregarded the squalid demeaning of her person. Of course she was bound to feel contaminated, she hated talk, whether it was well meaning or not; but there was no power on earth that could get her to read the book, or so much as touch it with her little finger. For her there was only one thing that mattered, as I understood only far too late – namely what *I* thought of it and what consequence *I* would draw from it.

## With the roses

Bettina stood in the garden, dabbing the murderous greenflies off her roses. Sometimes, when a bloom had been especially ravaged, she would mutter crossly under her breath. Next to the container with the insecticide was a tin bath of water with a syringe floating in it. Little Helmut was larking about, babbling and crooning. You couldn't imagine a finer opportunity for mucking about with water.

All at once he gave a blood-chilling scream. He had fallen into the tub. I heard it too and ran out with my hair on end with terror. By the time I got there Bettina had already dragged the little wriggler out of the water. Calmly she stood him in the sun to dry off. And to me, standing there looking haunted, afraid our adored offspring had come to harm, she said, with a glance at the dripping little man: 'Don't worry. It won't be the last time he gets a drenching.' And with that she went back to her greenflies.

## Guerrilla warfare

I wrote to Ganna to say that for the time being I wanted nothing further to do with her. She was to apply to Hornschuch on all financial and domestic matters. Five lines. But why 'for the time being'? Wasn't that half a step back already? And wouldn't Ganna, with her unerring sense of my weakness, draw courage from it for further stunts? For the time being! Puzzle me that one out, if you can; I can't. I know I'm not the 'never darken my doors again' type. Maybe it was my principle, inevitable in one who always sees himself confronting the two faces of the world, the No and the Yes. There are mysterious insistences and persistences at play, and the mental and intellectual is as close to the traitorous as thinking is to not-doing.

Ganna didn't accept the breach. Her letters were sweetness and light. Since I didn't reply, she wrote an extensive defence of her literary work and had it sent to me, along with reviews from reputable critics, via Dr Mattern. Since I still didn't respond, she instructed other intermediaries to plead her cause with me. I said to her people, if you eat garbage you first need to give your digestive system time to clean itself out. For a while Ganna kept silent, but before long the demands for money started coming again. Her allowance was too small for her to be able to live off it. The clothing and schooling of our two daughters cost several times more than what had been allotted for the purpose. Our old friends the '*imprévus*' cropped up again. Considerable 'backlogs' had been run up; she had instructed Dr Mattern to send me the 'vouchers'. Some of the backlogs dated from the time before the divorce; clearly, it had not come up to expectation.

I asked her why official seals and promises which for me had an absolute validity shouldn't equally apply to her. I rejected the demands, but the continual ranting made me ill; I wanted quiet, peace from her. Medical opinion prescribed a lengthy stay in Marrakesh. I wrote to inform the children; Ganna begged me for a meeting before I left. I gave in to her pressure and agreed. Then one wasn't enough, it got to be several. Ganna, riddled with anxieties, petitioned me for money, the housekeeping book put in an appearance, the numbered bills were produced, the 'vouchers' turned up. I could have said: what does it all have to do with me, I've paid and overpaid your bills and on the first of the month you'll have my next instalment, ciao. But I wanted quiet, I didn't want bickering and kvetching behind my back; I had enjoyed some unexpected successes that year, I was on the point of leaving on an expensive journey and even though I had intended to put something by for an emergency, I thought: damn it, and said very well, I was prepared to give her 10,000 schillings, of which she could have 8,000 right away. A couple of weeks later I opened a newspaper where one of her journalist friends worked, and saw an interview with her all about how she had to fight for money for her youngest child. Obviously she had got talking in front of some irresponsible fellow, and when she saw her froth set in the form of newsprint she was suddenly afraid and fired off a cable to me, where for the umpteenth time she swore by all that was high and holy that she was not to blame. I remained cool, but to chastise her for her lie I now held back the last 2,000 I had promised her. By now she had forgotten that the money was a gratuity and she demanded the rest, as if it had been a debt owing to her. She had already promised the money to a third person, and once again threatened to take me to court. Having received such a significant sum of money from me already, without any entitlement to it, she saw my pliancy as proof of her entitlement; above all it removed the least doubt in her about my Rockefeller-like wealth, her enjoyment of which had been hindered by the stupidity and wickedness of her lawyers. The deed was made the object of ceaseless study. She carried it around with her wherever she went by day, at night it lay on her bedside table. She knew its terms by heart and even so she immersed herself in it like a devout Jew in his Talmud. She was looking for a point she might attack. She found it soon enough in the clause relating to her monthly allowance. Her representatives had before the divorce argued that she should take a one-third share of everything I earned. This, however, I had rejected emphatically; I knew Ganna and saw that such a condition would have given her an opening for incessant nosing-around and demands for me to furnish her with my accounts. In its place a lifelong appanage had been agreed upon, at a fixed amount that was described as equivalent to one-third.

And at this point she brought her dissatisfaction and her appeal to bear. As usual, she insisted she had been deceived. She declared the clause was unjust and invalid. She demanded a third of my *actual* earnings. When it was pointed out to her that the deal she had secured was better, because years might come that would give her cause to regret her agitating, she laughed disbelievingly. She could afford to; she after all still had her lien. If and when hard times came over me again, then she could simply revert to the fixed allowance; and if I refused, she could foreclose on the Buchegger estate. For the moment, though, getting a share of my earnings not only seemed more lucrative to her, but the inspection and supervision of my financial circumstances gave her an entrée into my life and allowed her to establish herself in it as a controlling instance. With this in mind, she set up an extensive network of spies. She had herself informed about my expenditure, the standard of living of Bettina and myself; she knew at all times how many servants were in my employ, how many guests I had; she kept tabs on the size of my editions and the sums I realized for sale of translation rights to my books abroad; and on the basis of such material she raised her noisy claims, appealing always to morality, humanity and justice. Since I wouldn't get involved in any dealings with her, the flood of memoranda started up again and lawyers' letters. Presumably it was the extension of the house that had got her into renewed financial trouble. But in order to avoid that, she had taken out mortgage after mortgage. Matters grew ever murkier and more desperate. My only concern was Doris. She was now fourteen; the money earmarked for her largely went on Ganna's hopeless efforts to pay off her debts, and so I finally agreed to raise the sum for the child considerably, while reserving the right to end the arrangement if it became the basis of legal argument. This reservation angered Ganna. She saw in it evidence of suspicion on my part. The agreement was drawn up in March. In March I paid the increased sum for the first time. By October Ganna thought I owed her for the first quarter as well. An avalanche of letters. Two new lawyers appeared on the scene. At Hornschuch's, the files of Herzog vs. Herzog were menacing the ceiling. He shook his head in perplexity. In perplexity he came to me, in perplexity stood in front of Bettina, and said: 'I don't understand this.'

## Bettina homeless, myself under pressure

How could I have allowed it to happen: I didn't notice that Bettina lost heart, lost hope and, worst of all, lost trust. I didn't notice that she turned away from me in pain; felt lonely, disappointed, betrayed as never before. Didn't notice that she no longer took pleasure in the house, that the flowers died under her hands, that the beautiful things faded away. Didn't notice that she was cold, that her fingernails were often blue with it. With far-sighted care, she attended to the upbringing of little Helmut, concentrating on not showing him any excess, avoiding displays of feeling; but the fact that I was the deterrent instance of what not to do – I didn't notice that.

Had Ganna succeeded – already succeeded – in destroying our strong and tender union? Bettina was never one to cry easily. She doesn't follow Kierkegaard's saying that it's dishonourable for a Christian to live without tears. Everything takes place out of sight, behind a smiling face. She is like the goose-girl in the fairy tale, who makes the prince go and hide in the oven before she agrees to lament her woes. And I very much doubt that she made up her mind in the oven. Not-noticing was made all too easy for me. I remember one occasion when I almost awoke; in a letter she suggested in a shy, veiled way that she often had bold notions of independence buzzing round her brain; and when she thought of the freedom she had had when she was growing up, then she felt like dropping everything and fleeing into the world, relying on herself only. Her confession surprised me, but in my obtuseness I didn't understand it. I knew her too poorly. Never would she have managed to say: enough, let's separate. Remote from believing in her irreplaceability, the way most women do, she knew nevertheless that I wouldn't have got over her desertion – not even understood it. Rarely can a human being have been as generously considerate and forbearing as she to me. She took it as given that I needed her. Well, she let it happen. I needed her and used her, as I needed and used everything in my life, everything that protected me, confirmed me and gave me quiet. Including her. I know she felt my love for her. This love she was all too familiar with, there was a whole block of it, a mountain of love; but it was trackless, wild, inaccessible, strangely savage. You needed to master it somehow; learn to look after it, find your way around in it, sometimes find it in the first place. But had she ceased loving me? Sometimes I put the question to myself, the way a hypochondriac in his imaginary agonies thinks of death. Because Bettina was not able to love without respect – that was clear to me. The early admiration she felt for her father shaped her subsequent relationships and her life as a woman. Since her subtle sensuality only responded to stimuli in the imagination, in love she can only exist in a lofty spiritual realm. And without love she is incapable of existing at all. I should have realized why she felt alienated in her own home. She did her domestic chores, she procured peace and quiet for me, she looked after Ferry, Elisabeth and Doris when they came to stay, she was happy to see her own daughters when they came in the holidays; but all of that seemed somehow to take place outside of herself. Now I see that. A person who does his duty, as well as he can, but only his duty, may be an example and a paragon to others, but to himself he will be a burden and a curse; in solitary hours the artificial props snap, and a sea of sadness will close over his head.

Now I can also understand her growing need to spend time away from the house. She wanted to collect herself, to regroup. She hiked in the mountains on her own; on occasion she travelled to Vienna to shelter with her friend Lotte Waldbauer, or to Salzburg for a couple of days to stay with her old composition teacher. She enjoyed the speed and separation of being in a car; often, after a sleepless night, she would go for a drive and leave a note on my desk saying she'd gone. Then I would miss her, a little as I missed my hat when the tempest had blown it off my head. She went out, she came back, to 'keep an eye on things' as she derisively put it, disappeared again, suddenly missed little Caspar Hauser and when she had him in her arms again she might have taken him with her, if it had been possible. She was no longer at peace, no longer felt herself in fortune's good graces, she felt homeless.

Yes, I missed her – missed her like my hat. There is a remarkable ignorance in men that makes them think they have a woman when they have a woman. Even the most sensitive of them fall for the crude mistake of the body. Even the most ethereal of them are animals that think the byre and the cave are taboo.

I have no other excuse than that my eyes and ears were commandeered by the pursuer. Things had come to such a pass that each time there was a letter from her in the post I would feel my temples throb. The notion of having to see her was a nightmare, but sometimes the incredible thing happened and on my visits to town I would go to see her, if only to prevent her from coming to me. I experienced the most terrible form of sleep there is. You lie there shattered, your chest sliced open, suffering unendurable agonies from the unexampled wickedness of fate. And you sleep. And in your sleep you deal with your fate. Resist, justify yourself, get nowhere, talk for nothing, your throat choked with pleas and wails, with rage and astonishment, and you wake up with a shattered head. While I worked, I felt like someone with two loaded revolvers pressed to his head, one on either side. When I left the house I would be frightened for my son. A limitless dread of the Ganna devils. I walked around, waiting to see what she would come up with next, where the next lightning would strike. It had been going on for years now and no end in sight. I fervently wished I could turn back time, so that I would never have met the woman. What right did she have to wreck my life, on whose instructions was it? What sort of being was she that she could overturn any human agreement with impunity and rampage through a world that she saw as hers to despoil, a mad world with mad agreements and mad battles?

But I am getting a little ahead of myself.


## Three decent people

Thanks to the canny logic that often inheres in events, it was at this time that the tax authorities discovered that Ganna had neglected to pay any tax since her divorce, and demanded immediate back payments. It was a very large amount, almost doubled by the fine slapped onto it. Ganna objected, but in the teeth of the State's determination to fleece its citizens there is no objection possible. The most she could do was secure a postponement. She ran to several lawyers, but m'learned friends were unable to help either. They tried the usual methods of obtaining further delays, thereby only adding to the costs and interest. If she had still had the money she was supposed, by the terms of the divorce agreement, to have set aside as an emergency fund, then nothing bad would have happened, she would simply have had to use it for that. But there was nothing left of the money. Nor could she load the house with more debt; the mortgage interest payments were eating into her monthly allowance as it was and her other debts were going up all the time.

In her predicament she quite naturally turned to – me. We had a meeting at which she begged me to take on her tax debt. She claimed one of her lawyers had told her it was the only way of getting the sum asked for down to manageable proportions. She had previously written to me along these same lines; I had taken soundings with Hornschuch, who sensed illegal manipulations and advised me against allowing myself to be lured into a possible legal minefield. But even if there hadn't been any risks, I still couldn't have got Ganna out of this pickle; I told her my circumstances had deteriorated so much of late that it was difficult enough for me to meet my existing obligations. She sniggered contemptuously. It was as if I'd asked her to pick up the bill for lunch. Then I made the ill-advised suggestion that I might be able to help her if she renounced her lien on the Buchegger estate; then I would be in the position of being able to borrow money against the property. To hear this, to stare at me with burning eyes and to burst into a long loud shriek were all one and the same for Ganna. She carried on as though the lien were the apple of her eye and I was trying to steal it. In her tantrum I kept hearing the one word: blackmail. My suggestion was blackmail to her. She was prepared for everything, but not that. The fact that I looked to her to abandon her most powerful lever showed her just who she was up against. I was simple-minded enough to stick up for myself. In addition to the lien she also had the deed, I pointed out, and quoted the saying of a lawyer friend of mine who had once said: a deed is like a razor blade, the least movement and you start to bleed. Of course, she retorted, with difficulty keeping the triumph out of her voice, the lien was part and parcel of the deed, and to seek to interfere with it was an attempt on her life. And while she went on froth-ing at the mouth and babbling about blackmail, I took my hat and left.

Several weeks passed, during which she wriggled piteously. The tightening screw of the tax people took her breath away. Little part-payments gained her brief periods of respite. In order to quiet the rest of her creditors, she had chosen the system of partial consolidation. She paid One out, and agreed to even more oppressive conditions from numbers Two, Three and Four. She took to hocking her allowance and the rent she made on the house for months in advance. The lawyers she had engaged and who ran round the houses for her, and put in applications (there were already three or four of them at this time), didn't want to do their work gratis either. She put them off by writing IOUs. I asked myself and I asked others how such a thing was possible; IOUs are not legal tender, how long can someone go on issuing IOUs? Till someone who knew explained: if you are in possession of a deed, you can string along one loan after another, since one lender doesn't need to know about the existence of others, and in this case takes Alexander Herzog Ltd for a flourishing business. Aha, I thought, so a deed isn't just a razor blade, but also a golden-egg-laying goose; good to know; I wonder what further qualities it will turn out to possess?

Even though it was a wretched life that Ganna was living, besieged by creditors, constricted by debt, under fire from the tax authorities, she could have taken all these calamities – which she was used to, to which she had fully adjusted – fatalistically in her stride, were it not for the serious threat to her ownership of the house. If there should be a forced sale, through foreclosure of the mortgages, she was lost. At least that was her mantra to herself, and at the thought she gibbered with panic. I had occasion to watch her, and more yet to sense how her relationship with property was taking shape within her. The house that was hers and the lien on the Buchegger estate both gave rise to ferocious feelings of possessiveness in her, puffed up with which she steered confidently over the surging waves of her life. As long as she had those two in her grasp, she felt inured to storm and shipwreck. The house she lived in and the estate that Bettina owned (as for me, I seemed to be a kind of chattel to be pushed here and there) – they were like a treasure found and one still only dreamed of; but one knows where it is to be found and all that is needed to secure it is the knowledge of the correct phrase or formula. An extraordinary serenity came over her at times, when she pictured to herself how eventually she would move into the fairy-tale palace by the lake and watch her rival legging it out through the back door with a hatbox or two.

Meanwhile, the pressures on her were increasing daily. After Drs Sperling, Wachtel, Greif and Tauber had all tested their teeth on the tough revenue nut without achieving any notable breakthrough, the fifth to be consulted by Ganna, one Dr Storch, was illuminated by a flash of genius. In the course of a protracted consultation with her he pointed out that, were she still living with me as my wife, she would not be facing any tax demand. Ganna nodded sorrowfully. She didn't need any learned commentary to remind her of the sorry circumstance. But the lawyer had something else in mind. He had carefully reconsidered the case, he said, and while reading the files he had come upon a small technicality. Technicality? Ganna was positively giddy with excitement; she asked, stammering, what the lawyer – now suddenly transformed before her eyes into a celestial cherub – had in mind with his mysterious remark. With a smile he told her. Everything seemed to suggest that – probably in the haste of the final official dealings – my German nationality had been left out of regard. Pressing her hand to her bosom and breathing hard, Ganna asks what consequences that might have. At the very least it provided grounds for challenging the divorce, replies Dr Storch. At those words, Ganna gives a start – a pleasurable start, admittedly, but a start nonetheless. She reminds the cherub that I had since contracted another marriage. To which the cherub replies that that didn't change anything. Whereupon Ganna, with the same voluptuous feeling of panic, gave a little scream: that means, oh my God, that means it's bigamy. Whereupon the cherub, dampening down her exuberance, asks her to be cautious in the use of such terms. For the moment, he saw in this interesting circumstance nothing more than the means to put a little pressure on the tax authorities.

Dr Storch's revelation had some point, inasmuch as my divorce from Ganna was only carried out before an Austrian court of law, and not a German. As I had been a resident of Austria for decades, the divorce according to Austrian law was initially held to be perfectly sufficient. Even so, Hornschuch had anticipated that difficulties might come about one day and had insisted that Ganna deposit a letter in the file in which she declared herself ready, whenever it might be asked of her, to agree to the German divorce as well. She had forgotten all about the letter. When we jogged her memory later, she claimed it had been extorted from her.

But to stick to the sequence of events: Ganna went home from the meeting with Dr Storch with her heart palpitating. She was utterly bewildered by her good fortune. The lawyer's cautiously advanced point was in her eyes as good as a victory in open court. A legal bit of jiggery-pokery meant the eradication of an irksome fact. A technicality meant: there was no divorce and Ganna remains the lawful Frau Herzog. She dealt with contracts she had no intention of abiding by as with servants she sacked if they stood up to her. Above all, though, she, the doting spouse, thought of the danger to which I was exposed. With a happy shudder, she reflected that by my second marriage I had committed a crime. As she walked out of Storch's office she could see me in a highly embarrassing pickle, if I still refused to co-operate; by the time she boarded the tram I was practically behind bars. The day before, she had learned that I was expected in the sanatorium where I had to check in two or three times a year for my condition. She knew Bettina would be accompanying me. So much the better, she thought, then we'll finally get the woman thrown out. She wanted as much as possible to spare me. She would break the news to me in a tête-à-tête, and with enormous restraint. Admittedly, after all that had gone before, she would have to be ready for the chance that I might refuse to see her; but in this case she trusted to the gravity of the news she had for me, seeing as it was about my honour, as she said, and my reputation. She could already hear my weeping pleading and see Bettina grovelling on the ground in front of her . . .

The morning my checking-in at the clinic had been reported back to her by whichever of her people did such things, she had me called to the telephone. She was informed the doctor had told me not to go to the phone; any negotiations were out of the question; my condition required extremely careful handling. In that case she had better speak to Bettina, an indignant Ganna replied; the matter she wanted to discuss could not permit of even one hour's delay, it was a matter of life and death for me. Bettina was told. At that time Bettina was not as inured to Ganna's ways of procuring conversations as she got to be later. She thought the vulgar commotion might have something in it and she went, reluctantly enough, to the telephone. Ganna was reduced to a stammer. She didn't want to give away her plan of battle; on the other hand she was incapable of masking her triumph as concern. There had been a catastrophic turn in the tax business, she trumpeted in Bettina's ear, more or less; we should all consult together; Bettina too should be in on the consultations; and of course the lawyers on both sides; delay was tantamount to suicide. Trying hard to remain restrained, Bettina asked what this was all about. Then – I could imagine her wide staring eyes – it bubbled out of Ganna: the divorce was invalid, my marriage to Bettina was unlawful, one of her sharpest lawyers, an eminent man as well, had broken the awful news to her; we all should quickly get round a table; three decent people; if three decent people sat around a table together to avert a disaster, there could be no doubting a satisfactory outcome; the first step would be to discharge the tax debt; other questions could be settled civilly and constructively. Bettina, dazed by the cascade of words, said: 'Is that it, Ganna? Thank you, I'll tell Alexander.' And, half-irritated, half-amused, she repeated to me all that Ganna had dinned into her. I shrugged. I had no idea of the consequences it would have.

## Thirty or forty lawyers

When her kindly peace call remained without echo, she poured her moral indignation into a letter. 'I am beside myself,' she wrote. I could hear the hollow voice and the accusatory emphasis on the two last words, with a stage pause left between them. What, they don't respond, the fools, she said to herself disbelievingly, they knock back the hand of friendship? Has anyone ever known the like, to run to their own destruction?

She won't allow herself to be accused of not having done what was humanly possible to avert the catastrophe from Bettina and me. In this spirit she writes a second letter to me, one of her masterly, Tartuffian, technical-ethical epistles. I don't reply, even though the bearer is standing by waiting. She instructs Dr Storch to clarify me as to the legal position. I throw his letter in the wastepaper basket. Immediately afterwards she has a falling-out with the ex-cherub, for reasons I can't divulge, and forms a new compact with one Dr Kranich, who also assails me with a lengthy screed, in which the tax matter and the divorce are cannily entwined. Dr Kranich is a onetime Socialist, as she has me informed by one of her agents, and she hopes his – albeit no longer current – political views will commend him to me. I don't reply.

She goes to the sanatorium. She is not admitted. She yells at the porter, she insults the nurse, she complains to the director. Still she is not admitted. Now she really thinks she has done everything to save me from disaster. A seventh lawyer, Dr Schwalbe (no one can tell me why yet another one), communicates to Hornschuch about the impending test of the validity of the divorce. Hornschuch's apparent sangfroid excites Ganna's fury. She senses some peril must lie behind it, the man is an obstacle, she needs to get him out of the way first. She composes a twenty-three-page foolscap screed against him and has it delivered to the Bar association. She accuses him of dereliction of duty and of acting without instruction; to force her to agree to the divorce, he had without my orders and without my knowledge determined that her allowance be stopped. Blackmail again, hallo, hallo, is anyone home? Blackmail, are you there? No, I'm here. Hornschuch is compelled to take her to court for defamation. I am asked to appear as a witness, and of course I can't avoid saying the accusations were frivolous and baseless. My appearance impresses the judge; I get a little carried away with myself; I paint a picture of the unending persecution I suffer at the hands of the woman; basically I make myself into a sort of knight of the sorrowful countenance. Ganna is sentenced to a hefty fine, that's it. Since she doesn't have a penny that doesn't come from me, that doesn't come from my work, it means that I now have a fine to pay as well. Once sentence has been passed, Ganna comes up to me, pulls a pear out of her handbag and whispers dramatically: 'An Alexander pear . . . your favourite . . . ' What was it the last time? 'I'm giving you a divorce for your birthday . . . ' Always the same breathy pathos in the intervals of delusion.

In her grim compulsion to unmask and destroy the 'plot' between Hornschuch and Bettina, Ganna instructs an eighth lawyer, Dr Fischlein, to bring charges against Bettina, who, in company and before witnesses, had apparently accused her, Ganna, of being a liar. Another farrago of nonsense, product of hateful dreams; Bettina would never even say Ganna's name in public. But Ganna doesn't let facts get in her way, this is wash day, the lawyers are so many washerwomen, everything goes. The unreasonable couple (Bettina and I) won't be persuaded that all is lost, she says to herself; very well, they have only themselves to blame, my conscience is clear; and finally, with the assistance of a ninth lawyer, Dr Pelikan, she ignites the principal bomb: the legal questioning of the divorce, simultaneously challenging the legality of my marriage to Bettina. Hornschuch counters with a demand that she 'show cause', which goes as far as the administrative court and plunges Ganna into deep disquiet, because everything she has undertaken against Bettina and me strikes her as lawful, and pleasing unto the eyes of God and man – whereas everything that is undertaken against her is a criminal violation, as she tells the world with her shrill cry. There is nothing for it; I have to go to Vienna to make preparations and pick up a legal opinion from a legal eagle that both divorce and remarriage were perfectly lawful. It costs time, it costs money, it costs nerves, it costs concentration. It does me in. I can no longer speak about anything else. Running into friends in town, I talk to them blurtingly and incomprehensibly about horrible things I am drowning in. I sit at a table in my hotel room for hours, laying patiences.

But then, for some reason, Ganna suddenly breaks off her vengeance, offers to withdraw her suit in return for some 'conditions', apologizes for her pitiful desperation. There's no more to it than that; it's a fit of weakness, the pyromaniac's momentary hesitation before tossing the lit match on the dry straw. The Count von Gleichen idyll appears in a new version; she offers to share me with Bettina. (How's that going to work – it would be like two cats sharing a mouse.) Ganna is to be the lawful wedded wife in Vienna, Bettina is to have the same role in Ebenweiler; their spheres of influence can be kept nicely separate. When this great-souled proposition is again met with baffled silence, she turns to a minister who has been presented to her as an enlightened and philanthropical sort, and asks him to effect a conciliation between us. God only knows what she said to him; the man of God writes me an extraordinarily pompous letter. I think to myself it would be wrong to ignore the words of a priest; but instead of keeping to ten lines (see Stanger-Goldenthal), I fill seven pages with a description of Ganna's character and my predicament.

Shaking off her fit of weakness or her crisis of confidence or whatever it was, Ganna swings into action with renewed vim. Who is the enemy most to be dreaded? Why, Hornschuch. So she tackles him first. She bombards him with suggestions to try and tempt him to deal with her. She treats him like a wildcat you throw a hunk of meat to from time to time, so that he doesn't bite you. She hates him with every fibre of her being, but the category 'lawyer' – in any guise – fills her with such superstitious awe that she loses her head and does the most irrational things. She conducts expensive long-distance phone calls with him. In the midst of her usual dealings and agenda, it suddenly occurs to her to travel to Ebendorf, where Hornschuch is now living, the seat of the district court, four miles from Ebenweiler. An amusing little jaunt. To spend six hours on the train, by night if need be, is a breeze to her. The woman has nerves like bellropes. The final justification of the journey is threefold. First, she wants to inveigle Hornschuch into her toils and get the better of him; she flatters herself that she will be able to persuade him of the justice of her cause. Second, the proximity of the district court is like a sort of aphrodisiac to her; of course she's already taken on a local lawyer, the eleventh or twelfth, a political enemy of Hornschuch's, through whom she hopes to bring down her detested foe. Third, she's made some useful acquaintances in the bar of the hotel where she's staying – all sorts of local politicians and small-town dignitaries whom she flatters, stressing her conservative views and involving herself in Party business. On cosy beer evenings she tells anyone who cares to listen – and of course, they're all dying of curiosity – tear-jerking tales from her tortured marriage, or of how a certain lady up in Ebenweiler has it in for her and is making her life a misery.

Between Christmas and New Year she tried another ambush on Hornschuch. She implored him to induce me to pay the allowance for Doris that I hadn't paid her – Ganna – for months now. The fact that I paid out every penny of the money on Doris discretion keeps her from mentioning. When Hornschuch reminded her of the fact, she replied with irrational fury that she was the mother and, if the money were not paid to her, she would see it as not having been paid.

'I understand,' Hornschuch replied with the smile that Ganna liked to call Mephistophelean, 'your daughter is a sort of walking promissory note that you can present to the father when you're short. Good idea!'

'No!' screamed Ganna, white with fury. 'What I won't have is Bettina deciding how much support my child gets from her father. It's disgraceful.'

'No one's talking about Bettina here,' remarked Hornschuch coolly.

She went on chuntering away to herself, then all at once she was as soft as a sponge that you throw in water, began sobbing and painted such a heart-wrenching picture of her situation that, as he admitted to me, he was speechless for a while. He said perhaps an accommodation could be reached between her and her creditors; to that end, she would have to admit her debts openly, the full extent of them, and above all she needed to get rid of her lawyers. That got him a good reception. She went wild. Conditions? No, Sir, she wasn't that desperate, nor for a good time yet. See off her lawyers? That was the last thing she would do. And leave herself open to Bettina's persecution? No, thank you very much. That was one thing she wasn't going to do. There had been an attempt to have her declared non compos mentis, but thank goodness that had failed. (She gave a cackling laugh and sent Hornschuch a penetrating look like a detective on the point of catching a murderer out.) How failed? asked Hornschuch sympathetically. Yes, she had looked up a famous psychiatrist, who at the end of a twenty-minute conversation had issued her with a splendid certificate of mental health; if Hornschuch cared to see it: voilà! And already she was rummaging through her bag for the piece of paper, which obviously filled her with glee, as a little sub-magician might be at the sight of a licence to practise issued by the great chief magician.

Since the meeting with Hornschuch had failed, she hired a sleigh and half an hour later reached the Buchegger estate. Our maid knew who she was and didn't admit her. We were just having tea, Bettina and I, with Doris, who was there for the Christmas holidays. We could hear Ganna ranting and shouting outside. Bettina drummed her fingers on the tablecloth and said: 'Don't go out. Please don't go out.' But I went out. I had to see the woman off. I shouted at her. What did she think she was doing? What she was doing? She had come for money. She was groaning, howling, gurgling for money. Interspersed with that, a few insults and reproaches. The sleigh stood a few yards off; the coachman on his box was continually shaking his head, which made an oddly profound impression on me. In the hall, the servants stood around in a state of shock. Infected by Ganna's yelling, I started yelling back. No one in the house had ever heard me yell before. There is only one person in the world capable of making me yell and that is Ganna. I no longer remember how I induced her finally to get back in the sleigh. I stood at the top of the stairs and waited till the horse caparisoned with bells and its head-shaking coachman had disappeared into the darkness. Back in the house, I called Bettina. She had locked herself away in her room. Doris stood in front of the tea table, looking at me with round, frightened, sympathetic eyes. I went to my room and threw myself on my bed.

But all this was mere skirmishing for Ganna. A little later, she had worked out that I owed her 25,000 schillings. I don't know where this nice round figure came from. It could as well have been half a million. Doctors' bills, tailors' bills, 'backlogs' from other years, '*imprévus*' by the dozen, expenses on the children, a column of figures like a lottery draw. It's my belief that merely writing down numbers gave her as much satisfaction as actual money. The local district court rejected the case for want of evidence, even though two diligent new lawyers threw themselves into the fray for her. Without stopping to think for a moment about the irrecoverableness of the debt and the frivolousness of her suit, Ganna told herself: if I can't obtain justice in this country, then perhaps there where, according to my passport and as Alexander Herzog's wife, I belong. She made for Berlin, found some willing lawyers – three of them – and presented her claim in a splendidly stylish brief. But lo and behold, the 25,000 were become 39,000, a leap explained by the addition of her tax debt. I saw with satisfaction that her charming number-drunkenness didn't get in the way of a certain residual accuracy in Ganna. At the same time, in Berlin, where she set up a sort of *dépendance*, and where m'learned friends were charmed down from the trees, she attached her suit to the attack on the divorce. She was, it seemed, in the right place. The uncertainty between the two countries in point of matrimonial law made this entertaining legal adventure possible; it was one of the many breaches where canny lawyers like to wedge their crowbars.

But she also enjoyed social success in the German metropolis. She got to meet people to whom she could sing her song of woe. Since none of them were acquainted with the facts, she found credit and sympathy at every turn. Doling out copies of her *Psyche Bleeds* to all and sundry, she confirmed her role as an ideal wife, who had been sent to the brink of starvation by a cruel husband and his chit. She assiduously visited writers' cafés, where she could advertise her noble unhappiness. 'Even the moneylenders start to cry when I tell them of my predicament,' she once said, to the understanding murmurs of a bookish set at table. It may even have been true. It's not out of the question that the soul of the contemporary usurer has opposed the trend of petrifaction to which all other souls have been subject, and has humanized itself since the days of Balzac and Dickens. The result of her sentimental journey to the Prussian Olympus, at any rate, was that I received many anonymous letters full of insults and insolent instructions to me to better myself. Plus of course lawyers' letters, too many to count. They struck me as scouting patrols before the battle, these resolute gentlemen marching out to meet me with fists clenched. One wrote to say simply that if I didn't pay up 39,000 schillings by a certain date, he would have my royalties confiscated at the publisher's. I threw the letter away, with two or three hundred others of the same type and import. I had to laugh. My lifestyle and the pyrrhic divorce had set me back so much with my publisher that the tiny hands would find nothing left to confiscate. (What a great word, 'confiscate'; especially made for the little hands.) But Ganna told her people that by some financial manipulation I had contrived to smuggle money abroad, and hence fabricated my debt to my publisher. A story that made it possible to drag him into court as well. On top of everything else, she was now bandying the bigamy charge about. A few friends who got to hear of it wrote to beg me not to let it come to that. But what else could I do? Whimper for mercy? Run to court and say: protect me from the lawyers, otherwise they'll eat me alive, arrest that she-devil, otherwise I'll be done for? Nonsense. The courts would have arrested me first.

One day I remarked to Hornschuch: 'Can you explain it to me – excuse the naive question – but all these lawyers, they're thoughtful, experienced, no doubt honest men; don't they understand what's going on and how they're being misused?' Hornschuch listened. He raised his eyebrows and looked at me with a sardonic smile on his lips. His way of not giving an answer was uncommonly eloquent.

At that time there were a mere sixteen or seventeen lawyers whom Ganna had retained, some of whom she had already paid off, or hadn't paid off and was afraid to dismiss. Today, the number is closer to forty; it's not possible to be exact since I've mislaid some of the names in the welter of paper. These people surely had to realize that the support they were giving the woman only served to exacerbate her addiction, not to quench it. What was it that drove them to give their brains, their knowledge, their time to a person who, with morbid determination, sought to twist the rigid paragraphs of the law to suit herself? Presumably they said to themselves: we'll take in the winnings once the other side can no longer speak and will pay any money to be left in peace. That characterized the jurisdictional uncertainty, the ambiguity of the laws, the deadly rigidity of the process, the remoteness of the ivory-tower judiciary, the *via dolorosa* of appeals – and on top of everything, helpless and tyrannical, the State, a Chronos devouring his own children.

It accomplished nothing and explained nothing when I or others attempted to come up with a clinical category for Ganna's case. An army of three and a half dozen lawyers is a one-off. The idea of a mysterious dependency suggested itself to me ever more strongly. It couldn't but be that, in the atmosphere of confidential talk, expectation, advice, attack, subterfuge, statement and counter-statement, Ganna found a source of erotic satisfaction, a replacement for intimacy with another being; replacement also for the pleasure of tormenting another being, and no less pleasurable if one thinks one is the undeserving sufferer. The time spent in lawyers' offices, the smell of ink, dust and blotting-paper unquestionably had an aphrodisiac effect on her. With each new lawyer she entered a sort of new marriage, a marriage of torment. When she talked to one of them – in court, in his office, in her house – a strange, saccharine flirtatiousness came out in her, a slavish gratitude that admittedly could at any moment curdle into bickering and quasi-marital dispute. It had become her habit to call her current lawyer first thing every day, to ask perfectly ridiculous questions, to make quite useless dispositions, as if she wanted only to hear his voice, as though to check that he hadn't been unfaithful to her overnight. The telephone was another source of pleasure. Telephone and telegraph were magical gadgets with which, short of essence and existence as she was, she forced an entry into the time and consciousness of people attached to her, borrowed time and consciousness from them, in order to exist a little herself. How deeply into chaos and old night one is taken when one follows such a soul's vagaries into its depths!

## Conversations in another world

One day, Bettina and I had to go to Munich to discuss the legal challenge to our marriage with a lawyer there. Helmut was sitting with us at the breakfast table as we were about to go. He was complaining forthrightly.

'Why are you going away again?'

I explained that it was necessary.

'But why do you both have to go, why not just Papa?' he persisted.

Bettina stroked his hair and said I wanted her to go with me.

He thought for a long time, then a roguish expression came into his blue eyes and he said to her:

'I think I know why.'

'Why's that then, darling?' I asked him.

To which he, full of pride: 'It's like with the animals.'

Bettina and I looked at each other in surprise.

'What do you mean, Helmut?'

And he, the twinkle still in his eyes: 'Safety.'

He was lost in thought for a while, and then:

'Isn't that right, Mama, the three of us are a proper family, you and Papa and me, we all belong together?'

'Yes, little Helmut, of course we do.'

'Was I there when you got to know each other?'

'No, darling.'

'Was God there, then?'

'Oh, yes, He was.'

'Did He laugh, then?'

'Why do you think He would have laughed?'

'Because He was looking forward to me, maybe?'

At that point the cat, which had been stalking around the table with tail up, jumped into his lap. He looked at it tenderly and asked, to indicate his human superiority, with a cooing voice:

'Have you got eyes? Have you really got eyes?'

'He makes it impossible to say goodbye,' Bettina said to me afterwards.

## Two women

Even before the eventful January day I am coming to, I had had the feeling there was something going on with Bettina. But I didn't have the courage to ask her. For some time now we had been living in a strange silence, side by side, almost like two convicts who have been cellmates for too long. What was alarming was that this was so unlike Bettina. On the day in question, Hornschuch had already rung in at nine to say that Ganna was back in Ebenweiler. She had hurried down from Berlin to attend a hearing at the district court. What was at issue was the suspended money for Doris, also the monthly allowance for the girl for the summer, during which time she had been staying with me in my house. By the letter of the deed I was in the wrong; in my own lay opinion I was being required to pay twice over, along the lines of the kraal's principle of 'revocability' – and 'revocability' in my present circumstances was more than I could afford.

In pursuance of her claim, Ganna had obtained a temporary injunction with the court, freezing my bank account in the little local branch in Ebendorf. It didn't much matter, I didn't have any great sums there, I had sufficient cash for the time being; I would just have to see about getting the next advance. Still, it was disagreeable; and it gave ill-disposed people more ammunition for their gossip, and sooner or later we would need to refinance the household anyway.

At nine o'clock Hornschuch had put us in the picture. Thereafter, it was blow upon blow, like the fifth act of a melodrama. At nine twenty, the court usher turns up with a summons. At nine forty-five, Ganna's Ebendorf lawyer invites Bettina and me by telephone to an 'amicable' discussion. At ten past ten a telegram from a Berlin lawyer with a demand to attend an all-day hearing on the such-and-such. At half past ten, a wild telephone call from Ganna: if we turned down the 'amicable' meeting, then all bets were off and nothing could avert the approaching calamity. I'd heard that sort of bombast before. Three minutes past eleven: express letter from a lawyer in Vienna, to the effect that Ganna Herzog had made over her allowance for the months of February and March to him. Eleven fifteen: a messenger with a note from Ganna repeating her phoned ultimatum, but in a form and using expressions that cause Bettina, now suddenly up on the brazen intricacies of the Ganna method, to shudder. The letter was addressed to her; she was the first to read it. She understands, full of repugnance, the knife-jabbing either-or in Ganna's letter, but the claws have never come so close to her as now. She wants clarity, and calls Hornschuch. This is no harmless chit-chat, he tells her; Ganna is talking openly down in the village, wherever she meets her saloon bar friends, not only about the bigamous relationship in which I am allegedly living, but also about the 'wangled' leave to marry Bettina. What she meant by that was the expedited permission to remarry which I obtained from the consulate – an utterly lawful procedure, but which to Ganna's criminally fouled brain lets it appear as though Bettina and I had obtained permission by false information and forged papers; a wonderful opportunity to squeeze off a *coup de grâce* in our direction. Bettina, who that morning is not feeling her best and brightest, is scared by the possible consequences: the malicious tittle-tattle, the confrontation with envy, jealousy and the burning embers of hatred. Hornschuch tries to ease her mind. She reads out one or two particularly informative sentences from Ganna's squib. When she hears his reply: 'Excellent: people will draw their conclusions from that,' she all but slams down the receiver. 'No,' she cries disbelievingly into the mouthpiece. 'They won't draw the right conclusions at all. You forget that the woman's name is Herzog.' Pause. Thereupon Hornschuch again, drawling: 'All right, then. Whatever you say.'

When I walk into the blue salon she's lying on the sofa, swathed in blankets, looking pale and chilly. On foggy days she's only a shadow of herself, and this day would be black as pitch, even if it were cloudless. I look mutely down at her; suddenly she says:

'I've decided to speak to Ganna.'

I look at her as if she were mad. Suddenly she pulls herself up into a sitting position.

'I'm going to ask her up, and I'm going to talk to her,' she repeats in a high treble which reminds me of Helmut's little squeaky voice, and which is always a sign with her that she's nearing the end of her tether.

'Why? What would be the use,' I begin.

'I've made a mistake,' the high voice jingles back. 'I can't absolve myself . . . I thought I didn't need to notice her . . . I was lazy, I was bad . . . It must be possible to get her attention with some human utterance . . . from woman to woman maybe . . .'

I stare at her in dismal surprise. 'Do you really think that will work? You know how I kept . . . over all those years . . .'

She interrupts me. 'At least I have to give it a try. I must be able to tell myself I tried.'

She jots down a couple of lines, and sends the gardener with a note to the inn in Ebendorf where Ganna is staying. A pleasurable shudder goes through Ganna when she reads the invitation to come up to the Buchegger estate. At last! Have the fools come to their senses? Have they seen the error of their ways? Or are they just running scared? She plunges to the telephone to talk to Bettina. She is so terribly excited, it's hard to understand what she's saying. She would love to have a conversation, she tootles, but not in the house, oh no, not that, but in some neutral place, to her heart's content, and of course with her lawyer present. No lawyers, says Bettina with crisp decisiveness, absolutely not; if Ganna has inhibitions about coming to the house, she will meet her on the road and walk with her. Ganna gives in. They agree a time. An hour later – by now it's a quarter to one

– when Bettina sees Ganna on the snow-covered village road, in violation of the agreement, in the company of her lawyer, she stops dead. Her posture expresses such rigid unapproachability that the gentleman decides to bow and turn back. Not without a tasteless remark. Since he's among the dozen or so lawyers working on Ganna's legal challenge, he thinks, hat in hand, he owes her a word of apology:

'I hope, dear Madam, you don't assume I am working against the happiness of your marriage.'

To which Bettina replies – addressing her words to thin air:

'I'd kindly ask you to leave the happiness of my marriage out of it.'

And with a gesture invites Ganna to proceed.

Robbed of her legal adviser and hence of her poise, Ganna is suddenly rather *piano*. Silently she shuffles along beside the striding Bettina. She is wearing a black, crumpled cloche hat and a mottled fur. In her hand she carries the capacious leather bag which goes everywhere with her. It contains all the files and documents she might require, much as a travelling salesman has his samples and price list. Whenever she runs into an acquaintance of any degree, she fills them in with tumbling garrulousness as to the state of her case, pulls out the deed, her bundled writs, the various legal opinions, the official documents relating to the Buchegger estate, comforting letters from her supporters, and waxes so prolix that she no longer remembers where she is, where she's coming from, where she's going, or whom she's talking to.

Bettina, chatting – although chatting is really the last thing she feels like – glances at her from time to time. It's thirteen years since she's last seen Ganna; since that teatime meeting of disagreeable memory. Think of everything that happened in between! A whole lifetime. Beautiful things, noble things, pure things, indescribable joys, little Caspar Hauser, who would have imagined it – but also bad things, wretchedness, bitterness and an irreparable loss. Whether the woman walking beside her can guess any of it? Surely not: she doesn't sense things, she grabs; people like that are purblind. She even walks like a blind person. How wretched she looks. If only it were possible to help her. It can't feel good to be in her shoes. Someone like that is quite unapproachable, rigidly stuck inside themselves . . .

As she shows Ganna in, helps her out of her coat, conducts her to the living room and offers her a small snack, which Ganna gobbles down with grateful little exclamations, she keeps looking at her. With the crest of orange-dyed hair under which grey strands peek out as from under a wig, she looks like a peculiar idol. You would hardly notice she's over fifty. Her form is compact, but a little thickened, her facial expressions and movements vibrate with an eerie force of will. The intensity of her regard is almost frightening. It shows an illimitable desire to dominate.

Eventually, Bettina and Ganna start talking. Suddenly Bettina takes Ganna's hand – her tiny, freckled, ancient hand, really, just exactly as she'd wanted to take it so many years ago – she takes it and she says:

'Woman! Woman! What are you doing! You're destroying everything around you! Take pity on yourself, why don't you!'

At that Ganna looks at her in shock, her mouth quivers, her eyelids tremble, she cries. She nods – a sort of pagoda – to herself and she cries, cries, cries.

'I have to,' she stammers, 'what else can I do?'

What else can she do! And again Bettina thinks: poor, poor soul, what is she that we are so frightened of her? Suddenly she has so much courage and confidence, she feels she can get anything she wants from Ganna. She chooses her words terribly carefully, so as not to hurt her. She is tender, considerate, sisterly, even though inside she is continually fighting down feelings of nausea and dread; but I mustn't give in to that, she tells herself, everything is at stake here. Also, she tells herself the woman must have something; there must be something to her to explain how the man lived with her for nineteen years. This something is what she wants to locate and dig up and touch and address herself to: there it is, woman, the thing you owe him: decency, dignity, reasonableness, gratitude – yes, a little gratitude, there it is, hold onto it, can you feel it? And with a mixture of childishness and superiority she proceeds to court Ganna – as an older, experienced friend might. But Ganna turns suspicious right away and, when Bettina talks about giving in, she arches her back with the customary retort: 'Why should I have to give in? I've been giving in all my life.' And when Bettina talks about my worries, which are hanging over her and me like heavy clouds, Ganna takes it as a bad joke and replies with her cunning I-know-better smile that she had certain information that I was hoarding a large fortune in foreign banks. Bettina claps her hands at this; she has to laugh, she can't help it, and that gives Ganna pause, and she stammers; something undefined in the regard and expression of the younger woman strikes her as being true – albeit in a dim and washed-out way, and almost fading back into oblivion again, because how can she live with such an inconvenient truth. It's impossible, she thinks, with a puzzling pout, as if she'd been offended by the contact with truth; perhaps his life is no bed of roses, and she murmurs a couple of mildly sympathetic words. But when Bettina reproaches her for the indignity of mounting a legal challenge to my divorce and our marriage, and says that she is doing herself irreparable damage in the eyes of all decent people, then she gets angry: 'Now I must draw the line there, Bettina, you're quite mistaken about that,' and she rattles off the names of a score of friends who are standing by her, and would be with her through thick and thin. Bettina cuts her off; suddenly she's the stern judge, slender and upright, stressing moral order, natural trust, without which the whole world would fall apart. At that Ganna is alarmed; she sobs pitifully and says she could do nothing else, people were so mean to her, every single day began and ended in despair, no one had as much goodwill as she did, or loved goodness and nobility as she did, she yearned so deeply for a little happiness and a little respect; what was she to do? What did Bettina want? Drop it, says Bettina, stop fighting! And she takes the sobbing woman in her arms, however difficult it is for her, feels her wiry hair, the utterly alien skin, the painfully other smell, the smell of unaired clothes that have lain around in suitcases, the smell of cheap powder and cheap scent, of trains and dirty hotel rooms; she takes her in her arms and talks to her sweetly: 'But you just keep making things worse for yourself. Everything you try to prevent keeps happening. It crumbles away in your hands and when you reach for it it turns against you, don't you know that?' Ganna, dissolved in tears, says through her teeth, yes, she thinks so too, she can see what mistakes she has made. She says it audibly and aloud; it's the first time in her conscious life that she's admitted to having made mistakes. Bettina pricks up her ears; she appreciates the gravity of what is happening, she thinks something true has happened, she won't let her go, she spends fully seven hours closeted with her, from one o'clock till eight at night, and they come to a sort of agreement, which is immediately put into writing and signed by them both. Ganna will be paid a part of the sums she is suing for and where the figures have not simply been plucked out of thin air, in instalments (Bettina itemizes the sums in question); the payments for Doris will go to her as previously; I will reach out my conciliatory hand to her, and we will support her in any way possible and cease to cut her. In return, Ganna promises to withdraw all pending claims, to lift the block on my account and other legal distraints, and expedite the divorce in a German court.

After this pact has been concluded, Bettina calls me into the room. Ganna walks towards me, her arms outstretched, wailing: 'Alexander, you look awful, what's the matter with you!' I ignore it, but catch my reflection in the mirror in passing. 'We've been busy,' says Bettina, and points to the piece of paper with the two signatures on her desk. I look at Bettina, look at Ganna, say nothing. Then Ganna comes out with a plea. She would like some money. She admits glumly that she can't even pay her bill at the hotel. Bettina shakes her head. 'First you must do what you promised, Ganna,' she says, motioning with her chin at the piece of paper on the desk. Meanwhile, not attending to her piercing admonitory look, I had pulled out my wallet and passed Ganna three notes, a full third of the sum she should only have been paid after fulfilling the points on the agreement. Bettina turned away with a despondent look. She understood the idiotic mistake right away. I might have known: if Ganna has money in her hands, she'll forget the agreement, signature, promise, oath, the lot. Bettina understood my gesture – what was there about me that she didn't understand – thus: begone, begone, begone; money, begone, woman, begone; but, she wondered, is it possible to be so thoughtless, so unthinking, so destructive with regard to the nervous resources and humanitarian work of another?

I walk Ganna to the door. She stops on the doorstep and looks at me with big eyes full of reproach and complaint. I bow, take her hand and press it to my lips. Bettina is barely able to disguise her astonishment. What is he doing now, she thinks, why is he kissing her hand? Well, this is too much for her to understand. Again, it's a case of 'begone, begone, begone'. It's a farcical gesture of respect, by which Ganna becomes a stranger to me, a stranger in this house, a stranger in my world. An instinctive act in the form of an empty ceremony that means nothing but the last inner break with Ganna.

## The devil rides over the ruins

The upshot of this turbulent happening was – nothing at all. My account was not unblocked and the distraints not taken off. There was no mention of the German divorce. But surely you don't think Ganna was responsible for the breach of promise? Please. She washed her hands so assiduously in innocence that the bubbles got everywhere. Did she not give her lawyer in Ebendorf 'appropriate instructions'? Did he not overweeningly, for 'certain jurisprudential technicalities', refuse to carry out her instructions? Are you sure that Hornschuch didn't offer 'passive resistance' for obscure motives of his own? Hornschuch? What did he do? We're not told. The mere claim is sufficient. Then, in a pedantic memorandum to Bettina: 'Everyone knows that I am entirely scrupulous in all my dealings. I indignantly reject the claim that I didn't stick to the terms of our agreement; there can be no doubt that in this, as in every previous instance, it was the other party that is in violation.' Thus Ganna. And finally, the latest sanction, a veritable somersault of condescension: she can only make up her mind about granting the German divorce at the end of a trial year, once she has been convinced that my offer of peace and friendship is in good faith. The badger slips out of its sett, leaves its little malodorous pile and grins to itself when the dogs bark.

Bettina, though, felt like someone who with mortal daring and the last of her strength has carried a person out of a burning house, only to be spat at by them afterwards. She was unable to get over it. She suffered a strangely Bettina-esque collapse, very quiet, very discreet, but every bit as bad as a serious illness.

In sum: fourteen court orders, twenty-two payment orders, eleven forced sales, three official valuations of the Buchegger estate, four suits for defamation, two suits before the wardship authorities, five temporary injunctions, distraint of my car, forced sale of my desk, fifty-seven lawyers' letters in the space of six weeks, the blocking of my account with my publisher since I am unable to pay Ganna's monthly allowance any more and my earnings have dwindled to next to nothing; Ganna goes to court against my publisher; Ganna in Berlin, Ganna in Munich, Ganna in the district capital, Ganna in Ebendorf, always unexpected wherever she goes, as though she travelled everywhere by aeroplane; always with sword drawn, always gurgling in the fists of usurers; offers of conciliation, financial plans; yelling I had better make it up to her, or else . . .

Not one stone was left standing on another.

Ganna's legal bills alone amount to a fortune. When I think that these monstrous amounts are there to pay for her mercenaries in her war against me, that the money I scrape together month after month literally by the sweat of my brow all goes to the avenging fury to keep her army of lawyers together, then the whole world has turned into a grisly farce, a dance of death starring forty law offices and their entire staffs of typists and stenographers, legal drafters and researchers. When I turn to Ferry and ask him to try and make his mother see sense before it's too late, he drives up from Milan where he works as an engineer in an automobile factory and implores her by all that's holy to desist from her lunacy. She goes wild. She accuses him, her own son, of being in Bettina's employ. When news of it reaches my ears, it makes me feel as though the devil is shaking my living soul out of my body.

But a wonderful thing has also happened since then. From a certain vantage point, it was a big experience for me. It began with Bettina saying to me one day: 'You know, you're not up to this. It's killing you. Take a look at yourself. From now on, I'm going to take the whole matter in hand myself.' Such resolutions, with her, were the outcome of lengthy and mature reflection. They were always followed up. Once she had taken a decision, she saw it through with implacable consequence. Her force of will has something shining and compelling about it. A busy nature through and through; only facts command her respect; at bottom her spirit doesn't like dreamers; and I have often noted to my surprise that, while seeming to dream, she was actually thinking – and not in any loose sense of the word, but with philosophical stringency and in strict chains of logic. Suddenly the feeling had come over her that, in spite of her better self, she had led a pampered princess's life for years of balmy ease, a life on the sidelines; she flushed red with shame. From one moment to the next she changed. That was her gift; that was the miraculous thing about her before which I stood awestruck and uncomprehending. To anyone who lives entirely in contemplation, transformation in action is a mystery. From one moment to the next she dropped everything as if it had never existed – her music, her violin, her books, her correspondence with friends, her pretty things – everything that made life tolerable in the wild uplands, as she had called it in brief fits of irritation. Yes, even little Caspar Hauser was forced to get by on his own; and without holding anything back, without allowing herself any pleasures or distractions, she gave herself over to this one thing. She went to work radically. She studied the contracts, the documents, the relevant laws and ordinances. She sat closeted with Hornschuch for hours, whole days at a time. She replied to the writs and the lawyers' letters, dealt with the courts, with the tax authorities, oversaw the finances and reformed our whole household, as to whose sloppiness her eyes had finally been opened, with the strictness of a paid cost-cutter.

Day and night she was on duty, to protect me from ambushes and sudden attacks. Every attack from Ganna she warded off with an adroitness and care as though she had been in jurisprudence for decades. Her clear intellect, her intuitive understanding of real life always showed her the one and only way that could be followed. There was no danger she was afraid of, she shunned no strain, she didn't try to keep her time, her sleep, her health; the moral courage that filled her to the fingertips seemed to give her an almost masculine appetite for struggle. She went to Vienna to deal with persons of influence whose support might be important; she went to Berlin to take on a lawyer and to put my publisher in the picture as to what really was going on; and however speedily and instantaneously she made up her mind, still she never neglected to tell me what she was doing and to obtain my consent, so that the Ganna corner – suddenly alarmed – weren't able to claim that she was running my affairs by herself, without my knowledge and approval. She weighed up everything in her mind, she caught the tiniest advantage; with nervous vigilance she did everything to take the wind out of the enemy's sails. The whole woman was fight and flame. It was a spectacle the like of which I had never seen nor hoped to see.

And yet it had a frightening, even an alarming aspect too. Bettina was tied to me in a different way from the Ganna world. In the spirit of the anti-Ganna, I could say. She was the absolutely sane human being. The person destiny gave me so that I could share in truth and reality, instead of perishing in lies and illusion. That was the purpose of everything we'd gone through, if an existence like mine could ever be crowned by anything like a purpose. And now – was it a trick of fate, was it a higher testing, whose outcome still hung in the balance – now the anti-Ganna was being drawn into Ganna's orbit, was being asked – against her inner nature – to fight with Ganna's weapons, to confront her, to shadow her in her darknesses and thickets. Could that all be to the good? Was it good of itself? 'My Diana, tenderly rapt,' I had once written about Bettina; but would I not end up becoming the murderer of my tender goddess? True, Diana is the huntress, but her hunting-ground is not populated by phantoms, she doesn't hunt nightmares, she doesn't suffer her course to be set by Ganna ghosts – if she did, she would herself become the quarry.

And then, as if events were only waiting to confirm these endlessly frightened thoughts, I started to see Bettina's slow physical collapse. She became sensitive, irritable, prone to sudden fevers; she lost weight; sometimes she gave the impression some unknown toxin had been administered to her. Her mainspring was broken. In my service. Through my fault. In a certain sense, through my fault. So Ganna was the stronger after all. The nightmare had bewitched my Diana on her campaign and made her lame. From the dreadful moment I first saw it, just three weeks ago now, I had only one concern, which was how to lead Bettina back out of the poisoned land. But when I talked to her about it, she laughed at me. The courage that inspirited her was like a glass bell, melodious, uncontaminated, ringing pure.

Yesterday, 26 June, I received for the fourth time a summons to give the oath of disclosure which Ganna was trying to extort from me. I content myself with recording what happened. It was all to do with the alleged hidden fortune I am supposed to have tucked away somewhere. On previous occasions, I had objected to swearing such an oath. Once, taking Bettina's advice, I had gone away; another time I brought a doctor's letter. I have never sworn an oath in my life. It struck me as monstrous, a violation of honour, of sense, of all human feeling, that I was to use the name of God to assure Ganna that I did not own the treasures that she, in really the most literal way, wanted to squeeze out of me. I admit I was foolish enough to be afraid of it, as of an attempt on my life. Bettina shook her head over me. She said: 'What's the matter, what's so frightful about it? You don't have anything to hide. It's just an empty formality.' I answered that it was much more than a formality; it was an act of duress, in which the spoken word became fact; and by swearing it you gave yourself utterly into the hands of someone like Ganna. She would never drop her suspicion; every single day, every time I spent a banknote, she and her associates would sniff it; she would nail me to the sworn oath every bit as much as to my signature on the marriage contract thirty years before. Bettina said: 'Perhaps you're right. Then the only other possibility is that you go away somewhere. Go away.'

But where was I to go? Back up into the mountains? [. . .] If such a way doesn't lead to death or to an utterly changed life, then it is a farce. After the conversation with Bettina I wandered around the house and garden all afternoon, I was unable to read, to work, to think, I couldn't even properly see. Basically it isn't that endlessly foolish oath that frightens me, it's all the futility, all that endlessly foolish futility that is destroying my life. [. . .]

But in the end it's just words on paper, which can be turned and twisted and perhaps challenged by a higher instance. There remains a residue of division and human frailty. The other day I said to Bettina this whole enterprise feels as though I have a hammer that will not do what I want, which is to drive one nail into another, smashing the head of one, the point of the other.

So what do I need? A hand to help me past an obstacle whose nature I cannot ascertain. A human breath to imbue me with the spirit of understanding. Understanding would surely illumine me like a flash of lightning ripping apart the sheet of darkness. And then the devil riding over the wreckage of my life would disappear with a howl into the gulch of his hell. A slightly overdone image. But then I've lost all sense of measure. [. . .]

# Afterword

*My First Wife* first saw print in Amsterdam in the autumn of
1934, with the firm of Querido. Its blacklisted German Jewish
author, sick for some time with heart and kidney trouble, diabe-
tes and general exhaustion, had managed to complete it and
secure its publication with this newly founded firm of exile publishers – having been at the last turned down by the somewhat
pusillanimous and anxious Bermann Fischer, the son-in-law and
heir to the German Jewish publishing firm of S. Fischer, which
had successfully published twenty-eight of Wassermann's books
in an association lasting thirty-two years (the retired founder,
Samuel Fischer, increasingly deaf and increasingly terrorized,
was himself to die on 15 October of that year) – but did not live
to see it, or to write his intended preface to it, having died punc-
tually on New Year's Day 1934 at the age of an even sixty. The
project he was revolving in his mind at the time of his death –
because his circumstances were such that he had to go from one
book to the next, without the least break, even while contemplating an old age of fear, penury, homelessness, dishonour and
exclusion from the literature of his native language – was, ironically, the story of Ahasuerus, the Wandering Jew.

At that stage, though, *My First Wife* was not yet a book. It was
a book within a much longer book (ostensibly, a little like Italo
Svevo's *La Coscienza di Zeno*, it was 'written' by one character,
the writer Alexander Herzog, at the insistence of another, the
doctor Joseph Kerkhoven), which was in turn the third volume
of a rather wandering and unfocused (and thereby all the more
accommodating) trilogy. There was *Der Fall Maurizius* of 1928

(*The Maurizius Case*), *Etzel Andergast* (confusingly titled *Doctor Kerkhoven* in English) of 1931 and *Joseph Kerkhovens dritte Existenz* (*Joseph Kerkhoven's Third Existence*) of 1934. The last-named is qualified by the German literary historian Peter de Mendelssohn as 'not a complete success; no one would claim that it was'; as for the trilogy, that was nothing but a 'superficial bundling-together' of works that were never 'intended to go together, formally or thematically', and were 'only loosely, even fortuitously, connected by continuities of personnel', and even then 'with the characters taking up completely different functions'. Henry Miller, a great admirer of *The Maurizius Case*, found the author 'baffled' – it's a strange idea – by his own 'sequels'.

It all sounds, in short, like too many other works by Wassermann, who all his life wrote too much, too quickly, too chaotically and abundantly (the tiny handwriting which he liked to claim saved him thousands of miles of script was actually rather a mixed blessing). Rotted brocade, historical melodrama, brilliance of details but paucity of overall design was a diagnosis he got all his life, from friends and critics alike (his long-serving, long-suffering editor, Moritz Heimann, even suggested he take a break from writing novels). In these last years, moreover, for reasons some of which will have become apparent, he was even more a driven man than ever. The saving difference is that, into his very last book, Wassermann smuggled the manuscript of – call it what you will, his novel, account, protocol, confession, masterpiece – *Ganna oder die Wahnwelt*, to give it its original title, 'Ganna, or the Mad World'. If the trilogy had offered some coherence, then surely Bermann Fischer would have shown more interest in keeping the three volumes of it together (even with Nazi blacklists and book-burnings); conversely, if *Joseph Kerkhovens dritte Existenz* had been all about Kerkhoven, Wassermann would hardly have knocked himself out as he did (he suffered a major heart attack after the last of his meetings with

Bermann Fischer in Vienna in November 1933) to get it published. The 2,000-odd pages of the trilogy aren't the point; the
200-odd pages of *My First Wife* are.

What seems overwhelmingly likely to have been the case is
that Wassermann, knowing he was dying and wanting to put
out what was quite obviously the major story of his adult life,
but – for reasons of pride, because he was something of a public
figure, to protect the feelings of some of the survivors, perhaps
not knowing how else to do such a thing – in such a way that it
remained at least deniable, or half-hidden, 'gave' it to the character of Alexander Herzog. He built, if you like, a haystack for
his needle. Because, as anyone reading it then or now can tell
instantly, *Ganna* or (now) *My First Wife* is the true account of
Jakob Wassermann's first marriage to Julie Speyer of Vienna,
with almost nothing omitted or changed. It is, de Mendelssohn
says, 'exactest, most scrupulous autobiography', 'authentic to
the last detail', 'the true confession of the death-marked author,
Jakob Wassermann'. Readers who knew the couple smirked or
shuddered, according to taste. They confirmed (it's easy to
imagine): this is her all right – and him all right. When 'Sami'
Fischer's wife, the meddlesome and generally wrong-headed
Hedwig, read *Joseph Kerkhovens dritte Existenz*, her suggestion to
Wassermann – which speaks both to its self-sufficiency and its
shock value – was that he leave out the *Ganna* section! (Still,
even that response confirms me in doing the opposite: omitting
the trilogy.) But there it is. Wassermann's last baggy novel didn't
mind; his shapeless trilogy had nothing to say. It was not, finally,
so much a framing device as a pair of shutters, or a lid. The pity
of it is how well Wassermann's stratagem worked. Until I blun-
dered upon *Ganna*, and was promptly electrified, I had no idea
such a thing existed; I had never heard of it. (Has anyone ever
written so rivetingly about marriage?) Relative to its quality,
urgency and interest, the 2008 German edition of *Joseph Kerk-*

*hovens dritte Existenz* I worked from has no readers. It has the status of an obscure also-ran among a once-fashionable and successful oeuvre that has almost in its entirety failed to survive. Effectively, what Wassermann did was to keep his best and most anguished work hidden from view for the best part of eighty years. It is time it were seen.

Both the writing and the – however misguided – publishing bespeak a once-in-a-lifetime, if not actually a mortal, exertion. The circumstances of the only book that I think can stand comparison with *My First Wife*, Ted Hughes's *Birthday Letters*, are not dissimilar. Both books come wreathed in fiction: with Hughes it is the claim that these poems were 'birthday letters' written on Sylvia Plath's anniversary over many years; with Wassermann it is the wholly uninteresting, wholly forgettable framing narrative. 'In wartime,' as Churchill said – and both books belong, so to speak, to military history, as well as embracing wars, the First in the case of Wassermann, the Second with Hughes – 'truth must be protected by a bodyguard of lies.' Both books were fought off by their authors for as long as humanly possible. Both books would not have been published without the prospect of imminent death. Both books have an unmistakable and inimitable burn.

In progressive, 'zooming-in' order, it seems to me that *My First Wife* has three distinct claims on our attention. It is, first and widest, a story of a rare intensity and drama. It is, second, a story set at a pivotal juncture in the long struggle between men and women – at the very moment of *sorpasso*, I would say. And, third, it is the story of a man of some eminence and gifts, trying to be unimpassioned and truthful about what he did and what was done to him. Let me go through these three layers, these three distances, in reverse order.

*My First Wife* is almost wholly true. Nothing of significance has been omitted. There was such a family as the Mevises in turn-of-the-century Vienna, descended from a wealthy German industrialist, with six daughters and a dominant professor father; they were the Speyers, and they were indeed known 'all over town'; Julie Speyer was Ganna Mevis. In 1898, the then twenty-five-year-old Wassermann arrived in Vienna from Munich, following the publication of his first novel. He met Julie in circumstances like those related in the book (the agency of the well-meaning Frau von Brandeis), and the relationship developed, with Julie making the running, and Wassermann, as he relates, a mixture of awestruck, obliging, stoic and venal. The interview between Wassermann and his father-in-law passed off just as related. The wedding took place in January 1901. Honeymoon in Italy, pregnancy, return, shuttling around the Viennese suburbs – all as related. For three children, read four children (two boys and two girls – they were born in 1901 and 1903, 1906 and 1915). For meadow, read meadow. Ditto school foundation. For the extraordinary gift of a house on the edge of the city, read the extraordinary gift of a house on the edge of the city – and then, later, another one in the mountains, in Ebenweiler / Altaussee (for the generous Dutch businessman who couldn't settle in the area, read Salomon Deventer). For sister-in-law Irmgard, read sister-in-law Agnes (though there seems little sense in disbelieving that there was an affair. Infidelities on Wassermann's side were numerous, and – *pace* Herzog – not all that discreet).

Herzog's confusion in face of the war was Wassermann's. It was in 1915 that Wassermann first met Marta Karlweiss (Bettina Merck); by 1918 they were living together; in 1919 Wassermann finally asked for a divorce. Ganna writes an article about her husband; Julie a whole book: *Jakob Wassermann und sein Werk* (for his fiftieth birthday – 1923). She collects and publishes his letters; she collects and publishes his letters. The agonizingly slow separation, following a few summers in which Ganna and

Bettina 'shared' Alexander in the country, was real. The season-ally/economically conditioned hopping from place to place in Ebenweiler/Altaussee was real. Wassermann and Marta moved into the newly offered villa in 1923; 'little Caspar Hauser' – his actual name was Carl Ulrich – was born in 1924. Protracted legal manoeuvrings found their – provisional – end in a – for Wasser-mann – staggering, ruinous divorce agreement as late as 1926. Nor was Julie done. In her maniacal possessiveness, she launched wave upon wave of proceedings (even at the time of Wasser-mann's death, there were still cases pending). She wrote a *roman à clef* – *Psyche Bleeds* in the book, in actuality *Das lebendige Herz: Roman einer Ehe* (*The Living Heart: Novel of a Marriage*) – that came out in 1928. The blurb went like this:

With this work of fiction, the hitherto little known Viennese author-ess quietly, nobly and authoritatively takes her place at the side of her former husband, Jakob Wassermann, his equal not least in her valiant endeavour to truthfully plumb the deeply tangled relations between two human beings. *The Living Heart* is a novel about the end of a writer's marriage, of how – by ill luck, external circumstances and intrigues on the part of another woman – it was possible for a great man to become sundered from his family. In the midst of emotional storms, the char-acter of the first wife attains an unforgettable scale.

Astonishingly, Julie thought the book would win him back. Lawyers – 'thirty or forty lawyers' – clustered in several coun-tries, in several jurisdictions. The only satisfaction for the dying Wassermann was naming them for predatory or carnivorous birds: pelican, stork, crane and so forth.

I offered my sense that *My First Wife* is set at a pivotal moment in the relations between men and women. By this I mean not only that it is set in Vienna at the time of Freud, and that it plays in the decades either side of the First World War – the decades, if you will, of Women's Suffrage – but also that it ends a certain kind of late-nineteenth-century male fantasy about women and society and money and art, namely that it was possible by adroit use of the last of these to make an impression on the first three. Originally, the idea – French, as all these things originally are – had been that there was an opposition, an enmity even, between the artist and his tasteless, foolish, moneyed public; the painter, the poet, the musician loathed and despised the bourgeois, and in return was *maudit*, 'cursed' for it. There was no niche for the artist in society and, if there was, he shouldn't take it. His superiority, his aristocracy even, resided in his nerve endings. He was an outsider. As the nineteenth century turned into the twentieth, and the children of the bourgeoisie became cultivated and even a little neurasthenic themselves, there was finally some accommodation between the two. Each had something to offer the other, something to tempt him with. The bourgeois felt scandalous stirrings of a latent creativity, and the artist, tired of outlawry, a hankering for comfort and possessions.

Individual authors – like Dickens or Byron – may have come to money before, but Wassermann belonged to the first commercially successful *generation*; they made writing look like a reasonable career option: Lion Feuchtwanger (1884–1958), Hugo von Hofmannsthal (1874–1929), Thomas Mann (1875–1955), Franz Werfel (1890–1945), Stefan Zweig (1881–1942), even Hermann Hesse (1877–1962), though his great success came later. The successful authors bought themselves imposing villas and cars (often more than one of each), kept secretaries and domestic staffs, holidayed exhaustively in the mountains or by the seaside, travelled the length and breadth of Europe and beyond, and thought of themselves as deserving members of the grande bourgeoisie. That is, they continued to lay claim to the inheritance of the French *bohémiens*, but in practical terms they expected a lifestyle of mahogany and silver and libraries. They demanded personal freedoms and the kudos of rebellion or unconventionality for themselves, but they also wanted presentable families (Thomas Mann's pretty mob in sailor suits) and beetling castles or plush architect-designed homes (or, as was the case with Wassermann, both). The days of dying in garrets or taking one's lobster for a walk were over. No, these writers were a startlingly worldly bunch. Stefan Zweig (who admittedly was born into a wealthy manufacturing family) owned Beethoven's desk and Goethe's pen and Leonardo and Mozart manuscripts, and lived, when he cared to, in a fourteenth-century bishop's palace above Salzburg that his lovely and capable aristocratic wife had found for him; Thomas Mann was immortally described by Hermann Kesten as '*hartnäckiger Villenbesitzer*' (an obstinate or determined or serial owner of villas); while, sounding rather petulant in his almost fetishistic litany of aspirations, Hugo von Hofmannsthal (himself the son of a banker) wailed: 'I finally want a house with Empire furniture, a smell of lavender, Old Vienna porcelain and music being played, where people can drop in, listen in silence, and maybe chat quietly, or not as the case may be.'

Jakob Wassermann, who had lost his mother at the age of nine, repeatedly run away from a broken home, known starvation and rags, was mostly self-educated, and felt his Jewishness more and differently than many of the Austrians with whom he mingled, didn't quite fit into such a scene. In terms of family, class, education, socialization, ethnicity, nationality, provincialism, he stuck out. Yes, he had the required 'demonic' touch – the allure of the French line of descent, Baudelaire, Rimbaud, Huysmans, Nerval, he was a reasonably early reader and admirer of Dostoevsky, and 'demonic' was also one of his favourite words, though with his risible Franconian accent he tended to mispronounce it as 'temonic' – only the noun that he paired it with when describing himself was '*Kleinbürger*', or petit bourgeois, an extraordinary coinage and an extraordinary notion. It would be something like glorying in being a 'demonic suburbanite' or even a 'demonic C2'. His lavish standard of living may have earned him envy and incomprehension, but it was the only thing that stood between himself and the abyss.

In terms of their respective typology, you can see Alexander Herzog as late-*poète-maudit* and Ganna as late-femme-fatale. The poor, gifted writer / orphaned seventh son will carry off the book-loving bourgeois-princess-cum-ugly-duckling. Then either she will remain an episode – a novella, so to speak – or else they will both be transformed, he by love and she by him. He will get over his coolness and disdain, she will discover wifely virtues. What other way can it be? It's a foregone conclusion. Only this story doesn't end with wedding bells and 'happily ever after' (it would be shocking enough if it did!). Art is short, life is long. Alexander fails to tame his Ganna; Ganna can neither mellow, nor hold him. He, with the beam in his eye, is fixated on the mote in hers; she, thinking she has him, lets him go. Neither can change, but both develop the full and terrifying range of their latencies. The strife gets deeper and wilder. We see it all. The poet finds himself over-matched by the bluestocking. She has resources and determination of which he had no inkling. She arms herself with finance, society, business, the law; she reaches into undefended places of his of which he had no idea. In the end, the demonic bourgeoise simply pulls rank, and has the *temonic Kleinbürger* on toast. He may sneer at the style of it – the carpet bag, the cloche hat, the dyed hair, the unaired smell – but he loses and loses and never stops losing: home, career, freedom, happiness. The book ends, and he hasn't finished losing.

There was a third heading: the sheer intense and true drama of the story. It's like the House of Atreus, or Oedipus, or Macbeth. It's that very rare thing, a twentieth-century tragedy, played out with twentieth-century resources and recourses, with courts and banks and publicity. 'In the depths, everything becomes law,' says (a little surprisingly) Rilke. Things get worse, as calmly and methodically as in a Hitchcock movie. It's not just what happens, it's every stage of that happening; you start with a lobster and a bayleaf in a pan of cold water. What began by looking to the forever canny observer Arthur Schnitzler as a cold and blatant case of a marriage of convenience on Wassermann's part, ends up with the man hounded, frankly, to death. It is the victim's portrait in poison of his killer. Ganna – Julie Speyer – outlived Wassermann by almost thirty years.

Michael Hofmann, 2012

## Bibliography and Acknowledgements

Barbara Hoffmeister: *S. Fischer, der Verleger. Eine Lebensbeschreibung* (Frankfurt, 2009)

Thomas Kraft: *Jakob Wassermann* (Munich, 2008)

Peter de Mendelsohn: 'Jakob Wassermanns letztes Werk' – afterword to *Joseph Kerkhovens dritte Existenz* (Munich, 1982)

Henry Miller: *Maurizius Forever* (San Francisco, 1946)

Jakob Wassermann: *My Life as German and Jew* (translated by S.N. Brainin, New York, 1933)

Julie Wassermann-Speyer: *Jakob Wassermann und sein Werk* (Vienna, 1923)

I would like to offer the Canton of Wallis/Valais my heartfelt thanks for awarding me a residency in Raron, where the translation was completed (though it seemed a shame not just to stare out of the window). Penguin were their usual brilliant selves – especially Louise Wilder, Anna Hervé and the wonderful Adam Freudenheim. Linden Lawson made valuable suggestions (I accepted them), as well as taking out many hundreds of evidently redundant commas that I left like crampons in the text.

M.H.

WITHDRAWN